AMONG THE UNSEEN

BY JODI McISAAC

The Thin Veil Series

Through the Door

Into the Fire

Among the Unseen

AMONG THE UNSEEN

Jodi McIsaac

Text copyright © 2014 Jodi McIsaac
All rights reserved.

Published by 47North, Seattle

www.apub.com

ISBN-13: 9781477819845
ISBN-10: 1477819843

Cover design by becker&mayer! LLC
Illustrated by Gene Mollica

Library of Congress Control Number: 2013954685

Printed in the United States of America

FOR WILLOW

PRONUNCIATION GUIDE

If you haven't figured out how to pronounce these words by now, don't worry: I haven't, either. But the guide below should give you a very general sense of how some people in the Irish-speaking world say these words. You are, as always, free to pronounce them however you like.

Brighid—*BREE yit*

Ériu—*AY roo*

Fionnbharr—*FYUN var*

Fionn mac Cumhaill—*FYUN mac COOL*

gancanagh—*gan CAH nah*

leannán sí—*LAH nawn SHEE*

Lia Fáil—*LEE-ah FOIL*

Manannan mac Lir—*Man na non mac LEER*

Niamh—*NEE uv*

Nuala—*NOO uh la*

Oisín—*USH een*

Ruadhan—*ROO awn*

sidh—*SHEE*

sidhe (plural of sidh)—*SHEE*

Tara—*TAH ra*

Teamhair—*T'yower*

Tír na nÓg—*TEER na NOHG*

Toirdhealbhach MacDail re Deachai—*TUR a lakh mac DOLL ray DAW hai*

Tuatha Dé Danann—*TOOa ha DAY DONN an*

AMONG THE UNSEEN

CHAPTER 1

gain, she told herself. Taking a deep breath, Cedar held her palms flat in front of her. Small white flames flickered in the air above them. She closed her eyes and willed the energy flowing through her arms to gradually build, causing the flames to shoot up higher. Slowly, she brought them down again. *Control it. Keep it steady.* She opened her eyes a crack and checked to see how she was doing. The flames held steady, dancing and flickering on her palms but staying right where she wanted them. *If only I'd had this power sooner*, she thought, then reprimanded herself, closing her eyes again and trying to concentrate on the flames. *Don't think about it. Don't think about them.*

But it was too late. The images started to pour into her mind, and no matter how tightly she squeezed her eyes shut, she could not block them out. Her adoptive mother, lying in the dirt, covered in blood. Eden's sweet, innocent face twisted in terror as Liam—gentle, kind, treacherous Liam—tortured her mind. Jane's blackened figure, burnt beyond recognition. Finn's convulsions of agony as Liam slashed at him again and again with a crystal dagger.

She opened her eyes and flinched. The field she was standing in was engulfed in raging white flames. The brightly colored poppies Finn had grown for her were snapping and crackling and crumbling into ash. She swore loudly, then raised her arms and concentrated on bringing the flames under control, drawing them in until only a puff of smoke lingered over the charred field. Her control over her new-found abilities had come to her so easily, so naturally when she'd used them to defeat the druids while standing on the Lia Fáil. And she could still wield her powers effortlessly . . . unless she let her memories get the better of her. "Just relax," Finn had told her. "Imagine that you're painting, and the flames are the colors." She appreciated the metaphor, but relaxing was harder than it looked. *Nuala is dead*, she told herself. *Liam is dead.* But they hadn't been working alone, and Cedar would not rest until she knew her family was safe.

She was queen now, as strange as that still sounded to her. And she could relax as soon as every last druid who had been working with Nuala was found and imprisoned. She had captured all the ones who'd attacked her and her family and friends on the Hill of Tara, sending them via sidh to Maeve's workshop. From there they'd been transported through another sidh to guarded cells in Tír na nÓg. Still, she had no idea how many others had been working with Nuala and Liam. She massaged her jaw, trying to unclench it.

Cedar took a grim look at the charred field all around her and decided she'd practiced enough with fire for the day. Drawing in another deep breath, she gently closed her eyes. When she opened them, the air in front of her was shimmering like a sprinkling of fairy dust. She exhaled slowly. Through the sparkling air she could see a gentle green glade at the foot of a misty waterfall, one of her favorite retreats.

Being queen came with a lot of benefits, but privacy wasn't one of them. So even though Cedar technically wasn't supposed to leave her own home without an entourage of guards and servants, she took advantage of the fact that she could go anywhere she wanted, any-time she wanted, without stepping foot outside her front door. Finn didn't like it, which was becoming a source of tension between them. She had thought he would become less protective now that their lives weren't in immediate danger, but he still got nervous whenever she used the sidhe to do a little exploring, even when she created one from Felix's house to Jane's apartment, which, to her delight, was becoming a regular occurrence.

Stepping into the scenic glade, Cedar sank down onto the tender grass, feeling the tension leave her body. She'd spent as much time as she could spare exploring her new kingdom, which was coming back to life after years of poisoning. She'd only discovered the glade last week, but it was already her favorite place to go when she felt overwhelmed by how much her life had changed over the past few months.

She stretched languorously as she watched the sunlight shimmer through the mist of the waterfall, feeling as if she were inside one of her own sidhe. The gentle roar of the falls helped soothe her stressed nerves. Perhaps she would bring Eden here later.

Today was Eden's seventh birthday, and Cedar had planned a surprise party for later in the afternoon, complete with balloons and cakes and Eden's favorite foods. She had invited all their friends and family here in Tír na nÓg. She knew it wouldn't be as much fun for Eden as celebrating with a room full of little girls, but she hoped the party would help her feel at home. There was just one thing Cedar couldn't duplicate: Eden's grandmother had always been a big part of the festivities each year. Cedar hoped Eden's memory of her gran's death wouldn't ruin her special day.

Cedar's thoughts lingered on Maeve, as they so often did when she was alone. The tears for her adoptive mother had finally come in this sacred and quiet glade, where she didn't have to be strong, or make decisions, or solve problems—where she could just *be*. She wondered what Maeve would think of what she had done and who she had become. Would she be proud of her? Or would she be angry with Cedar for embracing her true identity and moving with Eden to Tír na nÓg? Cedar would never know, but she chose to believe that she and Maeve had reached an understanding before she died. If Maeve could have only seen beyond her broken heart, beyond her obsession with Brogan, she would have realized that the Tuatha Dé Danann are a wonderful, noble people. Flawed, yes, but no more so than any other race.

As Cedar thought about Maeve, her mind inevitably turned toward Halifax and her old life there. She missed it more than she'd expected. She actually missed her work as a graphic designer, and felt nostalgic for the simple, small things like her morning walk to work along the harbor, casual office banter, and Friday work lunches at the local pub, which often lingered well into the afternoon. She missed the smell of warm concrete, the rustic beauty of a maritime autumn, and the sound of seagulls' cries over the water. And she missed her apartment, which had been a total write-off after Liam and his fellow druids had destroyed it in a fire. As she lay on the grass, staring up at the blue sky, she found herself craving a strong coffee and sesame seed bagel. Something familiar . . . something like home. Just one more time.

Her stomach fluttered nervously at the thought, but why not? It wouldn't be her first trip back to Earth since becoming queen. After her first chaotic week on the throne, she, Finn, and Eden had spent a few days at Brighid's island retreat. It had been strange at first, spending time with the woman whom she'd once deemed a rival for Finn's affection. But by the end she'd been reluctant to leave behind Brighid's huge personality and wild tales, not to mention her in-depth knowledge about the world that Cedar now ruled. Cedar had asked Brighid to come back to Tír na nÓg for a while, but the Elder goddess had only laughed and politely declined, saying that she'd be happy for them to visit her anytime.

Cedar had also paid a stealth visit to Maeve's grave in Chester to rip out the rosebush Liam had planted and set it on fire. Maeve had never asked for his affection, and Cedar hadn't wanted his token to despoil her mother's grave any longer. Finn had been angry that she had gone—and gone alone. But what he hadn't understood was that she'd needed to do it by herself. Even though the druid was dead, his betrayal still burned like an open wound. She had hoped that ripping out the rosebush would give her some sort of closure. It hadn't.

Finn would have called her reckless for even considering another trip to Earth. And maybe it was true—she *did* feel a little reckless. But she had lived there for her entire life; why shouldn't she go back and visit as long as she was discreet? It's not like she was going to open a sidh in the middle of a crowded street. Leaving the waterfall behind, she walked slowly back into the scorched poppy field. She knew she *did* have to be discreet, particularly when opening a sidh to Earth. She wasn't the only one who wanted to go there, after all. Now that she and Eden both had the gift to create the sidhe, there had been a clamoring of requests to reopen the passageways between Tír na nÓg and the land the Danann called Ériu. So far, Cedar had adamantly refused. There were still those who believed humans were a blight to be snuffed out, and she didn't dare give them access to Earth. Still, it was safe for her to open a sidh from her home, which could be accessed by no one but their immediate family. None of the other Danann need ever know.

It was still early morning, and Jane's new apartment, two floors below the one that had gone up in flames, would be a safe place for her to pass through. Leaving her sidh to the waterfall glade open for Finn or Eden to close, she created a new one to Jane's apartment. She plucked a poppy that had somehow managed to survive her fire mishap and tossed it through the shimmering air as a way of announcing her arrival, remembering the time she had walked in on Jane and Felix getting to know each other better in the living room. She tiptoed through. It was dark when she entered, which meant Jane was probably still asleep in her bedroom. Sinking down onto her old sofa, Cedar released a drawn-out sigh. All of Jane's belongings had been destroyed in the druids' fire, so Cedar had given her friend her own furniture, which she'd put into storage before the move to Tír na nÓg. Jane had graciously accepted the modern pieces, and then set about scouring flea markets for decor that was more "her thing." It felt strange, sitting in this new place with her old belongings. A metaphor for her life, she mused.

Maybe I should wake Jane? Her friend didn't hide the fact that she wanted to see her more often. Cedar felt the same way. Before moving, she hadn't realized how much she relied on Jane for advice . . . and sanity. Still, she didn't want to disturb her friend's rest. She switched on a lamp and then went into the kitchen and reached for the jar on top of the fridge, where she knew Jane kept an emergency stash of money. She slipped a bill out and wrote her friend a note—*I owe you $10. Was craving a bagel. Will come for a real visit soon! xo—Cedar*

That done, she headed down the stairs, luxuriating in the thrill of anticipation she felt at such a simple thing. Sleeping in on Saturday mornings was a foreign concept for Eden, so Cedar had made a habit of bringing her to the bagel shop down the street for breakfast. Cedar would sip coffee and have a sesame bagel with plain cream cheese and read the newspaper, while Eden would munch on a chocolate chip bagel with strawberry cream cheese, her nose stuck in a book. It had been calm and peaceful—two things that didn't play a big part in Cedar's current life.

Mike, the shop owner, was just opening the doors when she arrived. "Well, now, look who's come back!" he exclaimed at the sight of Cedar. "We've not seen you in here for ages! I thought you must have moved away. Where's your little one? The chocolate chip bagels are fresh out of the oven!"

Cedar laughed nervously. "We did move, actually," she said, trying to think up an alibi on the fly. "We're just here to visit some friends. But I'll take a chocolate chip bagel for Eden. And I'll have my usual." She smiled as she imagined how Eden would react to her favorite treat.

"Did you really?" he asked, handing her a cup of coffee and putting her bagel in the toaster. "Where you living now, then?"

"Uh, Montreal," she improvised, starting to think this hadn't been such a good idea after all. What if one of her old colleagues from work walked in? She'd left Ellison with virtually no notice, and Jane had told her about the rumors that were still swirling around the office. She just wanted a bagel, not an inquisition. "Can I get that to go?" she asked as she watched him slather on the cream cheese.

"Sure you can," Mike said. "I suppose you've got lots of people to visit while you're back?"

She nodded, then handed him the ten-dollar bill and said, "Keep the change. Nice to see you again!"

"Happy Thanksgiving!" he called, but she was already out the door.

She'd forgotten—it was Thanksgiving weekend here in Canada, not that such holidays were celebrated in Tír na nÓg. She thought about heading back to Jane's apartment, but it was a gorgeous fall day, warm for this time of year, and the cry of the seagulls and the smell of the ocean were too intoxicating to leave behind. She pulled her bagel out of the bag and took a bite, letting the taste and smell and feel of the warm bread assault her senses in the most wonderful way. The food in Tír na nÓg was exceptional, but this, this tasted like home. She found a bench close to the waterfront and sat down, watching as a lone sailboat drifted past. *Maybe we could come back for weekends*, she thought idly. *Just so we can spend our Saturday mornings here.*

A sudden movement caught her attention out of the corner of her eye. She whirled around, but there was nothing there. Still, she felt unsettled. It was risky coming back to Earth, and she knew it . . . Enemy druids could be anywhere. She stood up and looked around, but the only other person in sight was a solitary jogger running in the opposite direction. If she had her way, she would bring every single druid on Earth in for questioning, but that task seemed impossible. There was no central registry of druids, and even the druids themselves did not know where all the others were.

She kept her head down as she walked back to the apartment, hoping she wouldn't bump into anyone she knew. Time to be responsible, she supposed. Jane still hadn't emerged from her room, so she stepped back through the sidh into the poppy field. There she found Finn, standing with his hands on his hips, his eyes dark as he eyed the half-eaten bagel in her hands.

"We do have food here, you know," he said stiffly, waving a hand at both the sidh to Jane's apartment and the one leading to the green glen, causing the shimmering air to return to normal.

"I needed some comfort food," she muttered. "I can do the sidhe just fine, but the fire is still giving me trouble. Obviously." She looked ruefully at the blackened field around them, and then wiped a bit of cream cheese off the corner of her mouth with the back of her hand.

"Cedar, you can't keep doing that," he said. "It's not safe."

"I was careful," she said, not quite looking at him. "No one saw me."

Finn looked like he wanted to argue some more, but instead he asked, "You miss it, don't you?"

"I do," she admitted. "But I also love it here. It's just . . . a lot to adjust to, that's all."

He wrapped his arms around her and kissed the top of her head. "I know. It's a bit different than when we were first dating, isn't it?"

She smiled, remembering those carefree days. She had never stopped loving Finn while he was away, but she knew that they'd both changed. It was a peculiar place to be in—sometimes she felt like they had never been apart, and other times she wondered who this strange man was lying next to her, playing father to her child.

"It means so much to me that you're here," he said, his voice muffled by her hair.

She rested her head on his chest, taking comfort in the steady beating of his heart. These first few weeks in Tír na nÓg had been so busy for both of them, and she wanted more than anything to just spend a lazy day with him and Eden. "It means so much to me that *you're* here," she said. "Who else would regrow a poppy field for me—again?"

He laughed. "Nevan's outside waiting to walk to the Council meeting with you," he said. "Eden's still sleeping; I'll tell her you said happy birthday when she gets up."

"Okay," Cedar said, feeling a twinge of disappointment as she handed Finn the paper bag in her hands. "Here, I got her a bagel; it's her favorite kind. Maybe bring her by to see me after the meeting?"

"I don't think we'll be back in time," Finn said. "I'm taking her into the mountains this morning. There's a secret network of pools near the top of one of the peaks that my mum used to bring me to when we were hiding out from Lorcan. I thought she'd like to see it. We'll just get home in time for her party." He grinned in anticipation. Finn had been like a child on Christmas morning ever since their return to Tír na nÓg. He spent almost every day exploring his lost homeland, discovering what had changed since his childhood and introducing their daughter to his favorite places.

"Of course," she said, forcing a smile. Instead of joining them on their adventure, she would be spending her morning trying to sort through the politics of a world she didn't quite understand. "Well, we'll have fun together at her party," she said, giving him a hug before disappearing into her wardrobe, which had expanded considerably now that she was queen. Thankfully, she could get into most of her dresses without assistance—only the most ornate ones required Finn or Riona's help. Today she chose a pale yellow dress with short ruffled sleeves, something that wouldn't have been entirely out of place at a summer wedding on Earth. She fastened her hair up with a shell-shaped comb and slipped her feet into a pair of delicate sandals studded with yellow sapphires. Finn had already left the charred poppy field when she walked back through it, leaving through the door that led to the circular courtyard lined with willow trees. As queen, she could have chosen to relocate to the opulent accommodations in the Hall with her family, but Cedar loved the home Finn had made for them, and she knew how attached Eden had become to her tree-house bedroom—and her new grandparents.

Riona was sitting on a bench under one of the willow trees, watching the waterfall that spilled into a pool in the center of the room. She stood up when she saw Cedar and curtseyed slightly. Cedar rolled her eyes. "Will you *please* stop doing that? We're *family*, and it's extremely weird when you bow to me."

Riona laughed but made no promises. "It comes with the title, my dear, so you'd best get used to it. You look lovely," she added. "I hope all goes well with the Council today."

"So do I," Cedar said. "I'll see you at the party later."

When she reached the outer door of their home, Nevan was waiting for her, just as Finn had said, along with three tall guardsmen dressed in the dark green and silver uniforms that marked them as part of the Royal Guard. "Good morning," she said. They nodded back but made no verbal reply.

Nevan curtseyed. "Good morning, Your Majesty," she said. Cedar smiled at her friend, who looked more like a fairy than any of them with her platinum-blonde pixie cut and glittering white dress. Together they started walking toward the Hall, with one of the guards in front of them and the other two behind. Cedar could have used a sidh, of course, but she enjoyed these morning walks with Nevan, who was bubbly and talkative and had assigned herself the role of Cedar's—and Eden's—tutor in the ways of the Tuatha Dé Danann. Each morning as they walked to the Hall together, she told Cedar more about the history of her people and then would quiz her on the previous day's lesson. They met at other times for more in-depth lessons, but Cedar had discovered that Nevan was quite politically astute, and she always felt more informed—and better equipped to make decisions—after their walks. It was the ideal way to head into a Council meeting.

"Tell me about your parents, Nevan," Cedar said. "You mentioned the other day that they're Elders. The only Elder I know is Brighid—are they like her? Can you still speak with them even though they've gone back to the Four Cities?"

Nevan laughed, a tinkling sound that always brought a smile to Cedar's face. "I'm afraid Brighid is quite unique," she said. "She has the most outrageous qualities of both the Elders and the humans, which distinguishes her from both races. But all the Elders, my parents included, are different from us. They're a step more . . . godlike, I suppose. They're more powerful and dominant than we are. You'd probably consider them melodramatic. They each seem to exist in their own self-contained world, whereas those of us who are their descendants are more interconnected, both with each other and with humanity—or at least we were back when we visited Ériu more."

"Wasn't it hard for you when they left?" Cedar asked. She couldn't imagine voluntarily leaving Eden behind, knowing she would never see her again.

"Not really," Nevan answered with a shrug. "I wasn't a child anymore, and they weren't the kind of parents that you're thinking about. I wonder about them occasionally, but we didn't have a close relationship like you and Eden do . . . or even Finn and his parents. As awful as it sounds, it wouldn't really bother me if I never saw them again. And who knows? Maybe I will. They left us for the Four Cities, but that doesn't mean they'll never return."

Cedar thought about her own birth parents, Brogan and Kier, and wondered what her childhood would have been like if she'd been born and raised in Tír na nÓg. Would they have loved her like Maeve had loved her? Kier had sacrificed the last bit of her power to give Cedar the gift of humanity in the hopes of shielding her from Lorcan. That had to mean something, she thought.

They walked in silence for several minutes; Nevan was apparently waiting for another question, but Cedar was distracted, her attention drawn to the beauty that surrounded them. She couldn't believe how quickly the land had rejuvenated in the past few weeks. The grass beneath her feet was no longer dry and coarse; it was as soft and tender as the flowers that dotted the fields and filled the air with a gentle fragrance. The trees, which had been dead and barren, now hung with heavy blossoms. Some were even beginning to bear fruit. Cedar had been delighted to discover that the queen had her own orchard, a maze of trees and bushes that were now bursting with life.

In its natural state, Tír na nÓg was always in the height of spring. There was no fall or winter here, at least nothing that lasted more than a day or two. The plants would bloom, bear fruit, and when the fruit had all fallen or been picked, they would bloom again, a never-ending cycle of growth and beauty without the darkness of death and winter. This cycle would repeat until the end of time—or, she supposed, until a new calamity struck Tír na nÓg.

Cedar was lost in thought when she heard a voice call her name from behind them. The guards stopped first, and then stepped aside when they saw Rohan approaching. "Good morning, Your Majesty," Rohan said as he dipped his head toward her. "Good morning, Nevan."

"Good morning, Rohan," Cedar replied, with only a slight roll of her eyes this time. Perhaps Riona was right, and she should just get used it. To her surprise, Rohan grinned at her. He'd become much more lighthearted now that they were back in his homeland and he wasn't responsible for the lives of so many.

"Your father used to hate it too, you know," he said. "He was my best friend, and had been for many years, and when we were alone, he insisted that I call him Brogan. But he deserved it—the title, that is. And so do you."

Cedar smiled gratefully. "Thank you," she said. "Any news?"

"Always. Do you want the good news or the bad news first?"

"Um . . . the bad news, I guess."

"Deaglán is causing trouble again, even from behind bars."

"What's he doing now?"

"It's not what he's doing so much as what he's saying. The people are curious about you, Your Majesty. Deaglán is encouraging the rumor that you are Maeve's child, not Kier's."

"What?" Nevan exclaimed. "They still think she's part human?"

"How could they think that?" Cedar asked. "The Lia Fáil chose me. They all heard it at the coronation."

Rohan nodded. "Yes, but it will take some time to convince everyone that the humans are not our enemies. And everyone knows you grew up among them. Some think that you are the child of a human and a Danann, even though we all know that such a thing is impossible. They are concerned that the Lia Fáil was . . . mistaken."

Nevan looked disgusted, but Cedar slowly nodded. She, too, had heard the whispers. She noticed the conversations that were hushed the moment she entered the room, saw the sidelong, doubting looks. Even in the throne room she could sense it, when her lack of knowledge about the Tuatha Dé Danann was displayed by some question or topic she didn't understand. She saw the glances the Council members exchanged when Gorman, whom she had chosen as her steward, had to whisper a correction or explanation in her ear. For a while she'd asked Nevan, who was on the Council, to explain things to her telepathically—but she just looked spaced out while she listened to Nevan's explanations, so they had scrapped that idea after a few days.

"Let them talk," she told Rohan. "I don't want to address every little rumor about me. I'll just have to win them over with time. What's next?" She started walking again, with Rohan and Nevan beside her. She could think better when she was moving.

"Ah, that's where my good news comes in. We've finished questioning the druids that were involved with the attacks on you at Tara and Edinburgh Castle. We used the goblet of Manannan mac Lir to ensure their truthfulness, and it appears that all of them were acting on Nuala's direct orders. We found a starstone among Liam's things that matches the one belonging to Nuala, so we assume the plan was for him to recruit the druids and for her to work her persuasive spell on them through the starstone. With your permission, we'll release them."

Cedar frowned and tried to shove her hands into her pockets, only then remembering that she was wearing a dress. "I don't think so. Liam couldn't have been working alone. At least some of them must have been helping of their own free will."

"There's something else you should know. We've been trying to answer that very question, and we came across something very interesting. Liam *wasn't* working alone—not at the library, at any rate. His assistant there is also a druid. Her name is Helen Sullivan."

Cedar and Nevan both stopped walking and stared at him. "Can you give us a minute?" she asked her guards, who fell back a few paces, out of earshot. "There's another druid at Trinity College? He never mentioned that. Was he training her?"

"We're not sure exactly what their relationship was," Rohan said. "But Liam was more than just a librarian. He was Keeper of Manuscripts. It's a very old and prestigious position. He was in charge of the Book of Kells and the other ancient manuscripts in the college's library. Helen was the Assistant Keeper of Manuscripts, and since his 'disappearance,' she's been promoted to the top job."

"Where is she now?"

"Still at the college, as far as I know. I'd like to bring her in for questioning, but I wanted your permission first, and of course I'll need a sidh to go and get her."

Cedar exhaled loudly. "I *knew* he couldn't be working alone. Of course you can bring her in. Let's go right now!"

"What about the Council meeting?"

"That can wait," Cedar said. "This is more important." If Liam had someone helping him, she needed to find that person—*now*.

CHAPTER 2

Irial was lying on a rock, tanning his perpetually pale skin, surrounded by seals. This island off the west coast of Ireland was never exactly warm, but his body seemed to be acclimatizing itself to the winds and chills. He had felt exhausted of late, so this chance to soak up some rare late-summer rays was a welcome opportunity. He stretched his thin frame and opened one coal black eye, absentmindedly running his hand through his black curls. At a glance, he appeared to be a normal human youth, with strong shoulders, a tight waist, and powerful legs. And yet there was something unearthly about the way all his pieces fit together. Once you set eyes on him, it was difficult to look away.

"Ladies!" he called. "It's a beautiful day! Why don't you shed the coats?"

The seal next to him made a sound that he thought was supposed to be laughter—or it might have been a sneeze. It twisted its head and strained its neck, as if trying to push something out. And then the seal's skin split neatly down the middle, and a dark-haired, dark-eyed, and very naked woman eased her way out and lay down on the rock beside him, the sealskin tucked under one arm.

"Better?" she asked. Some of the other seals did the same, but the rest ignored him.

"Indeed," Irial said, giving her an appreciative glance. He'd already tried with this one—Syrna, he thought her name was—without

16

getting anywhere, but she did like to flirt. And flirting was something he'd been unable to do since realizing what he was, and what happened to the women who loved him.

"Shout if you see a human," she murmured, resting her head on her arms and closing her eyes.

"You'll have to keep watch yourself, my dear," he answered. "I have a date with you in my dreams."

"Are all gancanagh as lazy as you?" she asked, but he could tell she was smiling.

"I wouldn't know. I've never met another."

Syrna opened her eyes and turned to look at him. "Really? You've never met another like yourself?"

"Hard to believe, I know, when you selkies all live in colonies. But I'm afraid I'm one of a kind. At least, as far as I know. Maybe hundreds of other gancanagh are out there charming the ladies and doing who knows what else."

"They say you don't do that anymore," Syrna said, her darkly lashed eyes looking at him with interest.

Irial propped himself up on one elbow. He could tell that a nap was not in his immediate future. And maybe the truth of his self-imposed exile would cause her to reconsider his advances. "I don't."

"But you did," she pressed.

Irial shrugged. "Yes. But for the most part it was because I didn't understand what was happening. I was young and cocky—hard to believe, I know—and thought human women were just attracted to me."

"So what changed?"

I got tired of killing people, he thought to himself. "You know how it works," he said. "Wouldn't you have changed once you realized what you were doing?"

She didn't answer, just continued to look at him with a mix of interest and skepticism. He sighed. "All right, if you want to hear the whole story. I enjoyed the attention at first—who wouldn't? But then . . . well, it wears on you after a while. It wasn't normal, the way they would act around me. It's like they stopped being human and started behaving like animals. And if I was, uh, intimate with one—even if I just touched her—she'd go mad. I know a lot of human men would say I had a pretty good deal, but in reality . . ." He looked out over the ocean. "It was horrible. I'd rather be anything else."

"Oh, I don't think you're so bad," Syrna said with a wink. "At least you stopped. And it's only human women you affect, anyway. There are lots of other fish in the sea."

He nodded ruefully. She was right, but it had taken him too long to figure that out.

"How did you become a gancanagh, anyway?" she continued. "Maybe you have family somewhere who are just like you."

Irial laughed. To selkies, it was all about family. They couldn't imagine a life apart from their parents, their brothers and sisters, and their seemingly endless string of aunts, uncles, and cousins. On the rare occasion when a human managed to steal a selkie woman's seal coat and force her to become his wife, she only ever dreamed of home, even if she bore children for her human husband. As soon as she found her coat again, she would disappear back into the ocean, leaving her children behind. Having never known his family, Irial didn't understand this compulsion at all. But they had allowed him to stay with their colony—and for that, he was grateful.

"I don't know," he answered truthfully. "Maybe I do have a family somewhere, but I've got a few choice words for them if we ever meet. I don't even remember being a kid. All I remember is waking up under a tree. It must have been hundreds of years ago."

"If you've never met anyone else like you, how did you find out what you were?" she asked.

"I got on the bad side of one of the Tuatha Dé Danann," he said. "Toirdhealbhach MacDail re Deachai. He was a healer. He was spending time in a little village in Derry for some reason—I never had the chance to ask him why. Anyway, he seemed to know what I was just by looking at me. Pulled me aside and told me he'd not seen my like for hundreds of years. So I know there *were* more like me at one time." He snorted. "Nothing like being told you're a kind of succubus and that your skin is toxic to women. And here I thought I was just irresistible."

"And you haven't been with a human woman since?" Syrna asked, raising one dark eyebrow.

Irial shook his head, his pale cheeks reddening slightly. "I'm not that virtuous. But I've tried to stop, and the, er, urges seem to be getting less intense. It helps that I avoid human populations. Before I came here, I was living with a troop of pixies down near the Wicklow Mountains. And before that I was with the Merrow. I haven't seen a human in ages, and I'm glad for it."

"Well, we Unseen have to stick together, don't we?" she asked, rolling over so that her side was pressed against his.

"I like the sound of that," he said with a glint in his eyes. "Don't suppose you'll let me steal that skin of yours?"

"Of course not!" she said, sitting up and clutching the sealskin to her chest. Then she looked at him through long black eyelashes. "But I might let you borrow it . . . for a night."

❧

When Irial woke up the next morning, he felt like he'd been dropped from the top of a cliff and smashed onto the rocks below. Syrna hadn't been *that* rough with him, he thought. He sat up and immediately regretted it. They were in the abandoned fisherman's cabin near the shore where Irial slept at night, though he often spent his days with the selkies on the rocks or swimming in the waves. Even in their human form, the selkies didn't feel the cold as much as he did, and Syrna had tossed off the covers and was lying naked beside him. Her mouth was slightly open, and she was clutching her sealskin in her arms. He was about to reach over and kiss her when she gave a long, low moan. Her eyes fluttered open, and she looked at him in confusion.

"Good morning," he said, trying to ignore the aches in his body. "Are you okay?"

"I . . . I don't think so," she said. She tried to sit up, but winced in pain.

"What's wrong?" he asked.

"I feel . . . awful," she said. "I think I need to get back into the water." She got to her feet shakily and wavered on the spot. Without looking back at him, she walked out of the cabin and down the few steps to the shore. She slid back into the sealskin and pushed herself into the water.

Irial wrapped a towel around his waist, grabbed a handful of the seaweed the selkies had given him to help his body adapt to the cold Atlantic waters, and stumbled down to the shore. A few yards off, Syrna's head bobbed out of the water.

"Do you feel better?" he shouted. The seal shook her head.

He stuffed the seaweed in his mouth and chewed it slowly and methodically. Then he braced himself for the first icy step into the ocean. He could feel the seaweed working its way through his system, and gradually the water began to feel warmer. He swam out to Syrna. He didn't understand why they preferred to live as seals when they could be beautiful naked women, but then there was a lot about selkies he didn't understand.

"I feel dreadful too," he said. "We must have caught the same bug."

She gave him a strange look, and then turned and swam away. Irial followed her, struggling to keep up. They swam over to a gathering of dozens of selkies, who were lying on the flat, smooth rocks that jutted out into the water. He was surprised to see that many others were lying on the beach—usually they didn't get so close to the humans who lived on the island. Syrna climbed awkwardly onto the rocks and started talking with her kin. He couldn't understand their way of speaking, but something was definitely amiss. He pulled himself out of the ocean and tried to find a warm patch of rock to soothe his aching body. He sat and waited, uncomfortably aware that many of the seals' heads had turned to look at him. After many long minutes, Syrna waddled over to him. She stretched out of her sealskin but did not remove it completely. It fell grotesquely around her shoulders, keeping the rest of her body covered.

"What's going on?" he asked as soon as her head had emerged from the skin.

"It's the same with all of them. They feel as sick as we do."

"But they all seemed fine yesterday," he said.

"I know," she answered. "I mean, I've been feeling more weary than usual lately, but nothing like this."

"Do they have any idea what's causing it?" he asked. "Something in the water?"

"Maybe. We don't know." She lowered her voice and leaned in close. "I should warn you—some are saying that perhaps *you* brought the sickness here."

"Me? But I've been here for months, and this has just happened."

"I know. I told them it was highly unlikely, but I just thought you should know."

"Thanks," he muttered, but he knew what it meant. Another place he wasn't welcome.

"Just wait a bit," she said, as though she could read his thoughts. "It might pass quickly, and then they'll realize it has nothing to do with you."

༄

It didn't pass quickly. Two weeks later, Syrna came to him in the middle of the night. He was lying curled up under a pile of blankets in his bed in the cabin, shivering so hard his muscles ached. Never in his life had he felt this sick for this long. He felt Syrna's flipper on his shoulder. Even in her seal form, he could tell she was not well. She had lost her round, plump figure, and her skin hung loosely where once it had been taut. A green fungus was spreading over her black skin. He looked at her blearily, watching as with great effort she pulled her head out of the sealskin and spoke to him.

"You have to leave," she whispered. "Now. They are coming for you."

"What?" he mumbled. "Who?"

Syrna glanced around nervously. "Sri has died," she said. "They're blaming you."

Irial struggled to sit up. Sri was one of the matriarchs of the selkie colony. Half of the selkies here were related to her. This would not end well for him.

"Where will I—" he started to say.

"You must go find help—for all of us," she said. "You said you knew the Merrow. Of all the Unseen, they are the closest to our kind. Perhaps they will be able to send help."

Irial nodded and stood up shakily. "Be well, Syrna," he said. "And thank you for your kindness."

"Good luck," she whispered, before slipping back out into the darkness.

Part of him wanted to just stay in bed, to let them find him and do whatever they wanted to him. But he forced himself to stand up and dress. He crept out of the cabin, glancing over his shoulder at the dark waters of the Atlantic. He would have to cross the island, swim to the mainland, and then travel south along the coast to where the Merrow had their underwater kingdom. It seemed like an impossible journey in his weakened state. But the only people here who could help him were human, and he had sworn to stay away from them. He followed the dirt road that cut through the island, which was divided into tiny square fields by a giant checkerboard of ancient limestone walls. He occasionally stopped to rest on one of the low walls, which had marked property boundaries in these parts for centuries. Cottage lights winked at him, taunting him with the promise of comfort, but he gritted his teeth and carried on, trying not to think of the warm welcome he would receive from a human woman. He cut through a stony field to avoid a house by the edge of the road and collapsed against a large granite boulder that seemed as out of place in these parts as he did. As he struggled to catch his breath, a gray mare, ghost-like in the moonlight, sauntered up to him from across the field.

"Hello, beautiful. I don't suppose you'd let me ride you?" he whispered sardonically. To his surprise, the mare sank down on her front knees and prodded him with her muzzle. Irial stared at her for a moment, and then grabbed a fistful of mane and hauled himself up onto her back.

"Need to get to the Merrow," he murmured, not sure if she could understand him. He knew they needed to go east to cross the island, but she was taking him north. He tugged on her mane to try and direct her, but she just snorted and continued on her chosen path. He gave up. At least he wasn't walking anymore. He held on tighter as she started to canter, jumping the low rock walls that were meant to contain her. Then they started to climb, and he realized she was heading for the ancient stone fort that stood in a semicircle on the edge of the island's westernmost cliff. He shuddered. Was she going to throw him off? The mare carefully maneuvered the rough steps that led to the prehistoric fort, keeping to the well-trod human path. The fields surrounding the ancient stronghold were littered with razor-sharp chunks of limestone that had been embedded in the ground like a sea of spears with the express purpose of discouraging any attack made by horse.

When they reached the top, she stopped, and he slid from her back into a heap on the ground. They were surrounded by a great curved wall on three sides, the fourth open to the chill air and a three-hundred-foot drop to the ocean waves that crashed below. The wind ripped through him like a thousand knives, and he curled into a ball. The mare prodded him again with her muzzle, and he stood reluctantly, trying to use her body to block the wind. "Why are we here?" he asked. And then he saw it.

"A púka," he breathed. The púka was in his horse form, a majestic black stallion, with a gleaming coat and eyes of red fire. But the fire in them had dimmed, and the púka lay on his side, his breathing heavy and labored. His flanks were covered in patches of white foam; his mouth was lined with dried blood. Irial looked back at the gray mare, who was nervously pawing the ground.

"I'm a friend," he said to the púka. "Can you speak? Can you take another form, perhaps?" The púka just looked at him out of dim red eyes filled with fear and panic. "This isn't right," Irial muttered as he ran his hands over the creature's body, looking for some sign of injury. "You should be able to speak to me." He had only ridden a púka once, but he'd never forget the experience. At one time the púka had been legendary in this land for offering wild late-night rides to weary travelers. If you were lucky, you stayed on the púka's back until the end. If not . . . well, you never knew where you might end up. He hadn't thought there were any more of them, and he wondered if this was the last. A chill ran up his spine. Maybe the púka was suffering from the same mysterious illness that was plaguing him and the selkies.

"Can't you speak to me?" he moaned. "The selkies are sick too; I'm trying to find out why. I need to get to the mainland."

At this, the púka raised his head a little. His body spasmed, and Irial could tell he was trying to stand. "No, stay down," he urged. But the stallion would not obey. He lifted himself up on his front legs, and then, with a monumental effort, he got to all fours. He let out a snort through his nostrils, and a plume of smoke drifted from them. Irial approached him hesitantly, slowly reaching out a hand to grasp the wild black mane. His grip tightened automatically, and he flung himself onto the púka's back. Then, before he could register what was happening, they were moving in a blur of sound and color, the wind rushing in his ears like the roar of the ocean. Irial could not make out where they were or where they were headed. He closed his eyes and hung on for dear life, wishing the journey would end quickly.

And then it did.

He landed roughly on the ground, rolling several times before coming to a stop. For a few moments he just lay there and tried to catch his breath, every bone in his body feeling as if it had been shattered. He gathered his wits and looked around, trying to figure out where the púka had left him. The black horse was nowhere in sight, which worried him. If he couldn't find it, he couldn't help it—even if he somehow managed to help himself.

As he circled around in the moonlight, he started to recognize his surroundings. He had been here before. He was in a small circular meadow, just enough space to hold maybe a dozen humans . . . or a hundred pixies. The trees were unnaturally thick around the meadow. It was perfectly quiet, but Irial knew it was not always this way. "Faelon?" he called out into the surrounding trees. He paced around the meadow. "It's Irial. I need your help! Faelon? Is anyone there?"

He did not even know if Faelon was still the leader of the pixies, as he had been when Irial last visited this place. But surely one of the sentries or night-dancers would hear him. The last time he had shown up unexpected, a whole troop of pixies had surrounded him and brought him to their king for questioning. Ultimately, they had allowed him to stay, at least until that unfortunate encounter with the woman hiker. The pixies could easily hide themselves from human eyes, but Irial was like a homing beacon for human women. He shook off the unwelcome memories, but his eyes kept straying to the barely discernable mound at the edge of the meadow where they'd buried her.

It was no use. He could not venture into the forest now; he was beyond exhausted and would only get lost in the pitch darkness beneath the trees. He would have to wait until morning . . . if he survived that long. He fell down onto the soft grass and was asleep within seconds.

When he awoke, his clothes and hair were damp with dew, and for a moment he wondered if he had died and gone to the Otherworld. The dewdrops sparkled in the early morning sunlight like a generous dusting of pixie magic. But then he felt the aching in his body, the same sensation that had plagued him for the past two weeks. He sat up gingerly, and headed toward the pixies' hidden home in the forest. But as he approached their hideout, he started to feel uneasy. They should have seen and heard him by now. It hadn't been so long since his last visit that they would have forgotten him, so it was unlikely they'd mistake him for a mere human. "Faelon?" he called again. He stopped and looked around. Had he gone the wrong way? No, he was sure this was it. The tall oak to his right was where Faelon held court, and the bushes that came up to his knees were the ones the pixies often decked out with glowing lights for evening soirees. But the place was empty and void of any sign of life. "Hello? Is anyone here? Faelon! Caldes! Dathel!"

Just then he heard a rustling in the leaves, and his body relaxed. But instead of the flutter of wings and the sound of high-pitched voices, the sounds that emerged were distinctly human. An old woman with long white hair that fell to her waist walked out of the forest. She was bent over, carrying a basket filled with herbs and plants and chunks of bark. Her hands were dirty, and one nail was bleeding.

"They're all gone," she said.

The woman was obviously human, and Irial's instinct was to turn and run. But she spoke as though she had answers.

She let out a dry laugh. "Don't you worry about me, boy. I'm far too old to be attracted to the likes of you, though I'll still keep my distance, if you don't mind. As long as you don't lay your hands on me I think I can resist."

"Who are you?" he asked.

"My name is Maggie," she answered. Then she narrowed her eyes and looked closer at him. "You don't look too good." She scowled. "Another one. I was afraid of this."

"Another one?" he repeated. "Who else?"

She waved a hand at the forest around them. "The pixies. They left the day before yesterday. Thought it was maybe a curse on the land. I don't know where they were heading or how far they'll get— some of them could barely fly anymore."

"How do you know? You're a human . . . Did they let you see them?"

"I am human, yes, but I am also one of the fili," she answered. "So some of your kind—the magical kind, that is—show themselves to me from time to time. You might as well come with me. I've been collecting more herbs for Martin; perhaps they'll help you."

"Martin?" Irial didn't move.

"You'd know him as Logheryman, if you know him at all."

"The leprechaun. He's sick as well?"

Maggie nodded tersely, and then headed back through the woods. At another time he would have been able to race ahead of her, but now he struggled to keep up. The forest was dense, and he moved slowly, leaning on tree trunks for support and climbing awkwardly over fallen logs. Every once in a while Maggie would veer from her path and stoop down to collect a handful of some type of plant or flower—they all looked the same to him, but she examined each leaf, petal, and stem closely before adding it to her basket. Finally, when he thought he could go no farther, they emerged into another clearing, this one with a small house at its center.

"Is this where you live?" he asked, leaning heavily against the closest tree trunk.

"No," she answered. "'Tis Martin's house. Come inside and I'll do what I can for you."

He made his way through the front door and collapsed on the sofa in the front room, unable to keep a moan from escaping his lips. Maggie clicked her tongue in concern and tossed him a blanket from across the room. He knew she didn't want to get too close, and he was glad for it. He needed her help, and she wouldn't be able to give it to him if she were driven mad with desire, which could very well happen even though she was old enough to be a grandmother.

"I'll be right back," she said. "I'm going to check on Martin." Then she disappeared into the back of the house.

Irial stared at the white ceiling of the simple cottage. They were all sick—the selkies, the púka, the pixies, and now the lepre-chauns—or at least *a* leprechaun. Even if he did make it to the Merrow, he suspected that they, too, would be suffering from this mysterious illness. But Maggie seemed fine, even though she had obviously been caring for the leprechaun. Were humans somehow immune? But what kind of sickness would affect only those from the Unseen world? And how had it spread so quickly? He was shiv-ering under the heavy wool blanket. Could *he* have caused this? As far as he knew, he was the only one who'd spent time with all the various afflicted species of the Unseen. But no—he hadn't seen a púka in years, let alone the one who'd given him a ride the previous day, and though he had heard of Logheryman, he had never before met him or any of his kind. He struggled to piece it all together. Then a sharp voice interrupted his thoughts.

"Martin! You get back in that bed this instant!"

Irial turned his head in the direction of Maggie's voice. A thin, grizzled man who he could only assume was Logheryman was limp-ing his way toward him. Dressed in a threadbare robe, he was lean-ing on a carved wooden cane. His face was gaunt and unnaturally gray, and his hair looked as if it had been falling out in chunks. He wavered and almost fell, but Maggie pulled his arm around her shoulders, muttering about "fool ideas" and "stubborn leprechauns."

"The time for looking after me will soon be over, my dear," Logheryman said as he allowed her to lead him to the large armchair across from Irial, and then arrange blankets over his lap. He laid his head against the back of the chair, as though holding his neck up required too much effort. But his eyes were clear and cogent when they settled on Irial.

"A gancanagh, she tells me," he said. Irial nodded. Logheryman regarded him silently for a moment before continuing. "Where did you come from?"

"The selkie colony on Inis Mór," Irial said. "It's the same there—they're all sick. I came to find help. I was trying to get to the Merrow, but the púka brought me here . . . well, to the pixies."

Logheryman raised a gnarled eyebrow. "The selkies as well? And the púka? Is it ill?"

"Yes," Irial answered. "I don't know where it went, but it must have expended a great effort to bring me this far."

"Dead, probably," Logheryman said in a hollow voice. He and Maggie exchanged a long glance. "How the tables have turned. Twice in recent days they have come to us for help, and now we must go to them."

"Who?" Irial asked.

Logheryman ignored him. "Maggie, my dear, would you mind fetching my boots?"

She scowled at him. "I will do no such thing! You're in no shape to go anywhere, magic boots or not!"

The leprechaun rolled his eyes. "I won't argue with you there," he said. "But this lad is much younger than I am, and he seems to be in slightly better shape. He must be, to have survived the journey from Inis Mór. A few thousand miles more won't kill him."

"And where will you be sending him, then?"

"They always knew how to contact me; they never told me how *I* could contact *them* if I were ever in need," he said, his words tinged with bitterness. "But I once sent them to a building in Halifax, care of my thousand-league boots. Her friend, the one who was burned, lives there now. Her name is Jane. She'll know how to find her."

"Find who?" Irial asked, thoroughly confused.

"Queen Cedar of the Tuatha Dé Danann," Logheryman answered. "I never thought I'd hear myself say it, but if anyone can help us, it's her. She seems to have made a habit of beating the odds."

CHAPTER 3

Cedar asked Nevan to convey the message that something urgent had come up and she wouldn't be at the Council meeting today. Then she and Rohan headed home, followed by her contingent of guards, so that Cedar could change into what she called "her civvies." Rohan told one of the guards to round up Murdoch.

"It will be too conspicuous for you to show up in Dublin surrounded by guards," Rohan explained. "But I'll feel better if at least two of us are with you."

Cedar didn't object, as long as it didn't delay their trip. But by the time she had slipped into her faded blue jeans and Rolling Stones T-shirt, Murdoch had arrived, looking rather grumpy in slacks and a sport jacket.

"For the record, I'd like it known that I object to the idea of bringing the druids—any druids—to our world in the first place," Murdoch said.

"They don't know where they are," Cedar said. "For all they know, they're still on Earth. This one won't be any different. Besides, you've assured me that our druid prisoners are well guarded."

Murdoch fell silent, and Cedar turned back to Rohan. "Ready?"

"Have you been to Trinity College before?" he asked.

"No, but I've seen pictures," she said, closing her eyes and concentrating on the photographs of the old brick buildings that she'd seen online. She opened the sidh in the air in front of them, adrenaline coursing through her veins.

"This way," Rohan said, immediately closing the sidh behind them. They were in a large cobblestone square surrounded by gray brick buildings. Tall, leafy trees tinted red and gold lined the pathways that crisscrossed the square. College students armed with iPhones and heavy backpacks pushed by them. Murdoch moved closer to Cedar as they hurried after Rohan. They rounded a corner, and entered a building through a side door. Cedar didn't have a clue where they were, but she was sure Rohan had done his research.

"Have *you* been here before?" she asked as she followed him up a narrow flight of stone stairs that had been smoothed by hundreds of years of footsteps.

"Yes," he answered, offering no other explanation. Finally, at the end of a long, unremarkable hallway, they stopped in front of a closed door labeled with a sign reading, "Helen Sullivan, PhD. Interim Keeper of Manuscripts."

"Will she know who—*what*—we are?" Cedar whispered.

"If she's a druid worth her salt, she will," Murdoch muttered in reply. Without knocking, he pushed open the door, entering first and giving the room a swift once-over.

Behind a tidy, polished desk in the center of the room sat a woman Cedar guessed to be in her sixties. She had short-cropped gray hair and rather severe features, with angled eyebrows that gave her a permanent look of disapproval. She was dressed in a simple black pantsuit, and a single pearl dangled from a fine gold chain around her neck. She stood up as soon as they entered.

"Excuse me, this is a private—" She stopped suddenly, her steely blue eyes growing wide. Cedar stepped forward.

"Helen Sullivan?"

The woman met her gaze, unflinching, her eyes still wide. "So it's true. The Tuatha Dé Danann have come to Earth. I heard the rumors . . . "

"We need you to come with us. We have some questions for you," Cedar interrupted.

At this, Helen frowned, her arched eyebrows becoming more pronounced. "Does this have something to do with Liam? Do you know where he is?"

"He's dead," Cedar said bluntly. "But we can't talk about it here." She watched closely for Helen's reaction, but the woman had become still as stone.

"And where would you like me to go?" Helen asked after a long silence.

"Somewhere we can ask you some questions," Cedar answered.

"You can ask me your questions here," she said, sitting down in her chair and folding her hands on the desk in front of her.

"I must insist," Cedar said, a new edge to her voice. "There is too much risk of interruption here." She glanced at Rohan and Murdoch, who both nodded.

Cedar opened a sidh back to Tír na nÓg, to the compound beneath the Hall where they were keeping the other druids. Helen jumped to her feet at the sight of the sidh. "Is that . . . ?"

"Yes," Cedar answered.

Helen's lips were tight. "I will answer your questions, whatever they are, since you give me no choice," she said. "But you must understand, I cannot be away from my work for long."

Cedar raised her eyebrows. Three Tuatha Dé Danann had just walked into her office, and this woman was worried about her work? Someone had priority issues—or was hiding something. She jerked her head toward the sidh. "Let's go."

Walking through it, Cedar let the other two Danann follow with Helen. As Rohan closed the sidh behind them, Cedar watched Helen assess her surroundings. While it did not appear that they were underground, they were in fact in the dungeons under the Hall. This place reminded Cedar of an old abandoned train station, cavernous and empty, with a gray, arched ceiling soaring above them. A series of archways lined each side of the chamber, and at first glance they appeared to be tunnels leading off in various directions underground. Two uniformed guards stood at each end of the chamber. Murdoch took the lead and they followed him down one of the tunnels, stopping at a solid wooden door set several feet within the wall. He took a large brass key from his pocket and shoved it into the lock. The door swung open to admit them.

Helen had remained silent up until now, but with one sweeping glance she took in the small room, which was outfitted plainly with a bed, a wardrobe, and a desk. "What is this?" she asked.

"It's where you'll stay until you tell us everything we need to know," Cedar said. Murdoch closed the door with an audible slam, and he and Rohan stood on either side of it.

"It looks like a cell to me," Helen said, wrinkling her nose in distaste. "I had heard the gods were arrogant. You have some nerve."

Cedar bristled. "What do you know about Liam's plans?" she asked, not wanting to waste any more time.

"Liam's plans for what? I don't know what you're talking about."

"You're telling me that you and Liam worked together every day, and he never once tried to recruit your help for his plan to steal the Lia Fáil and put Nuala on the throne?"

Helen's eyes narrowed. "Steal the Lia Fáil? The Stone of Destiny? No, he did not. And I find it hard to believe that he would be capable of such a thing. Liam was an excellent man and a fine scholar."

Cedar looked at Rohan, exasperated. He pulled a small silver goblet out of one of his inner pockets and handed it to her.

"You've heard of the goblet of Manannan mac Lir?" Cedar asked as she passed the goblet to Helen.

The druid nodded. "Heard of it, yes. But I did not know it actually existed."

"I'll ask you again," Cedar said. "Were you helping Liam and Nuala?"

Helen hesitated, staring at the goblet, which she was now turning over in her hands, examining it from every angle. Then she gripped it tightly and looked Cedar in the eye. "No."

The goblet remained intact, and Cedar frowned. Perhaps she had asked the wrong question.

"Did Liam tell you about his plan to prevent me from becoming queen?"

"No."

"Did he mention the Lia Fáil?"

"No."

"Did he talk about the druids returning to Tír na nÓg?"

"No."

"Do you know who Nuala is?"

At this Helen hesitated. "I had heard that some of the Danann were in our world. One of them, a woman, apparently contacted some of the druids. If that was Nuala, she didn't contact me, and it wouldn't have made a difference if she'd tried. I do not wish to be involved in the internal quarrels of the Tuatha Dé Danann." She gave Cedar a pointed look. "How did Liam die?"

"He was killed."

"By you?"

"Not entirely."

Helen raised an eyebrow at her. "I have answered your questions. I was not involved in any plot against you. I demand that you release me at once."

Cedar glared at her. "Both Nuala and Liam are dead. We know they weren't working alone. You were Liam's assistant—you worked with him every day. Do you honestly think I'm just going to let you walk out of here?" *I was fooled once,* Cedar told herself. *I trusted Liam so quickly, even when the others didn't, and he nearly killed Eden and Finn. I won't make the same mistake twice. She didn't even blink when I told her Liam was dead. She knows something she's not telling me.*

"I was his assistant *at the library*, not in some plot to take over the Otherworld. I wasn't even sure this realm existed until I was forced here . . . That's where I'm assuming we are, anyway. Look, your goblet is still whole. I have told you no lies."

She was telling the truth; the goblet was smooth and solid in her hands. Helen tried to give it back to her, but Cedar refused to take it. "I'm not done," she said. "Why were two druids working at the library of Trinity College Dublin? There aren't many druids left, so it's pretty odd that two would be working at the same place. Was he your mentor?"

"No, he was not." Helen sniffed. "Druids have an interest in ancient things. If you did your research, you'd realize that many druids are scholars of the ancient world. Our library possesses some of the most ancient and rare manuscripts in existence. It's not unusual that such treasures would draw more than one druid. Now, you must return me to the college at once."

"You seem unusually attached to your work," Cedar said.

"I am responsible for a priceless collection of artifacts. There is no one else there to keep them safe, so I *must* return!"

Cedar frowned at Helen's strangely worded comment. "I find it hard to believe that there is no one else in the entire library who can keep these things safe. Do you mean that there are no other *druids*? Why would that be important?"

Helen's jaw was clenched as she answered. "My work is very sensitive. Only I can properly oversee it. You do not understand the consequences."

Cedar kept an eye on the goblet, which was still in one piece in Helen's hand. The druid was far more flustered now than she'd been all day. Cedar knew she was on to something.

"Tell me about these consequences."

There was a long pause. "I can't."

"You can't or you won't?"

"It does not concern you. It is a sacred trust, given to the druids and no one else!" "What kind of sacred trust?"

"It is nothing. Nothing of importance."

At this, the goblet shattered, and Helen jumped back as the shards fell from her hand to the floor.

Cedar raised an eyebrow. "Now we're getting somewhere." She bent down and scooped up the shards. "I am queen of the Tuatha Dé Danann," she whispered to it, feeling a chill as it reformed in her hand. Then she handed it back to Helen.

"I told you I was not involved with any plot against you or anyone else. That is the truth," Helen said emphatically. "I didn't know what Liam and this Nuala woman were planning. And I *certainly* didn't help them. I have done nothing to harm you or your people."

"Did Liam know about this 'sacred trust'?" Cedar asked.

She saw Helen's eyes flicker toward the goblet before answering. "Yes."

"Tell me about it."

"No."

"Hiding things from me is not going to get you sent home sooner."

"Is it 'hiding things' to not tell you every detail about my life and work? You might be queen of the Tuatha Dé Danann, but you are not *my* queen."

Cedar took a step forward, so that they were standing eye to eye. "Liam was very kind to me. He offered to help us in our quest for the Lia Fáil. He told me stories about my adoptive mother, a druid who raised me—until Nuala killed her. He helped me understand her. He asked me to trust him, and I did. And then he betrayed us all in the worst possible way. He tortured my daughter and the man I love. He tried to burn us all alive. He would have allowed Nuala to start a new world war on Earth. I've learned how skilled druids are at keeping secrets—secrets that end up hurting innocent people. So forgive me if I don't exactly trust you . . . particularly not when I know you're hiding something from me."

She left the room, feeling a grim satisfaction at the sound of the heavy door clanging shut behind her.

CHAPTER 4

Jane rolled over and looked sleepily at the clock beside her bed. Ten a.m. She considered going back to sleep for an hour, but then she remembered that Felix was coming over today, and she didn't want him to find her still in bed—though they'd likely end up back there, anyway. He came over most Saturdays, if he could tear Cedar away from her official duties long enough to make a sidh for him. Jane allowed herself a wide grin as she stretched and sat up, running her hand through her short hair. She'd decided she liked it super-short after losing it all in the fire and then growing it back with one of Brighid's amazing spa potions. But she'd ditched the dirty blonde as soon as she came home from Cedar's coronation, choosing instead an ink black—for the time being. Her tattoos had all been burned off in the fire, and she already had appointments booked to get them replaced. Felix had laughed and said she changed her appearance more than Finn, and *he* was a shape-shifter. But he also said it was one of the things he loved about her, and he couldn't wait to see what she came up with next.

Jane's grin grew even wider at the thought. No one else in her long history of convoluted relationships made her feel like Felix did. She'd dated some strange guys in her time, but an Irish god took the cake. And even if he hadn't been a gorgeous, immortal being who could heal wounds with a single touch, she would have been just as smitten. Felix thought everything about her was amazing—not weird, not amusing, but fascinating. They could talk for hours, even though their conversations almost inevitably led to the bedroom . . . or the living room floor . . . or the kitchen table. It was as if she were the center of his universe. She couldn't remember ever feeling this way, and hoped that—this time—the relationship would last.

She headed into the kitchen to make some coffee, and laughed when she saw the note from Cedar. She often worried about how her friend was handling the pressures of royalty, but whenever they got a chance to talk—which was far too rare, in Jane's opinion—Cedar assured her that everything was fine. Which, of course, just made Jane worry more. She hadn't been allowed back to Tír na nÓg since Cedar's coronation. Cedar had made the sidhe off-limits, so she couldn't exactly have her best friend popping in and out as she pleased. Even Felix's regular visits to Earth had to be done in secret while Cedar struggled with the question of who should be able to use the sidhe, and for what purpose.

Jane stayed dressed in the negligee Felix had given her, a delicate lavender silk and black-lace number she would never have bought for herself. Still, she had to admit it looked damn good on her. She sipped her coffee and checked her email and social media, while at the same time keeping an eye on the starstone she and Felix used to communicate when he was in Tír na nÓg. She had it wrapped around her wrist like a bracelet so she'd notice right away when it started to glow. Usually he gave her some advance warning when he was on his way, but she liked being surprised once in a while.

Jane was wondering whether she should shower now or wait for Felix when a barely audible knock came from the direction of the door. She paused and cocked her head, wondering if it was maybe at a neighbor's door down the hall. But then it came again—a slow thump that sounded more like the fall of heavy footsteps than the staccato beats she was used to hearing against her door. She set her coffee cup down and padded over, peering out of the peephole to see who could possibly be visiting on a Saturday morning. She knew it wouldn't be Cedar or Felix—they both traveled by sidh and had a key as backup. At first, she saw nothing. Then she noticed a shadow on the hallway floor. From its shape, it looked as though a figure was crouched against her door, just out of sight of the peephole. Her breath caught in her throat and she paused, not sure what to do. She was about to head back to her room for a robe when she heard a plaintive voice from the hallway. "Please," it said, and the voice—though it was weak and sad—sent a shiver of pleasure down her spine. She quickly undid the safety bolt and swung the door open.

A young man was lying in a heap on the floor. He was wearing strange, old-fashioned boots with block heels and shiny silver buckles, along with faded jeans and a simple black T-shirt that clung tightly to his body. He was crouched so that she could only see the back of his head, a mass of black curls. Her heart rate, already higher than normal, started racing. And then he lifted his head and looked at her, and she gasped, unable to tear her gaze away. Something in the back of her mind triggered a warning, but everything else started to fade away as she continued to stare at him. There was an unearthly look about him; his eyes were black and wide set, he had a pronounced cupid's bow that drew her eyes immediately to his lips, and his skin glowed like moonlight reflecting off the ocean.

"Please, let me in," he said. The sound of his lightly accented voice was like sinking into a warm bath. "But don't touch me," he continued. "You can't . . . touch me."

"Who are you?" Jane asked once she regained her facilities of speech. "Are you hurt?"

The man struggled to his feet, and Jane put out an arm to help him. He convulsed and moved away, almost falling over again. "You mustn't!" he said, and she took a step back. He staggered forward into the apartment, and then turned around to face her. Standing up, he was even more arresting. He had broad shoulders and a narrow waist, and his black T-shirt emphasized the sculpted muscles of his arms and torso. He fixed his gaze on her, and she felt herself blushing. He looked away. "I need to talk to Queen Cedar," he said. Jane took a step toward him, but he raised a hand to stop her. "Don't come any closer," he warned. "They told me you would know how to contact her."

"Who are you?" Jane asked again. "How do you know about Cedar?"

"We need her help," he said, then wavered and fell to his knees again. Jane rushed to his side, her eyes wide with alarm.

"Should I call an ambulance?" she said, but he shook his head. "Here, let me help you onto the sofa," she said, and before he could move away, she took hold of his bare arm and tried to hoist him to his feet. He jerked away from her grasp, and she lost her balance, falling right on top of him. For a moment she just lay there, stunned. Then the most incredible feeling started to flood her veins. It was as if someone had injected a vial of pure sunlight into her brain. She could barely breathe through the pleasure of it. It distinctly reminded her of the one time she'd tried Ecstasy in university. She had liked the feeling too much, and had vowed never to do it again. But *this* feeling . . . She didn't want it to stop. She wanted more. She wanted to disappear into the body of the man beneath her; she wanted to join their souls so that no one could separate them.

She felt him twitching under her weight, and sat up. "You," she whispered. "You're the one."

"Oh no . . ." he moaned, staying on the floor.

"You're the one I've been waiting for my whole life," she exclaimed. She couldn't explain the feelings coursing through her, but she knew they were real. Lying on the floor in front of her was the most perfect man in existence, and fate had sent him directly to her. There was no one else in the world, just the two of them.

He moaned again, uttering soft curses under his breath. With effort, he sat up. She reached out to help him, but he snarled at her, "Don't. Touch. Me." She stopped, stung.

"That wasn't supposed to happen," he muttered. "The queen. Please, I need to speak with her at once. How can I contact her?"

"Cedar?" Jane asked in a plaintive voice. Why was Cedar always the center of attention? "You want to talk to Cedar? She's nothing special, you know. I mean, sure, they made her the queen, but it's really just because her father was king. She's not even really in charge over there; the Council does most of the work. I don't think she can help you. Why you don't tell *me* what's wrong? I'll do *anything*."

He answered her through gritted teeth, as if speaking was causing him physical pain. "No. I need to speak to the queen and no one else. I'm sorry . . . I warned you not to touch me. I didn't mean for this to happen. But . . . if you truly love me, you will take me to her."

"I *do* love you!" Jane exclaimed. "But I don't understand why you keep talking about *her*! She doesn't have anything to do with us! And besides, I can't take you to her. The sidhe are closed."

"But they've been reopened—at least, that's the rumor. Logheryman told me you are her best friend. You *must* have a way of contacting her."

Jane felt hot tears pricking the corners of her eyes, and she began to sob. "Do you love her?" she wailed, her body convulsing.

He ignored her. "What is that?" he asked, his eyes on the starstone attached to Jane's wrist. "Is that . . . a starstone?"

"This?" Jane said, tearing off the bracelet. "No, it's nothing. Just a cheap trinket."

"It's glowing," he said. "Is the queen trying to contact you? Answer it!"

Jane felt panic rising in her throat. She knew what the starstone meant—someone else was about to come between her and the man she loved. "I don't want to answer it! I don't want him to come here! He will just ruin everything!"

"He? Who? Another of the Tuatha Dé Danann? *Answer it!*"

"No!" Jane wailed, whipping the starstone across the room. "No one will come between us!"

The man collapsed fully onto the ground and covered his face with his hands. "This isn't happening," he muttered. She flung herself onto him, wanting to feel that burst of sunlight again. He tried to fight her off, but she was stronger. She was about to bring her lips down to meet his when another person's voice made her swivel around in surprise.

"Jane?"

Felix was standing in the living room, a bouquet of purple and yellow flowers in his hand, the shimmer of a sidh behind him. The look on his face was one of shock—and betrayal. But it had no impact on Jane, who shifted defensively in front of the man who was splayed across her floor.

"What's going on?" Felix asked, looking past Jane, who was still in her negligee, to the man behind her. The man started to speak, but Jane cut him off.

"Get out," she snarled at Felix, rising to her feet. "It's over between us. I've found someone new, and we love each other very much. Now *go.*"

Felix's face twisted with pain, and his cheeks turned bright red. He tossed the flowers to the ground and opened his mouth to speak, but then he took another look at the figure lying on the floor. He stared at him for a long moment, then walked around Jane and peered down at the man's face. He let out a long, heavy sigh.

"Hello, Irial," he said. "I didn't expect to see *you* again."

CHAPTER 5

Cedar paused outside the door that led to the common room of her home, where the guests were already gathering for Eden's birthday party. She had gone from the dungeons to her room so that she could swap her jeans and T-shirt for a light blue gown. She took a deep breath, trying to switch gears from queen and interrogator to mother of the birthday girl.

"She's telling the truth about Liam," Rohan had pointed out as they left the dungeons, leaving a guard at Helen's door. "She didn't know what he was doing."

"They're druids," Cedar had retorted. "We don't know what they're capable of. They managed to get inside Eden's head, so how can you be sure they haven't learned how to trick the goblet?" Besides, Helen was definitely hiding something, and she wasn't going anywhere until Cedar learned what it was.

As she slipped in through the door, the chatter in the room died down and several of the guests took a step back and bowed.

"Stop bowing!" she said, a smile spreading across her face. "It's a party, for goodness sake!" She wound her way through the room to Eden, who was sitting beside Finn at the head of a long table weighed down with pink and yellow flowers and several trays of food. Friends old and new surrounded them. Finn's twelve-year-old sister Molly was the closest in age to Eden. The two got along well, and they shared the experience of having been born and brought up on Earth. But Cedar knew that if this party had been held back in Halifax, Eden would have been surrounded by a gaggle of little girls, not stuck in a room full of grown-ups.

"Happy birthday, baby!" she said, giving her daughter a big hug.

"Thanks," Eden said, but she didn't look at all pleased.

"Um . . . do you like the balloons?" Cedar asked her. "I got them from home; I didn't think they'd have balloons here, and I know you like them."

"They're okay."

Cedar stood up and clapped her hands. "Thank you for coming to celebrate Eden's seventh birthday!" Everyone in the room cheered and clapped. "Please, sit down and enjoy the food!"

The guests found seats and turned their attention to the feast, loading up their plates. Cedar had asked Seisyll and Riona, who had volunteered to help, to prepare Eden's favorite dishes. Some of the party guests had never been to Earth, and they were examining the offerings with interest—ham and pineapple pizza, spaghetti with meatballs, and macaroni and cheese. Finn filled a plate for Eden, but she just pushed the food around her plate with her fork.

"What's the matter, Eden? Are you feeling sick?" Cedar asked, but Eden shook her head. "How were the ponds in the mountains?"

"They were great!" Eden said, brightening up for a moment. "I want to go there again!"

"I'm sure we can," Cedar answered. "I'd love to see it."

Eden's face fell. "Well, it's kind of me and Daddy's special place. Would it be okay if just the two of us went there?"

"Oh," Cedar said. "Of course. I'm sure he'd love to take you again."

"So, Your Majesty!" boomed a voice to her left. Gorman was looking at her with an air of great amusement. "You skipped out on holding court today—again."

She smiled back at him, trying to look relaxed. "I'm sorry. Something important came up."

Rohan, who was seated next to Gorman, laughed. "Your father was the same way," he said. "Constantly giving his guards the slip to go off hunting, which he greatly preferred to meetings. Used to drive them mad."

"Not that you ever tried to stop him," Riona said, giving her husband an affectionate look. "You were as bad as he was."

"Well, he needed me to come with him so I could close the sidhe, that's all!" Rohan blustered.

"Mum, where is Felix? He said he'd be back in time for my party," Eden asked.

Cedar looked around—it was true, Felix wasn't anywhere in sight. "I don't know, baby," she said. "Back from where? Where did he go?"

Eden suddenly looked guilty, and she wouldn't meet her mother's eyes. Cedar fixed her with a sharp gaze and lowered her voice to a whisper so that only Eden and Finn could hear her. "Wait a second. Did you open a sidh for him? You *know* you're not supposed to do that." She gave Finn an exasperated look. "Did you know?"

"No," he said, frowning. "It must have been while I was setting up for the party. Eden, I'm surprised at you."

"He said it was important," Eden muttered. "I thought it would be okay."

Cedar leaned close to her, still keeping her voice low. "It's not okay, not even for Felix. I'm assuming he went to see Jane?" Eden nodded. "He should know better, and I'm going to talk to him. Lots of people are going to want you to open sidhe for them, honey, and you have to say no to them all—even people you know."

"But he said you open sidhe for him all the time!" Eden protested. "And how else is he going to see Jane?"

47

"Shh! Felix and Jane are a very special exception to the rule, but you need to let Mummy deal with it, okay? I don't want you to open any sidhe unless I'm with you. It's for your own safety. Did you leave the sidh open for him?"

Eden nodded again. "It's in his house," she said with her head bowed. Cedar decided to drop the issue, but she planned to have some firm words with Felix later. The last thing she wanted was for people to think they could use Eden as their own personal travel agent.

The conversation around the table flowed easily, and as soon as dinner was finished, Seisyll floated a large pink frosted cake in front of Eden. Seven delicate white candles stood in a circle in its center. "Riona tells me that the custom on Ériu is to light the candles, and then have the child blow them out," Seisyll said. "Would you like to do the honors, Your Majesty?"

Cedar hesitated for a moment, and then said, "Of course." She tried to steady her racing pulse. She just needed to focus, to concentrate—and to avoid blowing up her daughter's birthday party. Slowly, she raised a hand, keeping her eyes focused on the cluster of wicks in front of her. The power built up inside her before flowing through her fingers in a gentle, controlled stream. There was a whoosh and a short burst of flame, and then she dropped her hand and released the breath she hadn't realized she was holding. All seven candles were lit, and she hadn't burned anything down. Finn winked at her from across the table.

"And now we sing!" Riona said, getting to her feet. She led them all in a round of "Happy Birthday," and the guests clapped as Eden took a deep breath and blew out the candles. As soon as she was done and Finn was serving the cake, Eden looked at her mother and asked, "Can I be excused?"

Cedar frowned. "Already? But don't you want to have some cake?"

"Can I just take it to my room?" Eden asked.

"What's going on? You've been acting very rude."

Eden's face grew dark, and she lowered her head. Cedar drew her chair closer to her daughter's and leaned in. "What is it, baby?"

Raising her eyes to meet her mother's for a moment, Eden quickly looked away. "It's just . . . I mean, I know you planned this party and everything, but all it does is remind everyone that I'm different from them. The Tuatha Dé Danann don't *have* birthday parties."

"They don't?" Cedar asked. She automatically looked at Finn for confirmation, but he was still passing out slices of cake to their guests. Eden shook her head.

"And all the human food, and the balloons, and everything. It's not how it's done here, and I want to be like them. I *am* like them!"

"Of course you are," Cedar said. "I just thought you might be missing your friends and school and the way things were back home."

"Maybe I should be, but I'm not. I don't want to go back. I like it here. And I don't want to feel like I stick out any more than I already do."

"Well, what about Molly? She's in the same situation as you. Maybe you guys can help each other out."

"Yeah, but her parents lived here, like, forever before they went to Earth. They know *everything* about the Tuatha Dé Danann, and they've been teaching her since she was born. She already knows way more than I ever will. And no one looks at her and thinks, 'Oh, there's that human girl.'"

Cedar reached out to hug her daughter, but Eden pulled away. "Can I just . . . go now?" she asked. Mutely, Cedar nodded, watching as Eden slipped through the golden door, heading for her room.

Finn returned to his seat. "Where did Eden go?" he asked.

Cedar stared at him. "Why didn't you tell me that people don't have birthday parties here?"

He looked taken aback. "Well, I knew you really wanted to do this for her . . . and I thought she'd like it."

"Well, she didn't. And now I feel like an idiot for not picking up on it."

Finn reached over and covered her hand with his own. "I'm sorry. I should have told you that we don't really do birthday parties. It doesn't make much sense when you live so long."

"It's okay," Cedar replied. "I thought she'd like it too. We always used to have a party for her at home. My mum would make a big meal like this and a fancy cake—one that would take all day just to frost. But I should have asked about the customs here. I know how badly Eden wants to fit in."

Seisyll, who had apparently overheard their exchange, patted Cedar's arm and said, "Don't worry too much about it. Eden's just trying to figure out who she is. Eventually she'll learn to celebrate her human upbringing *and* her identity as a Danann. She just needs to sort it out."

Cedar gave her a grateful smile. "Thanks. Sometimes I feel like she's seven going on fourteen. One second I'll see her clutching one of her stuffed animals from home . . . the next she doesn't want anything to do with Earth. I feel like I'm walking on eggshells trying to figure this out."

"I'll go talk to her," Finn said, standing up. "I know for a fact that some of her presents are very unhuman—maybe that will convince her to come back to the party."

Before he could leave, they were interrupted by the arrival of one of Cedar's guards, who had been stationed outside the house. "Pardon, Your Majesty, but there is a boy at the door who says he must speak to you. I told him to leave, but he insists he has an urgent message."

Cedar stood up, intrigued. "Of course," she said. "Send him in."

A moment later a thin boy with a shock of curly red hair stood nervously in the entranceway. He looked to be about ten years old, and Cedar wondered idly if Eden had met him. He was breathing heavily, as if he had just run a great distance.

"I have an urgent message from Toirdhealbhach, the healer," the boy said once she reached him, his voice hushed. "He begs you to come to his house at once. He says your friend, the human, is in great danger."

The room was silent, and Cedar wondered if anyone had over-heard him. The boy looked around nervously. Cedar drew closer and knelt down. "Jane?" she whispered. "She's here in Tír na nÓg?"

The boy nodded, then whispered back, "She's at his house. He sent me to get you."

Cedar stood up quickly, and then raised her voice to address their guests. "Sorry for the interruption, everyone, but it seems I have to step out for just a minute. Eden's taking a little break, but she'll be back to open her gifts. Please, stay and enjoy yourselves! I'll be back as soon as I can."

"You'd better come with me," she said to the boy. She motioned for Finn to join them and ducked through the doorway that led to the inner rooms.

"What's going on?" he asked as soon as the door closed behind them, giving the messenger a curious look. Cedar told him what the boy had said.

"Can you come with me to close the sidh that Eden opened to Jane's place?" she asked. "I still think it's a good idea for you to talk to her after that. She shouldn't be alone right now. I'll stay with Felix for a while to see what's up with Jane."

Finn nodded. "Do you know what's wrong with her?" he asked the boy.

"No, sir," the boy replied. "Only that I was asked to come here and tell the queen that her friend was in danger."

"It must be bad if Felix brought her back here," Cedar said. She frowned as she opened a sidh that led just outside Felix's house. "It's okay," she said to the boy, who was looking at the glimmering patch of air with alarm. He and Finn followed Cedar through the sidh to the cluster of boulders that concealed the entrance to Felix's house. Cedar pressed on a round stone, and one of the boulders slid away to reveal a curving staircase. The air around them grew brighter as they descended, and she could hear the boulder sliding back into place at the top of the stairs. The first time she had visited Felix's house, she had laughed and called it the "man cave," although it was certainly more spectacular than any cave she had ever seen. The walls were smooth slate gray, and the rooms were all airy and expansive.

The still-open sidh to Earth was visible in the front room of his house, shimmering in the air. Finn walked over and closed it with a wave of his arm. Then he gave Cedar a tight hug. "Good luck," he said. "You take care of Jane, and I'll take care of Eden. Hopefully we can do something to salvage her birthday."

"Okay," Cedar said. "Keep me posted." Finn headed back up the staircase to let himself out.

The messenger boy was still hovering nearby. "He's back here," he said, and Cedar followed him toward what Felix called his "halls of healing," a labyrinth of small rooms connected by silver doors and glowing white hallways. According to Felix, it had been built by his grandfather, Dian Cecht, one of the Elders. Felix's mother, also a healer, had added on several rooms, and Felix had been refining each of the rooms' special abilities. Some rooms increased relaxation, others numbed pain, and still others lowered the body temperature or had anti-inflammatory properties.

The hallway was illuminated by floating orbs of light that drifted along the ceiling. The boy stopped so suddenly Cedar almost ran into him. "He's just in there," he said, pointing to a door on the left that was open a crack. He stayed in the hallway while she pushed it open.

The sight in front of her was pure chaos. Felix and Jane were in the center of the room. For a split second Cedar thought she'd walked in on a personal moment again, but then she realized that Felix was trying to restrain Jane. Her hair was plastered to her head, and her face was red and shining with sweat. She was fighting him as hard as she could, straining toward the bed in the corner, where a young man lay supine. "Let me go to him!" she was yelling in a shrill voice.

"Jane?" Cedar asked, her jaw dropping.

Her friend turned at the sound of her name. "You," she said, her voice filled with venom. "You've come to take him away from me, haven't you? I won't let you! Don't go near him!"

"What the hell is going on?" Cedar asked.

Felix jerked his head toward the corner. "He's a gancanagh. Jane's infected."

Cedar had never heard of a gancanagh. She looked at the man on the bed. He appeared to be young, maybe in his twenties, with pale, smooth skin and a tumble of dark curls. He was beautiful, and she felt something stir pleasantly inside her. At first she thought he was unconscious, but then he opened his eyes and looked directly at her.

"The queen. At last," he whispered.

Cedar moved closer to the bed, ignoring Jane's wails of protest. She was about to ask the stranger who he was and where he had come from, when Jane finally managed to wrench herself free of Felix's grasp. She rushed toward Cedar and slapped away her hands.

"He's mine. Don't touch him," she snarled.

Cedar's eyes widened. "What's going on?" she asked again. "Why are you acting like this?"

"I love this man. He is mine. And that—*beast*," Jane spat, jerking her head at Felix, "is trying to keep us apart."

Cedar looked in horror at Felix, who was rummaging through one of the cabinets lining the wall, his jaw clenched. "Don't let her touch him," he said to Cedar, not looking up. Just as he said it, Jane tried to make a lunge for the man on the bed, but Cedar grabbed her arm and held it tight.

"Let go!" Jane snarled. "You're hurting me!"

"Talk to me!" Cedar pleaded. "What do you mean, you love this man? Who is he? What about Felix?"

But Jane didn't have a chance to answer, because Felix had crept up behind her and held a handful of crushed petals under her nose. She started to jerk away, but it was too late—she inhaled deeply, and then her eyes closed and she fell backward into the healer's arms.

"Thank you," Felix said to Cedar. He settled Jane in an overstuffed chair in the corner. "That'll keep her down for the moment."

"What's wrong with her?" Cedar asked.

"Irial is a gancanagh, a male succubus," Felix said, his eyes still fixed on Jane. "Not like the leannán sí that bit Finn," he added when he noticed the look on Cedar's face. "The male and female succubi are quite different—the only similarity is that they attract and ensnare humans. He didn't need to bite her. Irial's skin is toxic to human women—it drives them mad with love. He says he came to Jane looking for you, and she touched him. At first . . . well, I wasn't sure what I was seeing, but then I recognized Irial."

"You've met him before?"

"It was a long time ago. I was at a festival in Derry, visiting a, um, friend. This was before the sidhe were closed, obviously. I hadn't seen one of his kind in years, so I thought they were extinct. Anyway,

I recognized what he was right away. Either he was incredibly cruel, or he didn't have a clue what he was doing."

"What was he doing?"

"He was out in public in a human town, for starters. Just walking around the festival as if he owned the place. There were women all around, and any one of them could have brushed against him by accident. As I watched, he started chatting with one, this pretty young girl with a basket of flowers. She was holding out a flower for him to buy, and he was reaching for her hand. That was when I intervened."

"Intervened?"

"I basically threw him over my shoulder and removed him from the situation. Then I gave him a lecture I'm sure he hasn't forgotten."

"But he didn't know what he was? He wasn't trying to hurt the girl, was he?"

"No," Felix said. "He knew women liked him, but he never stayed in one place long enough to find out what happened to them after he left. He was devastated, and I don't blame him. Why these creatures even exist in the first place is beyond me."

"So what will happen to Jane?"

Felix's tone was grim. "If I hadn't found her, she would have gone mad with love and eventually died."

"*What?*" Cedar said, swiveling around to look at her sleeping friend. "But that's not going to happen now, is it?"

His jaw hardened. "No," he answered, but didn't elaborate. Cedar started breathing again.

She looked down at Irial, who was silently watching them. "What's wrong with him? Is he sick?"

"Ask him yourself," he answered. "It seems so. But I don't know why. He says he needs to speak to you. I'm going to move Jane into another room so that I can start a healing potion for her. I haven't had the time to properly question him yet. You don't need to worry. He can't infect you, only humans."

Felix hoisted Jane into his arms and left the room without sparing Irial another glance. Cedar drew up a chair beside the bed and sat down. Irial's dark eyes were fixed on her, and she felt a warm, tingling feeling in her stomach again.

"I'm sorry about your friend," he said, his hoarse voice sending a thrill up her back. "I really did try to warn her."

"Well, here I am," she said. "Why did you want to see me?"

"A great sickness has come upon the Unseen. Logheryman said you might be able to help us."

"The Unseen?" Cedar asked.

He gave her a strange look, and she assumed this was yet another thing she should know. "The magical beings of Ériu, like myself. The Merrow. Leprechauns. Pixies. And others."

"What kind of sickness?" she asked.

In a faltering voice, Irial told her about the strange illness that had fallen upon the selkies, and his travels, which had eventually led him to her. "Then I met this woman in the woods," he continued, "who said she was one of the fili."

"Maggie?" Cedar asked, relieved to finally know something.

Irial nodded. "She kept her distance, but she led me to Logheryman. He's the one who told me to find you. He said he was sure you could help us."

Irial looked at her with desperate, imploring eyes. He seemed so lost, so helpless lying there on the bed, and he had risked so much to find her. She reached out a hand to brush one of the curls off his forehead, but checked herself.

"Is Logheryman sick too?" she asked.

"Yes, and worse than I am, I'm afraid, which is why he sent me to search for you rather than coming himself. He gave me his thousand-league boots to make the journey. I don't think he has much time left."

"What do you mean? Is he dying?"

Irial nodded.

Cedar's heart constricted painfully. "Is it contagious?" she asked. "Will it spread to all of the Unseen? And then to us?" As far as she knew, she and Felix were the only Danann to have come in close contact with the gancanagh; perhaps if they quarantined themselves they could keep this sickness from spreading.

"I don't think so," he said. "When I found the púka, he was already sick. And the leprechaun too. The different species of the Unseen do not have so much contact with each other that it would spread that quickly. I do not believe that either the humans or the Tuatha Dé Danann are at risk."

"We're going to help you," Cedar said earnestly, leaning toward him. "You don't have to worry."

"Don't make promises I can't keep, Your Majesty," said a voice from behind her. Felix was standing in the doorway, his face still hard.

"What do you mean?" she asked.

He moved a few paces away and gestured for her to join him. "At this point I have no idea what's wrong with him—or with any of the other Unseen—if he's telling the truth," he said in an undertone.

"You think he's lying?"

"I don't know. The gancanagh are known to be . . . devious. It might just be coincidence that the beings he ran into were also sick." When Cedar continued to look unconvinced, he added, "Look, I know for a fact that he didn't stop getting involved with women after I told him what he was. There have been too many reports of women wasting away from a broken heart."

"And you think that's because of him?"

"There are signs," he answered. "I'm just saying that we shouldn't be so quick to trust him."

"But Logheryman sent him to get help," Cedar insisted. "He even gave him his thousand-league boots, and you know how much he values those. Are you saying there's nothing you can do?"

"No. But it will take time for me to figure out what's making him sick. And right now my priority is Jane."

Cedar couldn't argue with this. "Should I take her back to Halifax?"

"No. Her metabolism is running so high right now that she'll burn through the sedative I gave her quicker than I'd like. I need to figure out exactly what the toxin is doing to her, so I'll have to ask Irial a few questions. She's in the next room, and could wake at any moment. Will you stay with her?"

"Of course."

"Restrain her physically if you have to," he said. "She needs to stay away from him. I'll work as fast as I can."

Sparing one last glance at Irial, Cedar slipped into the hallway. When she pushed open the silver doorway to the next room, Jane was trying to sit up, looking around in confusion.

Cedar rushed to her friend's side at once. Jane blinked at her, and Cedar was reminded of Eden when she woke in the middle of the night and didn't know where she was. Then Jane's face crumpled and she started to sob. Cedar wrapped her in an embrace.

"I . . . need you . . . to do something for me," Jane whispered between sobs.

"Of course," Cedar said at once. "Anything."

"Please. Don't let him cure me."

"Oh, Jane," Cedar said, drawing her friend in closer.

Several minutes later Jane was still crying, but she jerked up her head when the door opened. When she saw Felix, her lips drew back in a snarl.

"Where is he?" she demanded. "What have you done with him?"

"Can I talk to you?" he said stiffly to Cedar.

Cedar joined Felix in the hallway, ignoring her friend's fevered protests.

"We can't leave her alone for too long," he said. "She might hurt herself."

"Did you find out how to cure her?"

"It can be done," he told her in a whisper. "I can isolate and remove the toxin, and she should recover. It's just . . ." He glanced at the closed door, through which Jane's sobs were still audible.

"What is it?"

"The toxin makes her believe she is in love with him, as you know. And obviously, it's very, very strong. So the withdrawal will also be very intense. She will feel as though someone she loved more than anything in the world has died. I'm afraid it will be very painful for her."

Cedar winced. She remembered all too well the pain she'd experienced when Finn left her, how she'd barely been able to function for months. For Jane to have to go through such intense pain just because she'd tried to help a stranger seemed like the worst kind of injustice.

"It's the only way," he whispered. "And I need to act fast."

"What can I do?" Cedar said.

"Just being with her will help. The process won't hurt her physically, but she'll be in deep emotional grief." He smiled sadly. "They say you can love even more after you know what it's like to lose, right? So hopefully . . ." He didn't finish his sentence, but Cedar could read the fear on his face. She tried to smile back at him.

"It's not easy," she said. "But yes, love can come back."

◠◡

Several hours later, Cedar lay staring at the ceiling, drenched in her best friend's tears—and her own. Jane was finally asleep beside her. Cedar had held her down while Felix forcibly injected her with the antidote to Irial's toxin. Jane had cried and screamed and cursed and begged them to let her die, but instead they'd only given her more until Felix was certain all of the toxin had been neutralized by the antidote. She closed her eyes and listened to Jane's even breathing, glad that her friend had finally found some peace in sleep. She thought about what Irial had told her; now that she knew Jane was going to survive, her thoughts were returning to the Unseen. What could possibly be making the magical beings on Earth sick? Felix had examined Irial thoroughly at her request, and had found no trace of disease or decay, no poison, no obvious wounds. He had checked for viruses, infections, enchantments—everything. There was nothing to explain it. Cedar rubbed her temples. There was also the druid woman to worry about, and whatever she was hiding. And Eden . . . Cedar had missed most of her birthday. She had talked to her earlier using the starstone, so at least she'd gotten the chance to say good night. Eden had excitedly told her about her new presents, which had included her very own lute—which taught its owner how to play it—and a tiny dragon figurine, which came to life whenever you put it in fire. Cedar had taken this as a sign that she was forgiven for the party fiasco.

Just a few minutes of sleep, she told herself, willing her body to relax. *And when I wake, I'll know exactly what to do about everything . . .*

The next thing she knew, she was sitting in a rocking chair on the veranda of the home where she was raised. The sun was sparkling off the bay, and she could hear the seagulls as they screeched and circled above.

"Here you go, dear."

Maeve was sitting in the chair next to her, her lap covered by a hand-knit afghan. She was holding out a tall glass tumbler of lemonade.

"Mum," Cedar whispered, accepting the glass. She took a sip and puckered. It was sour, nothing like the sickly sweet concoction her mother had always made for her as a child.

"Beautiful day, isn't it?" Maeve asked, looking out over the ocean.

Cedar followed her gaze. Instead of seagulls, a dragon was circling overhead, small bursts of flame occasionally erupting from its mouth. She looked down and watched as the long curved neck of a sea serpent emerged from the ocean. It stretched out, looked toward shore, and then disappeared back under the waves.

"Where are we?" Cedar asked, but Maeve didn't answer. She just kept gazing out over the ocean, rocking back and forth in the wooden chair.

"Your father used to sit in that chair, you know," Maeve said. "We spent hours out here. Just talking. He used to say it was one of his favorite places on Ériu."

"Are you . . . ," Cedar began, not sure how to phrase it. "Where *are* you? Are you . . . with him now?"

"I've gone on," Maeve answered simply. "It's nothing *you* will ever need to worry about, if you keep yourself out of trouble, that is. Tell me, dear, how are you doing?"

"Fine," Cedar said automatically, but then she felt words gushing from her mouth like a faucet that had been suddenly unblocked. "No, not fine. Not really. I'm worried about Eden; all she wants is to be Tuatha Dé Danann, but *I'm* not the one who can help her with that, since I'm just figuring it out for myself. I try to reach out to her, but it feels like she's pulling away from me. I keep thinking maybe she blames me for everything that has happened—for getting kidnapped, for you dying, and for everything that has happened since. But she doesn't like to talk about it; when I bring it up, she just pretends everything is okay. Then there's this druid woman who worked with Liam, and she says she wasn't involved, but she knows *something*—the goblet proved that. And now there's this problem with the leprechauns and selkies and who knows what else here on Earth, but Felix says he doesn't know how to help them. If I don't do something about it, though, I think they're all going to die. And I don't know how to handle any of it. And Finn . . . I'm so glad he's back, but I can't help but worry that I'm going to lose him again. It feels like it's too good to be true."

Maeve rubbed Cedar's back, just like she used to do when Cedar was a child. "There, there," she whispered. "You have a lot on your plate, it's true. But it's of your own making, Cedar. No one forced you to move to Tír na nÓg. No one forced you to become queen. No one forced you to get involved with these people in the first place. I warned you against it. If you had just listened to me, you would be living a normal, peaceful life. We all would. But you've always had to do things your way. I can't bail you out anymore. And if I give you advice, you'll probably do just the opposite. So . . . I'm afraid you're on your own."

Cedar sat very still. What else had she been expecting? That her mother would sympathize? Maeve was right. She *was* on her own. She stood up and walked down to the water, not looking back. Her feet pounded across the grass and she broke into a run, down the hill until she had reached the edge of the water. For what seemed like a long time, Cedar just stared at the horizon. Nevan had told her the Irish had once believed you could get to Tír na nÓg by sailing west. But Cedar knew that there was nothing between where she stood and the coast of Galway. Nothing but water. And maybe a sea monster or two. She wondered what it would be like to return to the days when she knew nothing about the Tuatha Dé Danann, when her daughter was just a normal little girl, when she thought she understood her place in the world. But she couldn't go back. Not anymore.

When she returned to the veranda, both chairs were empty. She didn't know why, but she felt calmer. She had spoken the truth to her mother, and had received a typical Maeve response in return—and she was still here. She walked around the side of the house to her mother's grave, under the reaching branches of the tree she had been named for. Both of her mothers were buried here, but today she had words for only one of them.

"You're wrong. You've always been wrong about me. But I believed you—I *still* believe you sometimes. I'm sorry you felt like your whole life was a disappointment. I'm sorry Brogan didn't love you. I'm sorry I hurt you by choosing a different path than the one you wanted for me. But I'm not sorry I chose it. I'm done living under that shadow. Done with feeling like I won't ever be good enough. Maybe you're right—maybe I will fail. Maybe I *won't* be able to help everyone who needs it. But I'm sure as hell going to try."

CHAPTER 6

Eden looked over her shoulder to make sure no one had seen her, and then closed the sidh behind her. The evening hung around her like a warm, heavy blanket. She closed her eyes and took a deep breath. The air smelled like freedom. The sky was deepening into indigo, and stars were beginning to awaken for the night. Not for the first time, Eden wondered if they were the same stars she'd seen on Earth the few times she'd been allowed to stay up late enough to see them.

She didn't need anyone's permission now. She sat down on the edge of a calm pool to watch the reflection of the moon rising into the night sky. Her parents thought she was sleeping, and she knew she'd get in major trouble if they caught her. She felt a twinge of guilt as she settled into the tall grass. But she liked it here . . . and the other places she had explored. Every single day she was surrounded by chaperones—either her dad or Riona or Molly or Nevan or her mum, when she had time. She liked being with them, but they all treated her like a child. And she didn't feel like a child anymore.

She picked a twig up off the ground and waved it in the air like a magic wand. Opening and closing the sidhe was cool, but she wished she could transform into an animal like her dad or move things with her mind like Riona's friend, Seisyll. "Abracadabra," she whispered, pointing the twig at the water. Unsurprisingly, nothing happened. "Hmph." She sat and stared into the depths. She didn't know why *she* always got in trouble for using her power, when no one else did. It was fine for her dad to turn into butterflies and for her mum to light birthday candles with her fingertips and for everyone else to use their powers whenever they wished, but she always had to ask first; she always had to make sure a grown-up was with her.

Well, I do have a grown-up with me, she thought. *Inside.* She could feel her there, the older Eden who had saved her mum from Nuala in the dream. Every once in a while, she would have a thought that wasn't quite her own or feel some strange emotion she had never experienced before. She wasn't sure, but she figured these things came from the older Eden. Did everyone have an older version of themselves inside? None of her friends back in Halifax had ever said anything about it. She wondered if it had something to do with being Tuatha Dé Danann . . . or if it was just her.

She lay back in the grass and crossed her hands behind her head. *I'd better not fall asleep here, or I'll really catch it*, she thought. She closed her eyes and tried to focus on the feeling inside her—the part that was her, but not quite. *Are you there?* she asked. She waited, trying to remember what had happened the other times she'd made contact.

Hey, Eden.

Eden's eyes flew open, and then she slammed them shut again. "Are you still there? Don't go away!" she said out loud. She could feel it stronger than ever, this second presence within her. It had never spoken directly to her before.

I'm here.

"What . . . who are you?"

You know who I am. You will be me one day.

"I wish it was right now."

She heard the other voice laugh. *Patience is a virtue . . . or so they tell me. But I'm afraid neither of us has very much of it.*

"Why can I talk to you?"

We're special, you and I.

"How?"

I can't tell you everything, now, can I?

"Why not?"

Was I really this inquisitive as a child?

"Mum says I ask more questions than there are answers."

And does your mum know you are lounging by the side of a moonlit pond far past your bedtime? It's a lovely spot, by the way.

"Thanks. She doesn't know. Are you going to tell her?"

I have no way of doing that.

"Can I become you sooner?"

Everything must take its proper course.

"What does that mean?"

It means, little one, that you have an amazing life right now. However . . .

"Yes?"

There is someone here in Tír na nÓg who might be able to help you, if you are interested. She could teach you how to control your power— and how to increase it. She can teach you how to focus. And that will help put you on your path to becoming me.

"Who is it?"

She's a druid, just like Gran.

"Is she one of the druids who attacked us in Ireland?"

No. She's very powerful, but she won't hurt you. Her name is Helen. Find her.

Eden felt the presence recede, like a wave pulling away from the shore. She stood and brushed the grass off her pajamas, then walked back to the tree where she'd first opened the sidh and placed a hand on its trunk. As soon as it started to glow she walked through it, quickly closing the sidh behind her. Her room was dark and mercifully empty—her parents had not discovered she was gone. She was tired, but her mind was whirring. She wanted to find this Helen woman right away, but she didn't think she could stay awake any longer. Tomorrow, when everyone else was busy, she'd find her. Then she'd get some answers.

∽

When Cedar woke, there was a bright light shining in her eyes.

"Sorry," Felix said as Cedar squinted and shielded her face with her hands. One of the light globes that had been floating in the hallway was now suspended over the bed where she and Jane had been sleeping. Jane was awake beside her, but lying very still as Felix waved his hands up and down about six inches from her body. Her eyes were bloodshot and puffy, and she was staring sightlessly up at the ceiling. Cedar clutched Jane's hand. She knew how horrible those first few days of heartache were. Felix stood up and took a step back.

"Well, it's all gone," he said. "I've double- and triple-checked. No more toxin. You'll be back to normal as soon as . . . well, soon, I hope." Jane managed a watery smile, and then rolled over into the fetal position.

"Can I talk to you, Cedar?" Felix asked. Cedar gave Jane a long hug and then climbed out of the bed, smoothing back her hair. Cedar was still wearing the blue dress from the previous day. Felix held open the door and they stepped into the hallway together.

"Is she okay in there by herself?" Cedar asked.

"She'll be fine," he said. "That is, she's not a danger to herself or others anymore. She's just . . . heartbroken."

"Are *you* going to be okay?" Cedar asked, placing her hand on his arm.

He was silent for a long moment. "Maybe. I don't know," he finally answered. "I know she wasn't being herself, but . . . Anyway, I had another one of the healers run the tests on Irial again, just in case the, well, situation was clouding my judgment. Same result. Nothing."

"I'm going to go to Logheryman's," Cedar said. "I'll see if he'll come back here so you can have a look at him too."

Felix nodded. "Do you want me to come with you?"

"It's okay," Cedar said. "You should stay here with Jane."

He nodded. Cedar stuck her head back into the room and told Jane she'd be back to see her soon. When she emerged from Felix's home, she squinted into the morning sun and saw that two guards were waiting for her. They bowed, and then fell into step behind her as she walked swiftly home.

When she arrived in the round courtyard, she found Finn sprawled out under the branches of a willow tree with a book. The sunlight was bouncing off the waves of his hair, and for a moment Cedar just stopped and soaked in the peaceful scene. Then he looked up and his face broke into a smile. He held out his arms. "Welcome home."

Cedar sat down next to him. He put his arms around her and nuzzled her neck. "Hello, my hardworking, never-sleeping queen," he said into her collarbone. She breathed in his scent and wrapped her fingers through his hair, feeling herself relax. She tried to pull herself closer, as if she could burrow into him and stay there for a while. "What's wrong?" he asked. "While you were sleeping, Felix told me that Jane's going to be okay; I thought you'd be elated."

"I am," Cedar said. "Although she's in a lot of pain. Did he tell you about Irial?"

Finn nodded and frowned. "I don't understand why Felix can't figure out what's wrong with him. He's never been unable to diagnose an illness or wound before. Though to hear Felix tell it, the gan-canagh aren't the most reliable creatures."

"He's a person, not a creature!" Cedar said. "And he can't make up the fact that he's really sick."

"Maybe," Finn said. "But let Felix handle it—he's the healer. You've got other things to worry about."

Cedar shook her head. "Nothing as important as this. I don't know . . . I just can't shake the feeling that something is really wrong. I believe him."

"Cedar, I know you want to prove yourself. You're going to be a great queen. You *are* a great queen. But you need to delegate—you can't solve every problem in Tír na nÓg *and* Ériu. You're going to burn yourself out. Leave this one to Felix."

"Felix has already told me there's nothing he can do," Cedar said, getting to her feet. "All he cares about right now is getting Jane back, which is good—they need each other. But Irial came to *me*. He said Logheryman is *dying*. So I'm going to go. I thought you might want to come with me."

"Where?" Finn asked, alarm spreading across his face.

"To Earth, of course. I'm going to go find Logheryman . . . and the other Unseen if I can locate them."

"Wait just a minute!" Finn said. "I don't think that's a good idea. Send someone else if you have to—*I'll* go. We still don't know if we've caught all the druids, remember? What if this is a trick to get you back there?"

"Look, I'll be careful," Cedar insisted. "But I'm not going to hide here forever. What kind of queen—or person—would I be if I just sat back and did nothing? That's the kind of queen Nuala would have been. These people came to me for help, so I'm going to try to give it to them."

"You need to stop taking unnecessary risks!" Finn said, getting to his feet as well. "You can't just do whatever you want anymore. Are you sure you're not *looking* for another crisis to solve?"

Cedar felt like he'd slapped her in the face. Her mouth moved soundlessly as she struggled to find the words to tell him how incredibly unfair he was being. When she found them, her voice was barely audible.

"Do you think I like it?" she whispered. "Do you think I liked it when Eden was gone, and I thought she was dead? Do you think I liked listening to the druids torturing her mind? Do you think I'm glad my mother is dead, and my best friend was almost burned alive? Do you think I enjoyed hearing you scream as Liam cut you open with that knife? I see these things playing over and over again in my mind—*that's* why I can't control the fire. Is that what you think—that I want more of it?"

Finn shook his head and started to move toward her. "Of course that's not what I meant—"

"Well, that's what you said," she snarled, then turned on her heel and stormed into their bedroom, shoving the heavy round door shut behind her. She threw open her wardrobe and tore off her dress, pulling her jeans and T-shirt back on. A small voice inside said that Finn only wanted to protect her, but Cedar couldn't stomach the idea of being safe and sound in Tír na nÓg while others—who were not so different from them—were suffering and dying. Why couldn't he see that?

She stalked out of the wardrobe and opened a sidh to Logheryman's house. She glanced at the door to the courtyard once more, and then stepped through the shimmering air, leaving their room behind.

Cedar's breath caught in her throat as she stared at the front of the house, which was just catching the early-morning rays of sun. The windows were draped in black, and a long black cloth hung on the front door. "No," she whispered before rushing forward and knocking on the door. Maggie answered it, and her face told Cedar everything she needed to know.

"Well, you've come. He said you would," the old woman said. "But I'm afraid you're too late. For him, anyway." There was a hint of reproach in her voice, and her face had lost its rosy glow. Maggie had helped them find the Lia Fáil, but Cedar had not been able to return the favor by saving her friend.

Cedar stepped inside the house. She struggled to find the right words as she clutched a hand to her stomach, which felt like it was filled with several large rocks.

"I'm so . . . so sorry," Cedar said in a small voice, unable to meet the other woman's eyes.

"You're alone?" Maggie asked, leading her into the sitting room.

Cedar sat on the edge of the sofa and nodded. "Irial arrived last night with the message. But Jane—my human friend—she had touched him . . ."

Maggie's eyes darkened. "Is she all right?"

"Yes," Cedar said. "But I should have come sooner. I'm sorry. He told us last night that Logheryman was sick, but I didn't think . . ."

There was a long silence. Then Maggie asked, "And how is the young lad? Is he still alive?"

"Yes, but he's not well," Cedar answered. "Felix—our healer—says he can't tell what's wrong with him."

"I'm not surprised," Maggie said. "I tried every remedy I know, and I've studied herb lore all my life. Martin was no novice, either, yet none of the things he suggested had any effect whatsoever."

There was another pause, and then Cedar asked, "Was it peaceful?"

"Aye, it was. Like fading into nothing, he told me in his last moments."

"You shouldn't have been here alone," Cedar said, shaking her head.

"You're here now, and that still means something," Maggie said. "I'm not so strong that I can bury a full-grown man without some help. Would you mind?"

"Of course," Cedar said quickly. Maggie led her into the bedroom, where a shrouded figure lay. They stood there for a moment, paying silent homage to their fallen friend. Cedar remembered lying in that same bed as she tried to rescue Eden from her own dreams—and ended up being rescued herself instead. She remembered Logheryman's swollen and bruised face after his encounter with the druids, and how he had led them through the woods to Maggie's house.

"I know your people used this place as a safe house at times," Maggie said, still gazing at the figure on the bed. "Know that you are always welcome at my home now . . . whenever you need it. I'm afraid I'm not as handy with magic as Martin was, but I will give you whatever help I can. There are so few of us who still believe."

Cedar felt a lump in her throat at the woman's kindness in the face of her own loss. She didn't know the specifics of the relationship between Maggie and Logheryman, but she suspected it had been more than a casual friendship. She wondered how long they had been together, and what the woman would do now.

"Thank you," Cedar said. "May I . . . may I look?"

Maggie nodded, and Cedar drew back the thin sheet covering Logheryman's body. She stifled a gasp. The leprechaun had always been thin and sinewy, but now he looked skeletal, like a mummy that had been recently exhumed. It was as though he really had faded into nothing. She gently lifted the sheet back over his face.

"Where would you like to bury him?"

"In the garden, I think. I believe he'd like to stay close to home," Maggie replied, shuffling out of the room to lead the way.

Cedar followed Maggie out the back door, watching as the older woman sank down onto a bench.

"He used to sit out here at night, smoking his pipe, listening to my stories," she said. "He never tired of them, always wanted more. This will be a good place for him to rest, beside this bench. I'll tell him a few more to ease his journey."

Cedar went into the shed to find a shovel. When she emerged, an old, rusted spade in her hands, Maggie was looking at her with a peculiar expression on her face.

"You're different from the rest of them, you know," she said. "Different from what the stories say, at least. Different from how Martin used to speak of them."

"How so?" Cedar asked. She plunged the spade into the ground, her newfound strength making it go deeper than she'd expected. She tugged on it to pull it out, and started again, more gently this time.

"Well, for one thing, you're here," Maggie said. "I think I can safely say that you are the first of the old ones to attend the funeral of an Irish leprechaun."

"I should have been here sooner," Cedar said again as she continued to dig.

"There's nothing you could have done," Maggie said. "If your man Felix couldn't help the young lad, then there was nothing to be done for Martin, either. You mustn't blame yourself."

Cedar felt ashamed of the tears that were filling her eyes. Despite Maggie's words, she knew she had delayed too long. She'd felt sympathy for the Unseen while she was listening to Irial's story, but now the problem was much more personal. "I'll do whatever I can to find out what's causing this," she said fervently. "I promise you that."

"And I'll do whatever I can to help," came a voice from the side of the house. Cedar looked up, her vision blurred by tears, and saw Finn walking toward her.

She almost dropped the spade. "What . . . what are you doing here?"

Finn crossed the yard in a few long strides and pulled Maggie into a long hug. They exchanged several words that Cedar couldn't make out, and then Maggie patted his cheek and headed back into the house.

Finn took the spade from Cedar. "Eden's with Riona," he said, forestalling her question.

She opened her mouth to speak, but he held up a hand. "Just hear me out. Then I'll leave if you want me to. You're not the only one troubled by the past. It still haunts me . . . those long days when I thought you were dead after you threw yourself at Lorcan. I can't describe how horrible it was. Sometimes all I can think about is keeping you safe. But I realize that you wouldn't be *you* if you cloistered yourself somewhere away while others were suffering. I wouldn't ever want to change that. And I'm sorry about what I said. I didn't mean it; I know you just want things to be normal, and that's what I want too. But I guess it's not quite time for 'normal' yet, is it?"

Cedar gave him a watery smile. Her T-shirt was sticking to her back, and she was pretty sure she had clumps of dirt in her hair from running her fingers through it. She was exhausted with grief—for Jane and Felix, for Irial and the Unseen, and now for Logheryman and Maggie. But the fact that Finn had followed her, that he didn't think she was crazy for doing this . . . it gave her a new hope. Together they had rescued Eden, and together they had found the Lia Fáil. Together they would find out what was killing the Unseen—and stop it.

"You know," Cedar said, "I have no idea what 'normal' even looks like for us. It's not like we can go back to the way it was, before all of this happened. Maybe this *is* normal for us now."

"Since you seem to have a penchant for saving the world, I suppose you might be right," he said. "But I stand by what I said about you burning yourself out. I don't know if even your heart is big enough to hold the whole world."

"I'm just—"

"I know," he said, kissing her forehead. "You're just doing the right thing."

He jumped into the hole Cedar had made and started deepening it. While he worked, Cedar went back into the house, where she found Maggie sitting on the edge of Logheryman's bed. She had uncovered his body and was holding one of his frail hands in her own, their fingers entwined. She stood up when she saw Cedar.

"Is it time?" she asked.

"Whenever you're ready," Cedar said.

"Oh, I'll never be ready," Maggie replied. "So we'd best just do it."

Cedar picked up Logheryman's body and cradled it in her arms. He weighed about the same as Eden, and she felt a sharp pang in her chest. She carried him back through the house and into the garden, where Finn was just finishing the grave. She stood at the edge and waited for Maggie, who came out of the house a few moments later, her arms heaped with heavy fabric. "I was making this quilt for him," she explained. "It's not quite finished . . . but I'll not be needing it for anything else." She nodded at Cedar, who passed the body down to Finn. After gently setting Logheryman on the ground and covering him with Maggie's quilt, he grasped Cedar's hand and climbed out of the hole.

"Good-bye, oldest of friends," Maggie said as Finn started to fill in the grave. "I never thought I, of all people, would outlive you. But the day I met you in my wee garden was the luckiest day of my life. There won't ever be another like you or a stranger or happier couple than the two of us."

CHAPTER 7

The last time Eden had been in the dungeons, it had been as Lorcan's prisoner. But she knew the woman who was being held there could help increase her power, help bring her closer to her older self. Eden double-checked to make sure she was alone. Her dad had told her that her mum was working, and that he was going to help her. He had left her with Riona, but Eden had told her grandmother she was going to her room to read for a while. It was the perfect chance for her to find the druid. After making sure the coast was clear, Eden opened a sidh to the cell she and Nuala had shared, repressing a shudder of fear. Then she tiptoed through it.

The cell was different from how she remembered it. It was warmer and had only one bed and a large wardrobe set against the wall. The room she had been held in was windowless, and yet there was a large window behind the bed, through which she could see fruit trees. She realized it must be an illusion, for the dungeons were far underground. A thin woman with long blonde hair jumped to her feet at the sight of Eden.

"Who are you?" the woman exclaimed, clutching her hand to her chest.

"Are you Helen?" Eden asked.

"No," the woman answered. "Who is Helen?"

Eden's face fell. "I'm looking for a druid named Helen. I thought she would be here, in the dungeons."

"Is that what this is?" the woman asked, looking around her. "Where are we?"

Eden frowned. "You're in Tír na nÓg, of course. Don't you know that?"

The woman merely gaped at her. Then she asked, "How did you get in here? Is that a sidh? Where does it lead?"

Eden closed the sidh and glared back at the druid. "You're in here because you tried to hurt my mum!" she said, backing toward the door. "You're not supposed to leave."

"Maybe I can help you," the woman said, slowly advancing on her. "I didn't know what I was doing; I was under a spell. I'm innocent! I swear it."

"Don't come any closer!" Eden yelled, her back pressed against the door. She wanted to open a sidh, but what if she couldn't close it in time and the woman followed her through? If she let one of the druids escape, she would be in big trouble. She pulled on the large iron door handle, but it wouldn't budge.

"You must be Eden," the druid said in what was obviously meant to be a soothing voice. "I'm not going to hurt you. I just need to go home to my family. You know what it's like to miss your family, right?"

It was the wrong thing to say. "You hurt my family," Eden said, her eyes burning. She pressed her hands to the door, and then stepped through to the other side. She saw the druid run toward it, but then heard the thump as the sidh was replaced with solid wood. She leaned against the door, breathing heavily. This might be harder than she'd thought. She crept down the short hallway that led away from the cell, peeking around the corner into a cavernous chamber. She had only seen it twice—when being led into the cell, and when being led out of it, to her death. At least, it would have been her death if her mother hadn't saved her.

It's like the inside of a castle, Eden thought, before realizing that technically she *was* inside a castle—or at least under it. Four guards were standing at either end of the chamber, and she whipped her head back around the corner. How was she going to find Helen?

Eden? she thought. *Um . . . older me?* She waited, but there was no answer. But then . . . she couldn't explain it, but she had this feeling that she was supposed to go down the hall. Not to the next door, but the one after that. The problem was that she wouldn't be able to get there without the guards seeing her, and they'd haul her butt back to her parents before she had time to say "trouble." Then an image flashed into her mind so vividly that she almost gasped out loud. It was the inside of a cell. It looked the same as the one she had just visited, except there was no window, and a woman with short gray hair was sitting at a desk in the center of the room. Eden had never seen her before, but she didn't waste any time; the guards could walk by her hiding place at any minute. She squeezed her eyes shut and focused on the image in her mind, and then put a hand to the wall until she felt the solid rock give way to shimmering air. She was about to step through the sidh when she heard a guard's voice call out, "Stop! Who goes there?"

Eden swallowed a gasp and leapt through the sidh, closing it at once. She wasn't sure how much the guard had seen, but there were only two people in this kingdom who could create the sidhe, and her mother had no reason to sneak around. Her heart was beating so wildly that it took her a moment to realize where she was.

The woman inside the cell—the same woman who had been sitting at the small wooden desk from Eden's vision—jumped up and gaped at her. "Who are you, child? How did you do that?"

"I'm Eden," she gasped, her breath still ragged from fright. "Are you . . . Helen?"

The woman sank back down into the chair at the desk. She was old, like a grandma, with short gray hair. Dressed in human clothes, she looked like she was ready to go to work. Eden watched her warily, waiting, ready to make another sidh back home if this was not the right druid after all. She could hear shouts out in the hallway; the guards must be looking for the intruder.

"Yes," the woman said at last. "I'm Helen. Why are you looking for me?"

Eden unclenched her fists, and her face broke into a smile. "Someone told me you could help me become more powerful."

"Who told you that, child?"

The smile slid off Eden's face. "Um . . . it's kind of weird . . ."

Helen indicated the bed in the corner. "Why don't you sit down?" Her voice had become gentler. "You gave me quite a fright, but I'm very pleased to meet you. And believe me, I've seen plenty of 'weird' things in my life. You don't have to worry."

Eden took a seat on the edge of the bed. Now that she was here, she wasn't sure how to explain it. She glanced nervously at the door, wondering if the guards would burst through. "Um . . . well, I've only been a Tuatha Dé Danann for a little bit. I mean, I haven't known about it for very long. We're new here, my mum and I."

"Who is your mother?"

"Well . . . she's the queen. Her name is Cedar."

Helen's eyebrows shot up, but her voice was steady when she said, "I see. And did she tell you to come see me?"

Eden felt her cheeks growing warm. "No," she muttered, looking at her knees. "She doesn't know I'm here. It was someone . . . inside me." She glanced up at Helen to see her reaction, but the older woman was still watching her calmly, so she continued, her words tumbling out in a sudden rush. "She's real! She's like an older version of me. And

I guess she helped me fight off Nuala a couple of times, though I don't really remember that because I was asleep. Once it was just me and Nuala, and the other time it was me and Nuala and my mum. She attacked my mum, but then I was able to save her by turning into older Eden." She lifted her chin with pride. Helen looked suitably impressed.

"But you don't remember this?" the druid asked.

"No," Eden admitted. "My mum just told me about it, and I guess Nuala said something about the first time it happened, when it was just her and me. But I can feel her sometimes, the older me," she added eagerly, as though to prove she was telling the truth. "It's like an imaginary friend, but she's inside of me. And last night she actually talked to me. She told me to come and find you."

"Did she, now? What else did she tell you?"

Eden was relieved that Helen didn't seem to think she was crazy or a liar. "It was really cool! She told me that you could teach me how to control my power, so I can become older Eden sooner."

"Fascinating," Helen said in a whisper. She stood up and started to walk slowly around the room, her forehead creased. Then she stopped and looked back at Eden. "Tell me, Eden, what is it like, living in Tír na nÓg and being one of the Tuatha Dé Danann? Are you happy here?"

"Oh yeah!" Eden exclaimed. "It's awesome. It's just . . ." Her voice faltered slightly.

"Just what, dear?" Helen encouraged.

"It's just . . . well, there aren't very many kids in Tír na nÓg, and the grown-ups think they have to keep an eye on me all the time." She rolled her eyes. "There's nothing dangerous here, but they still think I can't take care of myself. I mean, what's the point of being a princess if you can't *do* anything?"

Helen made a sympathetic sound. "I understand. That must be really difficult."

"Yeah," Eden continued. "I mean, it's not that I want to run the place, but I don't want to have someone with me all the time. It's totally impossible for me to get lost—I can come home whenever I want. It's like they don't trust me. They think I'm this little kid who doesn't know anything, but I know *lots* of stuff."

"I'm sure you do," Helen said. "In time, they'll see that you're not a little kid anymore."

"That's what I want!" Eden exclaimed. "I want to help do things, and protect the kingdom, and make sure no one hurts my family again!"

A strange expression passed over Helen's face, but then she said, "Those are all very good reasons, Eden."

"So . . . you'll teach me?"

"Yes, I'll teach you. But I need you to promise me something first."

"What?"

"Once I've taught you how to control and access your power, once I've shown you how to speak to the Eden inside you whenever you want and access *her* power . . . I want you to use your ability to send me home."

Eden had been leaning forward, soaking in Helen's words, but at this last part she sat up straight. "Home where?"

"To Dublin, Ireland. I'm a prisoner here, you see. Your mother is very angry with the druids because of something a friend of mine did. But *I* have done nothing wrong. Still, your mother insists on keeping me locked up here. Would you like it if you were being punished for someone else's mistake?"

"No," Eden said. "But if you've done nothing wrong, why won't my mum just let you go home?"

"Sometimes people don't think as clearly as you and I, especially if they are angry or hurt," Helen said. "And, to be honest, the

Tuatha Dé Danann usually do whatever they want, without thinking about others. But if you promise to let me go home, then I promise to help you."

Eden frowned. If Helen hadn't done anything wrong, why shouldn't she be able to go home? There was a clatter outside Helen's door, and Eden jumped. She had to go before she got caught.

"Okay," she said. "It's a deal."

Helen held out her hand, and they shook on it.

"I'll have to do some thinking about your lessons," Helen said. "Can you come back tomorrow?"

Eden nodded. "Yes. But I have to go now; I think the guards may have seen me." She opened a sidh in the air, glancing up to make sure Helen had noticed.

"Very impressive," Helen said with a small smile. "Oh, and Eden? I'm sure you already know this, but best not to say anything about this to anyone. We wouldn't want them to keep you from coming to see me. It will be our little secret, okay?"

"Okay!" Eden said. "See you tomorrow!" She made a sidh to her bedroom and poked her head through it. She looked around, and—with a final wave at Helen—stepped through and closed it behind her.

◦◦◦

"What do you plan to do?" Finn asked softly, once they were back home. They had stayed with Maggie for the rest of the day, listening to her stories about Logheryman and their wonderful, unexpected relationship. Then they'd walked her safely back to her own house before leaving.

Now she and Finn were sitting by the pond in their bedroom, their feet dangling in the cool water. Eden was out with Riona, picking berries. Cedar was glad, because it gave them a chance to discuss their plans without a hundred questions from their inquisitive daughter. She took a deep breath before answering Finn's question. She still found it difficult to accept the truth of Logheryman's death. Suddenly, the situation with the Unseen felt much more real—and much more urgent.

"I think we should go directly to the selkies," she said. "Irial said that the pixies are gone, and the púka who helped him disappeared. We know for sure the selkies are sick—he never made it to the Merrow, so we don't have any confirmation about them. I suppose we'll have to warn them, anyway, although I'm certainly not looking forward to that encounter." The last time they'd visited the Merrow, one of the Danann had killed their queen, and the Merrow had killed him in return. She didn't know if they would even talk to her, but she supposed she'd have to try. The Merrow had only been defending themselves; they didn't deserve to succumb to whatever illness was afflicting the Unseen.

Finn stayed silent for a long moment.

"You still don't think I should go," she said, feeling her stomach twinge. Cedar waved her foot in the water and watched as the fish swam past, oblivious to the sudden tension above them.

"I told you that I'm going to help," Finn said. "I was just thinking about Eden."

"I know," Cedar said. "If we tell her where we're going, she'll want to come . . . but I don't know what we'll run into out there, and she's already seen too much death. I think you should stay here with her."

"Oh? And you're just going to leave a trail of open sidhe around Ériu? Or were you planning on taking the train?"

"I could take Rohan," she mumbled. "He could close them for me."

Finn leaned in so that she couldn't avoid looking at him. "You'd rather bring my father with you than me?" he asked incredulously.

"Of course not," she said quickly. "But what about Eden?"

"You're right, she should stay here . . . with my parents. We won't be gone long. If you're going, I'm going with you. We're a team, Cedar. Besides, you wouldn't even know where to look for most of these beings. I spent years trying to find them and reach out to them, remember? They're very good at not being found, but no one knows where to start looking better than I do. Otherwise you'll just be shooting in the dark. It's not like Irial is fit to travel; he can't take you to them." He stared down into the pond for a few moments, his brow furrowed. "Felix should come too; he'll know the right questions to ask, and he can collect some more samples—if this actually is some sort of disease, which I'm starting to doubt."

"Good luck getting him to leave Jane," Cedar said. "But you're right—we need him. I just hope Eden doesn't mind being left behind."

"Eden will be fine," Finn said again. "We've got the sidhe, remember? And the starstones. If we're gone for longer than a day, we can come back to see her. And there will be a whole lineup of people who want to spend time with her. She'll hardly notice we're gone."

Cedar reached over and took Finn's hand. He laced his fingers through hers and squeezed tightly, bringing her hand to his lips. "Look, I know things haven't been easy," he said. "I know you've been under a lot of stress. And I'm sorry I haven't been more helpful. I've just been so overwhelmed with getting to know Eden and being back in this place. I never thought I'd see it again. And now I'm here, with my daughter and the woman I love, and it's like a dream come true. But I keep forgetting how overwhelming all of this must be for you."

"Thank you," she said softly. "There's been so much change. It's been hard. Wonderful in so many ways, but hard."

Finn nodded. "I know. The three of us have been through a lot. Just being a normal family without some crisis looming over our heads will take some getting used to. If," he said with a wry grin, "it ever happens."

"I want that more than anything," Cedar said. "I hope you believe me. But I have to—"

"I know," he said. "I wish it could be someone else this time . . . but I understand how you feel. I do. But when we get back, *I* want nothing more than to spend some uninterrupted time with you. And we're going to make this work, whether we're in Halifax or Tír na nÓg or somewhere in between."

Cedar smiled. "There's somewhere in between? Is there another world I don't know about yet?"

Finn grinned at her and flopped back down onto the ground, pulling her with him. "I was thinking Maui . . . or maybe that island of Brighid's in Thailand."

"Uh huh," Cedar said, rolling her eyes as she got up. "Let's go find Eden; it's past her bedtime. Then I'll ask Felix if he'll come with us. We should leave first thing in the morning."

"Think Rohan will let you go to Ériu without a full legion of guards?"

"He'll have to," Cedar said. "He forgets that I can take care of myself now."

Finn got a wicked grin on his face, and Cedar found herself momentarily distracted by the dimples in his cheeks. "Can you, now?" he said, before tackling her to the ground.

Cedar squealed and pushed him off, amazed that she was now strong enough to do so. But it felt good to laugh; it had been too long. She could tell from the look in Finn's eyes that he had more than "playing" in mind, so she quickly stood up. She couldn't get distracted now—not with so much at stake. "Eden," she reminded him. He gave an exaggerated moan and got to his feet.

They managed to catch Eden and Riona as they were walking home, carrying baskets weighed down with bright red berries.

"Mummy!" Eden squealed and ran to her.

"Mmm, looks good," Cedar said, taking a bright red berry out of one of Eden's baskets and popping it into her mouth. "What are you going to do with all of these?"

"Eat them," Eden answered simply. Her lips and fingers were already stained red.

Finn ruffled his daughter's hair, and then sauntered over to Riona. Cedar assumed he was going to fill her in on their plan.

"How's Jane?" Eden asked as they continued toward home. It had been impossible to hide Jane's sudden appearance and "illness." Cedar hadn't wanted Eden to think she'd leave her birthday party for anything other than a true emergency—though, to be fair, Eden had left the party first. But Cedar hadn't told her about the gancanagh. At that point, she hadn't really understood the full extent of what was going on.

"She's doing better," Cedar said. "She's spending some time with Felix, and he's helping her." She stopped walking and knelt down to Eden's level. "Listen, Mum and Dad are going away for a little bit. It might only be a day, but it might be longer. We'll probably be gone when you get up in the morning. You're going to stay with Rohan and Riona, okay?"

Eden's bottom lip jutted out. "Where are you going? Why can't I come?"

"It's just a quick trip to chat with some people on Earth. I hope we won't be gone long. You'd be really bored."

"I wouldn't be bored. I want to come."

Cedar was glad she hadn't mentioned the real reason they were going. There would be no stopping Eden if she thought she might get to meet a selkie or a pixie. "Sorry, baby, not this time. But I've got our starstone, so use it anytime. We should be gone for a couple of days at most."

Finn and Riona caught up to them, and Cedar remembered something else she had been meaning to tell Eden. "This might make you feel better. We met a little boy the other day, and he's close to your age. I thought maybe you could play with him while we're gone."

"Really? A boy *my* age? Who?"

"His name is Niall. His dad works with Felix. He's the one who brought us the message about Jane yesterday. He's nine. I asked Felix who he was, and he thought the two of you would hit it off."

"Atty's boy! Of course!" Riona exclaimed. "His mother and I were friends years and years ago, before we left for Ériu. I did hear that she had a son. I'll take you to meet him after your lessons tomorrow, Eden. I haven't seen Atty since we got back, so it will be an enjoyable visit for me too."

"Well, okay," Eden said, looking excited but nervous.

"Now come, it's time you were in bed," Cedar said as soon as they reached their home.

Half an hour later, after a story and several more questions about where Cedar was going, Eden was sound asleep. Cedar stood and watched her for a long time, her gaze lingering on Eden's long, dark lashes as they rested against her cheeks, and on the steady rise and fall of her tiny chest. She remembered how Logheryman's limp body had weighed the same as Eden's. She knelt down and gathered the child into her arms, holding her sleeping form tight. "Stay safe," she whispered.

When Cedar finally arrived at Felix's house, Jane was sitting up in bed, a cup of tea clutched in her hands, her eyes bloodshot. Felix was reading to her from *A Hitchhiker's Guide to the Galaxy*. He looked up when Cedar walked in. "How did it go?" he asked. "Did you bring Logheryman?"

"He's dead."

"*What?*"

"He was dead when I got there. Finn and I helped Maggie bury him."

Felix stared at her openmouthed, as though he couldn't quite understand what she was saying. Jane was looking down at her sheets, but Cedar could see the tears starting to drip off her chin. She didn't understand why Logheryman's death would make Jane cry—after all, she had hardly known the leprechaun. But then her friend lifted her chin and said in a strangled voice, "Is . . . is *he* going to die too?" Cedar didn't have to ask who "he" was.

"I don't know," she said.

Felix looked stricken. "I'm so sorry," he said. "My worry over Jane held you back. You could have left sooner."

"Well, now we know that this is serious, and for more than one species. Finn and I are going back to Earth in the morning to see what we can find out. We're going to go see the selkies first. Will you come?" she asked Felix, and he nodded slowly, her news about Logheryman clearly still hitting him hard.

"I'll come too," Jane said.

"Are you sure?" Cedar asked, surprised. "I mean, how are you feeling? You've only just recovered. Sort of. Have you?"

Jane's cheeks reddened, and she ducked her chin. "I feel like shit, to be honest, but I know from experience that sitting around doing nothing will only make me feel worse. Besides, I haven't been on a life-or-death adventure in what? A month?"

"This isn't going to be like that," Cedar said. "I just thought we might be able to figure out what's affecting the Unseen if we see more of them in person. Maybe one of them even knows what's going on."

"Maybe," Felix said, "but I suspect that whatever is ailing them is beyond my ability to heal. Which, I must admit, is a first. Excuse me; if we're leaving first thing in the morning I should go prepare some things. And I'll ask one of the other healers to keep an eye on the gancanagh while I'm gone." He hesitated before opening the door, giving Cedar a concerned look. "Just a heads up—the Council probably won't approve of this. They don't like getting involved in the affairs of other beings."

"Then they don't have to know," Cedar said. "I don't have time to argue with them. I'll just tell them I'm taking a couple of days off."

Felix looked doubtful, but he didn't argue.

"I'm so sorry, Cedar," Jane said after he had left the room. "That must have been horrible for you."

Cedar sat down on the edge of her bed. "It was," she admitted. "I feel awful for Maggie, all alone out there." She took in Jane's tear-streaked face. "How are you doing—really?"

Jane's eyes were fixed on the door through which Felix had just left. "I don't know," she said. "It feels weird. It's like, I know that I like Felix—I love him—and yet I can't feel it, y'know? All I feel right now is this huge sense of loss. It doesn't make any sense to me, but it's there."

"Does it feel strange to be with him?"

"Yeah. It's awkward," Jane said. "I know I should want to be with him, but I don't. Not yet, anyway."

"It'll pass," Cedar assured her, hoping it was true. "Your feelings for him will return, I'm sure of it. Just hang in there for a little while longer. Don't do anything crazy."

"Like go on a scavenger hunt for sick mythical creatures, you mean?"

CHAPTER 8

The first thing Cedar noticed was the wind. She could feel it, but it didn't cut through her like it once did—before she took that life-changing step onto the Lia Fáil. They were on the island of Inis Mór, off the west coast of Ireland. It was morning, but the sky above them was the color of smoke from a raging wildfire. Dark gray clouds were billowing in from the ocean at an unnatural speed. The ocean was also dark and stormy, whitecaps leaping toward them like the ocean's teeth preparing to devour its prey. All around them the landscape was covered in flat limestone rocks, thin grass, and weeds trying to eke out a pale existence between them.

"How do we find them?" she asked.

Finn led Cedar, Felix, and Jane down toward the water's edge. They stepped carefully along the rocks, slick with seaweed, and Cedar noticed Jane awkwardly accept Felix's steadying hand. The lonely cry of a solitary seagull echoed in the air around them, then fell silent.

"If we explore the caves, we should find them," Finn said. "Of course, they probably already know we're here. We'll see if they want to be found."

Apparently they did. As they made their way around a bend, Cedar caught sight of a small series of caves under an outcropping of rock. Large boulders jutted out from the stony beach on the far side. Several seal heads popped out of the water and gave several short barks before swimming toward shore. As the Danann and Jane reached the first cave, they saw a woman working her way out of her skin. Another, a male, was doing the same thing beside her. The others remained in their seal forms, but they gathered together on the rocks. Cedar tried to keep her expression unflappable, as if she witnessed seals transforming into humans every day.

Cedar waited for Finn or Felix to introduce their group, but then realized that *they* were waiting for *her*. She stepped forward. "Um . . . greetings from the Tuatha Dé Danann," she said, wondering if there was some intramagical community etiquette she should know about. "I'm Cedar. The queen," she added, in case it made a difference. "We heard you were sick, and we came to see if there was anything we could do to help."

The female selkie stepped forward, and—given that the woman was completely naked—Cedar tried to keep her gaze locked on her eyes. "Thank you," the woman said in a faint voice. "I am called Syrna." Her face was pale and her dark hair thin. Patches of it seemed to have fallen out. Even though she'd never met a selkie before, Cedar felt certain this was not their natural condition. "How did you . . . how did you know to come?" Syrna asked.

"A gancanagh named Irial came to us. He said he had been staying with you up until recently. He is sick as well . . . and so are the púka and the pixies and the leprechauns."

"Irial!" Syrna exclaimed. She glared around at the other selkies. "I told you he had gone for help."

"You told us he went to the Merrow," said the male selkie standing next to her. "How could he possibly have made his way to Tír na nÓg?"

"He was trying to get to the Merrow," Cedar said. "But he didn't make it that far. A friend of ours found him and sent him to us."

"Is he still alive?" Syrna asked.

Cedar forced a reassuring smile. He was alive when they left Tír na nÓg . . . but she didn't know how long he would last. "Yes. And we're giving him the best care we can. One of our healers is with him right now. We have brought our chief healer with us. This is . . . well, call him Felix," she said with an apologetic look at her blond friend. She might be a Danann, but she still had trouble pronouncing his real name.

Felix stepped forward. "I've examined the gancanagh, but there is no obvious reason for his illness. The leprechaun who sent him to us has died. Irial mentioned that one of your people has died as well. Have there been any others?"

Syrna shook her head. "Not yet. But Nuri, my grandmother, is very close, we believe." She gave Cedar a slight bow of her head. "It would do her great honor if you would visit with her, Queen Cedar."

"Of course," Cedar said quickly. "Why don't Finn and I go see her, and Felix and Jane can stay here and examine some of the sick?"

Felix immediately headed toward the back of the cave and started talking with the other selkies, who were pushing their way out of their skins to speak to him. Jane seemed to be taking it all in stride; she followed close behind him, pulling a pen and notebook out of her bag.

"My grandmother is very wise," Syrna said to Cedar. "She is the eldest of our kind. She has mentioned a theory about this sickness, but I must admit that I do not understand it. At first I thought it was maybe just . . . well, just the illness talking."

"I'm very interested in hearing your grandmother's theory," Cedar said. "Particularly since we have so little else to go on."

"You will have to swim to reach her, I'm afraid," Syrna told her apologetically. "She is far too weak to swim anymore. We have seaweed to numb the cold if you would like some."

"We'll be fine," Cedar said, hoping her Danann blood would be enough to keep her warm in the North Atlantic waters. She looked at Finn questioningly, and he nodded.

"It's cold, but it won't be unbearable," he said.

Syrna cocked her head. "Have you been here before?"

"Yes," he answered. "Just a few years ago. I spoke with Nuri then, and a couple of others."

Syrna nodded slowly. "She said she had met one of the Tuatha Dé Danann. That there was a war in your world, and a few of you had escaped."

"That's right," he confirmed. "But the war is over, and we've returned home. Some of the Unseen told me they wanted nothing to do with my people and our conflicts. Nuri said that the selkies would fight for us if the war came here to Ériu. Fortunately, that didn't happen, but I'll always remember her generosity. I'm anxious to see her again."

Syrna slipped back into her sealskin and slid into the water. Cedar was surprised when Finn started stripping down to his boxers. He shrugged when she raised her eyebrows at him. "My clothes don't have any magical drying properties," he said. "I'd rather not spend the rest of the day soaking wet." Feeling self-conscious with all the selkies in the cave watching her, Cedar did the same, leaving her jeans, T-shirt, hoodie, and shoes on a nearby rock. Syrna's head bobbed in the water as she waited for them to join her. Cedar hesitated at the water's edge. She had visions of her muscles seizing up in the cold—it would hardly be a good introduction for her as queen of the Danann if the sick selkies needed to jump to her rescue.

Cedar took a deep breath, and then stepped into the water after Finn, who had transformed into a seal. He was right—it was cold, but no more so than the ocean waters she had swam in as a child in Nova Scotia. The ocean floor dropped off more suddenly than she had been expecting, but she discovered that she could swim with ease, and the cold water felt good against her bare skin. She dove underneath the waves and looked around. It was as if she had entered another world. The water around her sparkled as shafts of sunlight broke through the clouds and shot through the waves, illuminating small creatures floating beside her and the waving sea grasses below. She kicked her feet and swam deeper, where she could see clusters of bright pink and green anemones growing on an outcropping of rock. She bobbed back to the surface for air, and then dove down again to follow a school of tiny blue fish that darted in and out of a growth of reddish brown kelp. She motioned to Finn and pointed, and he swam alongside her. Syrna was swimming ahead of them, leading the way. They followed her for several minutes, and Cedar was amazed that she wasn't growing tired. She had never been much of a swimmer before her transformation on the Lia Fáil, but this felt amazing. She dashed up to the surface to catch another breath and realized that Syrna was waiting for them on the shore, in front of the entrance to another cave. A great cliff rose up above them, and Cedar could see that this was the perfect hiding place for the selkie colony. No one could see them from the top of the cliff several hundred feet above, and if boats came too close, they could easily hide beneath the waves or in the caves at the back of the inlet.

"That was incredible," she said, climbing out of the water. "I've never felt like that before. It's amazing down there."

Finn transformed back into his normal form and shook the water from his hair. "I agree," he said. "You have a beautiful home."

Syrna seemed surprised at his transformation, but she smiled at his compliment, which returned some of her natural beauty to her gaunt face. "Irial used to wonder why we choose to spend most of our lives in our seal form," she said. "Now perhaps you can understand."

She left her coat behind a rock at the entrance to the cave, and led them inside.

Cedar wondered how Jane and Felix were getting on with the others. She knew Jane would have some sly remark to make about them walking around in their underwear. At the back of the cave was a cluster of five seals. The largest one was in the center, and the rest were lying around her, their sides pressed against hers. Syrna knelt down, and the four outside seals shifted their positions so that she could touch the one in the center. Cedar opened her hand and produced a small ball of fire. Warmth and light flooded the cave.

"I have come, Grandmother, and I have brought help. The Tuatha Dé Danann are here. Irial sent them," Syrna said.

Nuri raised her great head, which was mottled with gray. She barked at them, and Cedar glanced at Syrna in confusion.

"She can understand you, but she cannot speak any human languages in this form," Syrna said. "She feels that death is near, and she wishes to die as a seal. But I will translate. She greets you, and thanks you for coming."

"We are honored," Cedar said. "We're very worried about what is happening to you and the other Unseen. Your granddaughter told us that you might know what is causing this sickness. Can you tell us about it?"

There was a series of barks from Nuri, the meaning of which Syrna conveyed to them. "She says she has lived a long time, longer than any of the other selkies. And her mother and grandmother were both blessed with long lives."

Nuri laid her head back down, and the four seals huddled closer around her and Syrna, who rested a gentle hand on her grandmother's fin. "She is very weak. It is difficult for her to speak."

Gently lifting Nuri's head, Syrna cradled it in her lap, leaning in close to listen. Cedar could hardly tell that Nuri was making any sound at all, but after a moment Syrna straightened up and spoke. "She says you must find the druids, who have a sacred trust to protect the Unseen. There is a curse, and only the druids can break it."

A sacred trust. She had heard that phrase before. "What curse?" Cedar asked, her heart racing. "How are the druids involved?" Syrna bent down to listen, but her grandmother was now silent and still.

∾

"I want the truth, and I want it *now*," Cedar said as she and Finn appeared in Helen's room without warning. She had sent Jane home to her apartment in Halifax with Felix, hoping that the familiar surroundings would help them reconnect. Felix had taken some samples from the selkies, and he'd promised to take a closer look at them, though he didn't sound hopeful that he would discover anything new. Cedar had to agree—according to Nuri, the solution to the Unseen's illness was here in this room. She had realized that in the drama surrounding Jane and Irial and the Unseen, she had forgotten to tell Finn about finding Liam's assistant. She had filled him in quickly, and then they had headed straight back to Tír na nÓg.

When Cedar and Finn stormed in, Helen was sitting at her desk, writing in a pocket-sized black notebook. She closed the notebook and stood up in one smooth motion.

"The truth about what?" she said, her calm demeanor infuriating Cedar all the more. "I already told you I was involved in no plans to harm you or anyone you know. Or do you not believe this goblet of truth of yours?"

"The truth about your *sacred trust*," Cedar said. "There's a dead selkie who used those exact words. She said the druids have a sacred trust to protect the Unseen. She also said there's a curse—and that you can break it."

Helen stared at Cedar, her mask of indifference wavering. "What are you talking about? What has happened to the Unseen?"

"They're dying," Cedar answered. "Most of them—all of them, maybe—are sick, and now they're starting to die, one by one. We've been trying to help them. A gancanagh came to us a few days ago, very ill, to give us the news. A friend of ours, a leprechaun, has died. And I've just returned from the selkies on Inis Mór. They're all dying too."

Helen sat down hard on her chair, her hand covering her mouth. Then she let out a small moan and said, "So it's come to this already. We're too late."

"Who's too late?" Cedar asked. "What is the curse? How can we break it?"

Helen shook her head, her hand still over her mouth. When she stayed silent, Cedar wrenched the door open. "Find Rohan and tell him I need the goblet of Manannan mac Lir in here right away," she told one of the startled guards in the hallway.

"There's no need," Helen said quietly. She seemed to be doing battle with herself. Her mouth was a tight line, and she was folding and unfolding her hands in her lap. Twice she took a breath and seemed about to speak, and twice she closed her mouth. Finally, she spoke. "We are not permitted to speak about it—to anyone," she said. "But it appears the curse has come at last."

Cedar waited, trying not to interrupt with more questions.

"What the selkie said was true, although she probably didn't know the entire story," Helen continued. "I certainly don't, and I doubt anyone who's still alive does." She spoke slowly, as though carefully choosing her words. "Many hundreds of years ago, no one knows how long exactly, a spell was cast that bound the magical creatures of our land—the Unseen—to humanity's belief in the magical realm. As long as humans believed in that which they could not see, the Unseen would live in peace, avoiding the notice of their enemies." She shook her head slowly. "I'm sure it seemed like a prudent decision at the time, perhaps even a necessary one."

"Why was it necessary?" Cedar asked.

"They had enemies," Helen said simply. "The church, perhaps, or this could have happened even before Saint Patrick arrived in Ireland. But it is safe to say that there have always been forces in the world that wish to dispose of the magical creatures of old. I don't know who their enemies were, but the danger must have been great for them to make such a bargain."

"Maybe it didn't seem like that much of a risk to them at the time," Finn said, looking thoughtful. "If this happened centuries ago, no one would have imagined that humans would stop believing in the magical realm. Before science and technology came onto the scene, magic was the only way humans were able to explain the world around them. Belief in the hidden realm was part of their everyday life. It was part of who they *were*. So it must have seemed like a safe bet."

"So the deal was that the Unseen would die if humans stopped believing in magic? That's what's happening?" Cedar asked. "Logheryman was fine just a few weeks ago. According to Irial, he was too. Why would it happen so suddenly?"

Helen's blue eyes had a haunted look to them. "I didn't think it would happen that way. Of course, there are still *some* who believe," she added. "We druids, for example, but there are few of us. And there are other humans who believe in the old places where magic runs particularly deep. But it appears that there are no longer enough to sustain the power of the spell. It must have passed a certain threshold, which triggered the curse."

"But the selkies said you could break it," Cedar protested.

Helen shook her head sadly. "I'm afraid they were mistaken. Once, it would have been true. The druids were given the task of guarding the eight precious jewels that were used in the binding of the spell—or curse, depending on how you look at it. If the stones were destroyed, the bond between the Unseen and humanity would be broken, leaving them defenseless against their enemies. Keeping those jewels safe was our most sacred trust." She gazed at the floor, her face etched with sadness. "But we failed. Despite all our efforts, the jewels were stolen . . . and they've never been recovered."

"So maybe *that's* why the Unseen are dying—because these jewels were stolen," Cedar said. "Did it happen recently?"

"No. They were stolen in 1007, in the summer, to be precise," Helen said. "The jewels had been embedded in the cover of what is now known as the Book of Kells, but the book was stolen from the church where it was being kept. When it was found, it was missing the cover—and, of course, the jewels."

"Why was it in a church if the druids were supposed to guard it?"

"I have no idea. But I do know that at least one druid was always with the jewels, and one of us has remained with the Book of Kells ever since in case the cover is found. There were some missing pages attached to the cover, which might help identify it as belonging to the Kells manuscript."

"So that's why you and Liam were at Trinity College—to be with the Book of Kells," Cedar said, remembering what Rohan had told her.

"Liam was preparing to retire, though based on what you've told me, I suppose he had other plans. I was to take over as Keeper of Manuscripts after he left."

Finn had been following the volley of their conversation quietly. "So if the jewels are destroyed, the bond between the Unseen and the humans will be severed, is that right?"

"Possibly," Helen answered. "I am not sure how the spell works. But it stands to reason that after the bond is broken, they will no longer be subject to the frailties of human belief. However, they'd still be vulnerable to their enemies."

"But if no one believes they exist, it's not likely they have many enemies left," Cedar pointed out. "At least they'd have a chance."

Helen set her elbows on the desk and put her head in her hands. "In theory, yes. But it doesn't matter, don't you see?" she said. "The jewels are gone. The druids searched everywhere for them. I told you—there is no hope."

Cedar stopped pacing and looked down at the woman. "There is *always* hope," she said, feeling the fire build up inside her again. "What else do you know about the jewels? Do you know who took them? Where they came from? What they look like?"

"I don't," Helen said in a small voice. "The druid who was in charge of them at the time was killed. So we have no idea what happened. Only that they are gone and have never been found."

A slow smile stretched across Cedar's face as she realized what needed to be done. "We can save them," she said. "We'll find the jewels and destroy them."

"Haven't you been listening?" Helen said, her voice now sharp. "The jewels are gone. How do you possibly think you will find them?"

"By asking someone who can find any magical object—Abhartach the dwarf."

CHAPTER 9

Eden and Nevan were in the library room at the Hall, which Eden had taken to calling the "school room," since this was where she had her lessons—sometimes with Nevan, sometimes with Riona. When her dad had first shown this room to her and her mum, both of their jaws had dropped. It was completely circular, and instead of walls it had hundreds of bookshelves filled with leather-bound volumes and manuscripts, some of them taller than Eden, some so small they would fit in the palm of her hand.

Eolas, a skinny man with long, thin arms and huge blue eyes that seemed too big for his head, was in charge of the books. He reminded Eden of an insect, although she made sure never to say so. Whenever they wanted a book from the top shelves, he would float to the ceiling as though he weighed nothing at all. Eden looked for wings, but he didn't seem to have any. If he wasn't there, a ladder that reached all the way to the ceiling would float across the room, hovering just a few inches off the ground. Eden had wanted to climb it since the first time she set eyes on it, but Eolas had told her it was just for grown-ups. She wasn't allowed to touch the books, either, not even the ones she could reach, unless one of her teachers said it was okay.

"Guess what?" Eden asked Nevan. "I'm going to meet another kid my age later today." She told Nevan what her mother had said about Niall. "How come there aren't more kids around here?" Nevan looked up from the book in front of them. There was only a single table in the room, made from a dark wood in the shape of an X. She and Eden sat beside each other along one of the arms of the X. "Well," Nevan answered slowly. "It's partly because of the war. Those who stayed here were afraid that Lorcan would take any children whose powers he desired. But the Tuatha Dé Danann in general have far fewer children than humans; we always have. The birth of a child is a rare and special occasion. But it also means that the children who *are* here don't have very many playmates. "

"Do they all have special powers? Every one of us?" Eden asked.

"Eventually, yes," Nevan answered.

"But why do people have different abilities?" Eden asked.

"No one knows for certain," Nevan said. "Usually a firstborn child has the abilities of both his or her parents, and the other children just inherit one gift. Sometimes a child is born with an ability that neither of his or her parents has. There are patterns, but no hard and fast rules."

"So if you and Sam had a baby, it would be able to control the water *and* talk inside peoples' heads?"

"*If* we had a baby, that would be one possibility, yes," Nevan answered, amused.

"How come some kids get an ability that their parents don't have?" Eden asked. "What makes them so different?"

"I don't know," Nevan answered, shrugging her petite shoulders. "Perhaps it is meant to address an imbalance in our people. If more gardeners or musicians are needed, more children are born with those talents."

"Yeah, but who decides which kids get which abilities?"

Nevan's laugh bubbled out of her, and she reached out and ruffled Eden's hair. "We don't know how it all works, O inquisitive one. It might just be chance. But if you ask me, I think there are powers out there beyond us that direct the flow of our lives."

Eden sat and pondered this for a moment. She had thought the Tuatha Dé Danann were the most powerful beings in the universe. To think that there might be something beyond them . . .

"Shall we turn back to our lesson?" Nevan asked, interrupting Eden's thoughts. She turned reluctantly back to the book in front of them. They were learning about the Elders, which was interesting, but right now she was much more concerned with how you could get different abilities than the ones your parents had.

"This is Aengus Og," Nevan said, pointing to a picture in the book. "His greatest feats included—"

"Hey, I've seen him before!" Eden exclaimed.

"You have?" Nevan asked. "In another book, you mean?"

"No, in my dreams!"

Nevan shifted in her seat to stare at Eden. Eolas, who had been working at the other end of the table, suddenly went still, and the scratch of his quill was for once silent. "You have dreams about the Elders?"

Eden shrugged. "I didn't know that was who they were," she said. "But they're really nice. Always smiling and laughing. We have a great time together. But they're just dreams." She leaned over the book in front of them, suddenly much more interested. "Can I turn the pages?" she asked. "I want to see if the rest of them are in here too."

Nevan nodded, and Eden started eagerly flipping the pages. "Yeah, she's in my dreams too!" she said, pointing to a picture of a tall, smiling woman with blonde hair spilling to her ankles. "And this guy!"

Nevan stared at her in shock. "That's my father," she said in a small voice.

"Really?" Eden said. "Your dad is an Elder? How come you're still here, then? I thought all the Elders left. And I've never seen *you* in my dreams."

"My parents were Elders, but I am not," Nevan said, her voice still barely above a whisper. "I was born here, in Tír na nÓg. Only those who were born in the Four Cities can return."

"Huh," Eden said. "That's too bad. Do you miss them?"

Nevan ignored the question. "When you see the Elders in your dreams, do they speak to you?"

"Sometimes," Eden said, wrinkling her nose in concentration. "I can't remember exactly what they say, though. I think it's mostly just chatting." Then she noticed Nevan and Eolas exchange a long glance over the table. "It's okay, right? I mean, I can't control what I dream about."

"Of course it's okay," Nevan said hastily. "It's just . . . interesting. I've never heard of anyone dreaming about the Elders before. Even I don't have that kind of connection with them. I'm not sure what it means."

Just then the door to the library swung open, and Riona peeked her head in. "Am I interrupting?" she asked.

"Not at all, come on in," Nevan said with a wave. Her voice sounded casual, but there was a line between her eyebrows that hadn't been there before.

"Hi, Riona!" Eden said brightly. She had tried calling her Gran, but it didn't seem to fit, so she had just started calling her Riona like everyone else. No one had seemed to mind. She was glad, because none of the Tuatha Dé Danann seemed to use titles like "Mum" or "Dad" or "Uncle."

"Did Eden tell you what we have planned for the afternoon?" Riona asked. "I thought we'd head out soon—if she's finished with her lessons, that is."

Eden knew they weren't done, but Nevan nodded and said, "Yes, I think we've covered enough for the day."

"Great!" Eden said, jumping up. "See you tomorrow!" She and Riona walked back out into the bright sunshine. "Did you talk to them? Can we visit?"

"Yes," Riona said, smiling. "And I'm sure Niall is just as excited as you are."

Eden felt a nervous thrill run through her. Riona must have noticed, because she said, "I imagine it must be a bit boring to hang out with us adults all the time."

Eden shrugged. It *was* boring, except for the prospect of her secret lessons with Helen. She'd snuck into Helen's room this morning for her first lesson, after she knew her parents had left for Earth with Felix and Jane. But nothing exciting had happened; Helen had only asked her more questions about what her older self had said, how often she sensed her presence, what it felt like, and how she used her ability to open and close the sidhe. She took notes in a black notebook, and started drawing strange designs. Eden had tried to hide her disappointment, but Helen had noticed, anyway. She gave Eden another talk about the virtue of patience, and promised that tomorrow they would start some meditation exercises that would help Eden locate and tap into her hidden stores of power.

"Eden? Everything okay?" Riona asked.

"Oh, yeah!" Eden said, snapping out of her daydream. "Hey, is Niall named after the story of Niall and the Nine Hostages?"

Riona beamed. "See, you *have* been learning! Same name, different person, I'm afraid. Now, it's a bit of a walk; how would you like to go by pony?" Without another word, her grandmother transformed into a brown and white spotted pony. It gave her a nudge with its muzzle, and Eden giggled. But then she stopped. Ponies were for little kids.

"I'd rather ride a horse," she said. In a moment, Riona stood before her again, her eyebrows raised incredulously.

"Really? Have you ever ridden a horse before?"

"No," Eden admitted. "But I bet I can. I'll hold on real tight, I promise."

Riona didn't look convinced, but after a moment she said, "Okay . . . we'll try a horse, but I want you to grab the mane, and don't even think about letting go. And we're going to walk, not gallop, do you hear me? No kicking." Eden nodded to everything, and in a whirl of movement Riona transformed into a beautiful brown and white mare—though it seemed a bit smaller than a normal horse. The mare sank down on her front legs, and Eden scrambled up onto her back. Another thrill ran through her as the mare got to her feet and started moving forward. Eden imagined herself in a royal procession, and she even let go of the mane to give a wave to her imaginary followers. The mare stopped abruptly, and Eden rolled her eyes before grabbing onto the mane with both hands. She enjoyed the gentle sway of the horse's back as they meandered through a meadow and along a path lined with blooming cherry trees. When they reached a thickly wooded area, Riona stopped and knelt down, and Eden slid off her back.

"How was that?" Riona asked once she had resumed her normal form.

"It was great!" Eden said. "But we should go faster next time!"

Riona laughed. "We'll see. Who were you waving to?"

"Oh, no one. I was just pretending. Do you think I really will be queen of Tír na nÓg someday?"

"Maybe. But your mother will probably be queen for a very long time, so I wouldn't be in a hurry if I were you. You just concentrate on being the best possible princess you can be." Riona led the way to the edge of the forest, where it looked as if a huge tree had been uprooted.

It was lying on the ground, its exposed roots like a giant sea monster's gaping mouth and outstretched tentacles. Riona tapped one of the branches closest to them, and Eden involuntarily jumped back as the monster's mouth grew wider—wide enough for them to walk through.

"Are you sure this is where they live?" she asked, taking hold of Riona's hand.

"Don't be afraid," her grandmother answered. "Yes, this is the entrance to their home. A bit different from ours, to be sure." Still holding hands, they carefully climbed between the roots and into the tree trunk. As soon as they stepped inside, Eden felt a rush of wind, and suddenly she was standing outside a charming cottage covered in leaves and blooming red flowers.

"How did we get *here*?" she exclaimed, looking around for the dead tree.

"Everyone's home has its own little tricks," Riona said. She knocked on the front door, which was painted a cheery red that matched the flowers climbing up the sides of the cottage. The door was flung open from the inside, and a woman with a shock of curly red hair grabbed Riona in a tight hug.

"Riona! At last! I've been anxious to see you ever since you returned, but I know you've been ever so busy. But now here you are at last, and you've brought the girl, just as you said."

Riona disentangled herself and made the introductions. "Atty, this is Eden, my granddaughter. Eden, this is Atty." She looked into the house. "Is Niall here?"

"Yes, yes, he's just in the back. I'll call him over." Atty tilted her head back and hollered, "Niall!" There was no answer, so Atty grabbed Eden's hand and led her around the side of the house. "See those trees back there? He's just in there. He knows you're coming, so he'll be expecting you. If you need anything, just holler. We'll be inside having a long overdue cup of tea."

Eden started walking hesitantly toward the trees. She felt suddenly shy, and had to fight the impulse to run back to Riona's side. *Don't be silly*, she told herself. *You can go anywhere, anytime, remember?* She stepped under the cover of the trees and was looking around for the boy when a storm of small nuts rained down on her. She covered her head with her arms and squealed. When the nuts stopped falling, she looked up. There, several branches above the ground, was a boy with the same mop of red hair as his mother's. He was laughing down at her.

"Hey! That's not nice!" she yelled, balling her hands into fists.

The boy jumped and landed softly in front of her, as if he had just stepped off a low stool and not a branch twenty feet in the air. "Nice to meet you too," he said, and then took off running into the forest.

Eden stared after him for a split second; then she was in fast pursuit. But there was no catching up to him—he was only a blur through the trees, and then she couldn't see him at all. After a few minutes she stopped, panting for breath, and sat down on a nearby stump. She was about to head back to the cottage to ask Riona if they could go home, when she heard the sudden rustling of leaves. He was heading straight toward her, and she didn't see how he could possibly stop before slamming into her. She squealed and covered her head, but when she peeked between her arms, he was standing in front of her, motionless. And still laughing.

"I bet you think you're pretty fast," Eden said with a scowl.

"I *am* fast," the boy said. "When I'm fully grown, I'll be the fastest of the Tuatha Dé Danann. Want to race again?"

"No," Eden said. "I don't like racing."

"That's because you always lose," he said.

"Why are you so mean? I don't even know you."

"I'm not mean," he said, and he looked genuinely puzzled. "I've just never met a human before."

"I'm not human!" Eden said, standing up and stamping her foot. She stretched herself up as tall as possible and glared up at him. "Why did you say that?"

"Well, you were born on Ériu and raised by humans," he said. "That makes you pretty much a human."

"I was raised by the queen, you idiot," she said. "My parents are both Tuatha Dé Danann, and so am I."

"Yeah, but you've been in Tír na nÓg for what, five minutes? I've been here my whole life."

"It's not my fault where I was born! And you're not so special. So you can run fast—big deal."

"Oh yeah? What can *you* do? Do you even *get* abilities when you're from Ériu?"

Eden felt like punching this rude boy with his red hair and stupid opinions. "I'll show you what I can do. I'll race you after all. Back to where we started."

"You're on," he said, and without looking back he was off, leaving a cloud of dust and leaves behind him.

Eden grabbed hold of the closest tree trunk and concentrated. Then she stepped through the sidh and quickly closed it behind her. She was sitting calmly on the ground when the boy arrived moments later. He stopped and gaped at her. "Took you long enough," she said.

"Whoa," he said. "How did you do that?"

Eden smiled smugly as she stood up. "I can go anywhere, just like that." She snapped her fingers. "And I *don't* need to run. I'm a sidh-opener, just like my mother, the queen."

The boy stared at her for a moment longer, and then a sheepish smile broke across his face. He held out his hand to her. "Well, that's pretty cool," he said. "I know your name is Eden. Mine's Niall."

"I know," Eden said, but she took his hand and shook it.

They stood there looking at each other for a few seconds. Finally Niall shouted, "C'mon!" and headed back into the woods—at a slower pace this time. They spent the afternoon climbing trees and sliding down vines. Niall taught her the names of the plants that were native to Tír na nÓg, and showed her how to make music from the irendal flower, a huge golden plant with petals the shapes of horns. He brought her to a waterfall that fell from the top of a tall tree with diamond-shaped leaves, every branch ending in a clear stream of water. After they'd been outside for a while, he heard his mother calling, and they ran back to the cottage, where a tray of elderberry tarts and a tall pitcher of purple nectar awaited them.

"Can we stay longer?" Eden asked her grandmother between mouthfuls of tart. Riona and Atty shared a delighted glance.

"Of course," she said. "It must feel good to have someone to play with again."

"I think Niall is glad for the company as well," Atty said, reaching over and ruffling her son's hair.

"Atty, stop it," Niall said, squirming out from under her hand. Once the last elderberry tarts were gone, the two children raced back into the woods.

They climbed up a tree with thick, curving branches, and crawled out to the edge of one of them to see if they could make it dip down to the ground. It stayed as solid and straight as ever, and Eden wondered if it was enchanted, like the tree in her bedroom. She told Niall all about her tree-house room, which he thought was just as neat as his bedroom—designed to look like the mouth of a dragon. Then she had an idea.

"We don't have to stay here, you know," she said. "We could go anywhere."

Niall leaned in closer, lowering his voice conspiratorially. "You can open a sidh to *anywhere*?" he asked.

"Well, it has to be a place I've seen," she said. "But I've seen some pretty cool places."

"Like where?"

Eden thought. Where was the coolest place she'd ever been? "Well, the first time I opened a sidh it was to Egypt—that's a place that's really hot, with big old pyramids." But Tír na nÓg was probably way older than Egypt, so maybe Niall would think it was boring. "Or there's this place called Disney World, with all these great rides . . . but it's kind of just for humans, I guess. It's not as good as here. Um . . ." As Eden thought some more, she realized that she hadn't actually been to that many cool places—at least not places that would impress her new friend.

"I know!" she said the moment the idea struck her. "Have you ever visited the Merrow?"

"No," Niall said, his eyebrows lifting in surprise. "I didn't think they existed anymore. Are you saying you've seen them?"

"Yes, and they were very nice to me," she said. It was true; Queen Deardra and the other Merrow had delighted in plying her with sweets and showing her the wonders of their kingdom. It had all turned out rather badly, of course, but that had been Nuala's fault, not the Merrow's. She wondered if they would be happy to see her . . . or angry because she was a Danann. Maybe it wasn't such a good idea after all, but the look on Niall's face was enough to sway her.

"Can we really go see them?" Niall asked, and she nodded fervently.

His eyes were gleaming with excitement, but then he hesitated. "Are we allowed to? I mean, won't we get in trouble? Should you ask your parents first?"

"My parents aren't even here," she said. "They're off on some mission on Earth, I mean, Ériu. I'm sure they wouldn't mind." She felt a twinge of guilt at this lie, but what better way to prove she wasn't human than to show Niall what she could *really* do? "Besides, we don't need to stay long; we'll just say hello, and then come right back. Our parents won't even know we were gone."

Niall grinned. "I *knew* you were going to be cool! All right, let's go!" He jumped out of the tree, and—just to show off—Eden made a sidh that brought her from the upper branch where she was sitting to the forest floor.

"I need to think of where we should go," she said. "It's probably not a good idea to show up underwater. They have to give you a kiss first so you can breathe."

"A kiss?" Niall said, screwing up his face in disgust.

"Don't be a baby. It's no big deal," she said. "I know! We stayed in a little hut last time. It was really cool. It looks all run-down from the outside, but on the inside it's like the world's best aquarium. You'll see. Let's use this rock for the sidh. I don't need to," she hastily pointed out. "But it makes it easier." She placed her hand on a large gray boulder and thought hard of the dilapidated old shack where she and Nuala had spent the night. Then she grabbed Niall's hand and pulled him through before he could change his mind.

"Where are we?" he called once they had stepped through the sidh. Eden squinted at the shimmering patch of air behind them and it disappeared, like a tiny star collapsing in on itself.

"I told you, we're near where the Merrow live," she said, her hair blowing wildly in the biting wind that was coming off the water. They were precariously balanced on the rocky island, in front of the old fishing hut that served as the Merrow's guest room. It was darker than it had been back in Tír na nÓg, and Eden felt a chill that had nothing to do with the wind. She yanked on the door, relieved that it would still open for her. "C'mon," she said. "It's just down here." She pulled open the trapdoor and peered inside, then started to climb down the ladder, Niall just behind her.

When she reached the bottom, she frowned. "It's changed," she said.

She didn't recognize anything from her time here. It was cold, just like it had been outside, whereas before the air in the hut had been warm and comforting. The soft glow had disappeared too—the only light was filtering down from the open door to the hut. There were no trays of food or pitchers of sparkling water. It was a cold and inhospitable place, just as it appeared to be from the outside. She ran over to one of the round windows, hoping that they would at least be able to see an octopus or some of the brightly colored fish she had watched before. But the water outside no longer looked like a tropical paradise. Everything was dark, and she could only make out a few rocks and some waving seaweed. Niall came up beside her. "What are we looking at?" he asked. "Is this some kind of joke?"

Eden felt like bursting into tears. "It was all . . . different before. Honest!" she said. "There were fish and octopuses and it was really, really pretty!"

"Well, it's not pretty anymore," he said. "Just dark. Are you sure we're in the right place?"

"Yes! I'm totally sure. I wouldn't have been able to open a sidh here if I didn't know where we were."

Niall looked at her skeptically, then shrugged his shoulders. "So I guess it *did* change. I wonder why?"

"I don't know," Eden said. "It was only a few months ago. Maybe after Queen Deardra was killed . . ." She was starting to regret bringing Niall here, even if it had impressed him that she knew the Merrow. He didn't seem that impressed now, and they might be in real danger. It was, after all, one of her kind who had killed the Merrow queen. Maybe they had forgotten about the candies; maybe they had forgotten that she was innocent. She had been so stupid to come here with Nuala, thinking she would find her father. She'd watched the

Tuatha Dé Danann—including her father, though she hadn't recognized him at the time—and the Merrow do battle while she thrashed about in the water. She'd watched as the queen fell with a dagger in her throat. Then Nuala had pulled her back to the hut, and her mum had appeared out of nowhere to save her, until—

She shook her head to clear it of those horrible memories, memories she had tried to forget. Pressing her face against the glass to look once more, she jumped back with a shriek when something—*someone*—floated by.

It was a Merrow, her hair swirling around her head like a rainbow cloud, her tail a shimmering gold. But she looked wrong—she was mottled with a sickly green, and her eyes and mouth were open, her eyes sightless. She looked even worse than Queen Deardra had before Nuala found the red hat that had restored her to her usual beautiful self.

"Is it . . . dead?" Niall asked.

"I . . . I think so," Eden whispered. A sudden change in the current pushed the Merrow's body toward them, and they both leapt backward as her bloated face pressed up against the glass.

"Let's get out of here!" Niall said, his voice going up an octave.

Eden couldn't agree more. This no longer felt like a harmless adventure. She grabbed Niall's hand and concentrated with all her might on the air in front of her. As soon as the shimmering patch was big enough, they ran through it, and Eden closed it with more force than necessary, sending small sparks up in the air.

"Why was it dead?" Niall said. His pale skin looked more ashen than usual, and they both sat down hard on the forest floor behind his cottage home.

"I don't know!" Eden said, trying not to freak out. "They were all fine before! They had an amazing magical underwater kingdom, with all kinds of fish and plants and everything. Now it's all gone!"

"We should tell someone," Niall said. "What if no one else knows? They might need help."

Eden was silent. She knew he was right, but then she'd have to confess that she'd opened a sidh to Earth—and back to the Merrow, of all places. Her parents would be furious, and they'd probably figure out a way to keep her locked in her room forever. Or what if . . . what if they took away her ability? It had worked on her mum when *she* had been a baby—Gran and Kier had given Cedar the gift of humanity, and it had masked her Danann talents. Could they do that to her?

"I don't . . . I don't think we should," she said in a small voice.

Niall was watching her shrewdly. "You're worried you'll get in trouble," he said, and she nodded meekly. "I don't want you to get in trouble, and I would love to keep using the sidhe. But that Merrow was *dead*. We need to do something." He cocked his head to the side and frowned, as if he were thinking hard. Eden thought it made him look rather grown up. Finally he met her eyes again, and said, "You know Toirdhealbhach, right? The healer?"

"Yeah, but I just call him Felix. He's like my dad's best friend."

Niall laughed. "Felix! That's an odd name. All right, let's call him that. Anyway, *my* father is also a healer, so they work together sometimes. And sometimes they get me to run messages for them and stuff. I'm not supposed to tell anyone this, but I know that Felix has a gancanagh in his home, and that he's really sick. Felix has gone away for a few days, so my father is looking after this guy." Niall puffed out his chest.

"What's a gancanagh?" Eden said, stumbling over the strange word.

"It's kind of like a Merrow—I don't mean the tail and stuff, but it's kind of in between us and the humans. It's a magical creature, but it lives on Ériu."

"So . . . what about him?"

Niall shrugged. "I dunno. I was just thinking there might be a connection. Sick gancanagh, dead Merrow, both from Ériu."

Eden considered this. "Maybe . . . ," she said. "I know!" she said after a moment. She almost told Niall about Helen and their secret lessons, but stopped herself short. "There's someone I know who can help us. She knows a lot of stuff about Ériu."

Niall looked at her suspiciously. "Yeah? You won't get in trouble, though?"

"I don't think so. Look, why don't you see what you can find out from your father? Try and listen in on more of his conversations. And I'll ask my, um, friend what she knows about the Merrow. We'll be detectives, like Nancy Drew!"

"Who?"

"Never mind."

They headed back to the house just as Riona emerged from the back door.

"I was just about to call for you," she said when she caught sight of them. "Did you have fun?"

Eden nodded her head vigorously. "Oh yeah, tons of fun!"

"What did you do?" Riona asked.

"Oh, nothing. Just climbed trees and stuff. Had races." Eden and Niall glanced at each other from the corners of their eyes.

"Yes, your mother tells me you are quite the runner," Riona said, giving Niall an approving smile. He muttered something that sounded vaguely like "thank you" and shuffled his feet.

Riona and Eden stayed for dinner with Atty and Niall. A couple of hours later, when Eden thought she possibly couldn't eat another bite, Riona said it was time to go.

"I could . . . you know," Eden said, giving her grandmother a hopeful look.

"Make a sidh? You could, indeed, since you have a guardian with you. But I thought you might like to ride back," she said with a wink.

"I would, but maybe next time?" Eden said.

"Go right ahead, then," Riona said, taking a step back.

Eden winked at Niall and then leaned casually against the wall of his house. "Bye, Niall!" she called as she let herself fall through the sidh into the front room of her own house. Riona followed her, shaking her head in amusement.

"So did you like that boy?" she asked once Eden had closed the sidh.

"Yep," Eden answered. "Can we go see him again tomorrow?"

"If you would like," Riona answered. "*After* your lessons."

Eden gave a mock groan, picked a book up off the floor, and skipped toward her bedroom. There was a mystery afoot, and she and her new friend were going to solve it.

CHAPTER 10

Cedar and Finn had returned to their bedroom from Helen's room, and Cedar was practically dancing with anticipation. All they had to do was ask Abhartach to locate the jewels, and the Unseen would be saved. She wished she'd had this information in time to help Logheryman, but at least now no one else would need to die. She pulled a backpack out of her wardrobe and started thinking of what they would need for the next leg of their journey. She knew Eden must be having her lessons with Nevan in the library now, and then Riona planned to take her to meet Niall, so they probably wouldn't see her until they got back.

"Do you know where Abhartach is?" Cedar asked.

"Last I heard from Brighid, he was headed for MacGillicuddy's Reeks," Finn said. "There are folk stories about blood-drinking fairies in those parts, and I think he hoped to find some of his own kind there."

Cedar shuddered at the thought of a colony of blood-drinking dwarves. "Where's that?"

"It's a mountain range in County Kerry, Ireland." He watched her bustle around the wardrobe, a peculiar look on his face. "Are you going to let them go now?"

"Let who go?" she asked as she pulled on a clean T-shirt.

"Helen and the other druids," he said. "You can't keep them locked up forever."

"Why are you thinking about that now? We know what we have to do next! Aren't you excited?"

"If it weren't for Helen, we'd still have no idea what was going on with the Unseen. She's told us everything she knows. The other druids have cooperated too. I just thought it was maybe time to let them go home."

"We don't *know* that she's told us everything," Cedar pointed out. "Maybe she's just telling us what she wants us to know."

"Do you really think that?" Finn asked. "What could she possibly stand to gain? She clearly wants to get back to the library, so it's hardly like we won't know where she is."

"The reason she wanted to go back to the library so badly is that she thought the jewels had a chance of being returned there," Cedar said. "But now we're going to find them. We have no idea where she might go once the jewels are destroyed. Besides, why didn't she tell us the truth from the beginning? She only told us about the Unseen *after* we confronted her with what Nuri said. She knew we were on to her." Her voice hardened. "I don't know what her game plan is yet. But I still don't trust her. I didn't think Liam had anything to gain by betraying me, either . . . until it was too late."

"Helen's not Liam," Finn said quietly.

Cedar met his eyes with a steely gaze. "We don't know that yet." Then she softened. "Listen, we can talk about it more once we've found the jewels. We have to stay focused. Abhartach is—"

Suddenly Cedar felt the bottom drop out of her stomach. A look of horror spread across her face. "Oh no," she whispered.

"What is it?" Finn said, alarmed.

"He's a dwarf. He's one of the Unseen."

Finn's hand flew to his forehead. "You're right. Why didn't I think of that before?"

"He might already be dead," Cedar said. "We need to go find him now."

"Wait," Finn said. "He'll need human blood in order to find the jewels. Do you think Jane—"

"Absolutely not," Cedar said forcefully. "I'm not subjecting Jane to that again. He nearly killed her last time." She thought for a moment. "I used to donate blood in Halifax. We'll go there first and grab a couple of bags."

"It's the middle of the day—you're just going to walk in there and steal some blood?"

"It's Thanksgiving Monday," she replied. "It'll be closed. It's perfect."

"Okay, but even if we don't bring Jane, we'll still need Felix. Neither of us speaks ancient dwarvish, remember?"

Cedar rubbed her temples. "You know, sometimes I wake up for a moment and forget that all of this has happened. I'll find myself thinking about a client project for Ellison or Eden's schedule for the week. And then I remember that I'm the queen of Fairyland, I can shoot fire from my palms, and I'm about to break into a blood-donation center to steal blood for a vampire-zombie-dwarf living in the Irish mountains."

Finn laughed and rubbed her shoulders. "Just another day in the life of the Tuatha Dé Danann. You wouldn't want to go back, would you?"

"Depends on the day," she muttered. She exchanged her Keds for hiking boots and grabbed her backpack. "You said he's in the mountains somewhere—where, exactly? We can go straight there once we grab the blood."

"Apparently there's a fortress in MacGillicuddy's Reeks that the locals call Dun Dreach Fhola, which means 'the Castle of the Blood Visage.' That's where the stories come from, but I've never been there, and I don't know exactly where it is. All I know is that it's near one of the more secluded mountain passes. But that still gives us a lot of ground to cover—it might take us a while to find it. And it will be dark in Ireland soon. We'll find him faster if we wait until morning."

"What if he doesn't make it until morning?" Cedar protested.

"If we go now, we'll just spend the whole time wandering around in the dark. Even with your fire to guide the way, we won't be able to see more than a few feet in front of us. And I don't think we can count on the friendliness of whatever creatures live in those mountains. I'd rather not be ambushed in the dark, especially since I'm assuming you'll be leaving your guards behind again."

"I'd like to leave them behind forever," Cedar said. "Fine, we'll wait until morning, but I'm going to get the blood now. You coming?"

"Yes, ma'am," Finn said.

She opened the sidh into the far back of the donation room— the only part of the building she'd ever visited. It was empty, as she'd predicted. She stayed perfectly still for a moment, wondering if there were motion detectors. But when Finn strode in behind her, she relaxed. It was an older building, and it wouldn't make sense for their security technology to be state-of-the-art. Besides, she thought, who in their right mind would want to steal blood?

"Where do they keep it?" Finn wondered.

"I don't know," Cedar said. "This is the room where you donate it, but I don't know where it goes after that. It must be somewhere refrigerated, though."

They started searching, moving from room to room with Cedar in the lead, a ball of fire balanced in the middle of her palm. "Here, help me open this door," she said. "It's locked." Together, they shoved their shoulders into the door, which opened with a loud clang of metal. A rush of cold air greeted them.

"Excellent," Cedar said, stepping into the refrigerated room. Bags of blood hung on hooks on all the walls, labeled by blood type. She started hauling bags down and stuffing them into her backpack.

Finn's comments about the druids kept replaying in the back of her mind. *He* had been deceived by Liam just as she had been. Did he really think they should trust the next druid who came along to offer them help? Was he that naive? She pulled another bag down more forcefully than she'd intended, and it split open, blood spilling down the front of her shirt. She swore loudly, shaking her arms and sending red drops spraying around the room.

"I think we have enough," Finn said. "Let's get back."

Cedar had dismissed the fireball from her hand and was just about to open the sidh back to Tír na nÓg when all the lights in the room turned on. A security guard stood in the doorway, one hand on the light switch, the other bringing his radio up to his mouth. Then he froze.

"*Cedar?*" he asked. "What the hell are you doing here?"

Cedar couldn't speak for a moment. This was the worst-case scenario. She had been caught red-handed—literally—by someone she knew. And *not* someone who was apt to do her a favor.

"Troy! Hey! How's it going?" she said, forcing a cheery smile.

He scowled at her and stalked over. "I asked what you were doing here. And why are you covered in blood?"

"Um, well, one of the bags broke," she said, wincing. "Sorry."

Troy and Finn sized each other up, and then Finn stepped in front of her protectively.

"You told me you were gay," Troy said to Cedar, giving Finn a defiant glare.

"I am," she lied, not wanting to piss him off further. "This is my brother. Look, I know this seems weird, but we're just in town for the day and a friend of ours needed some blood. An emergency thing, you know. And we've got a doctor and everything, so it's all good. If you could just . . . not mention this, I'd really appreciate it." She tried to give him a coy look, but she knew the effect was probably ruined by the blood dripping from her hair.

"Whatever," he said, reaching for his radio.

"You know, you really don't want to do that," she said, stepping around Finn so that she was directly in front of Troy again.

The security guard stuck out his chest. "Oh yeah, and why's that?"

"Because we'll be long gone by the time your reinforcements come," she said. "And then you'll look like an idiot." She refrained from adding "more than usual."

"You're not going anywhere," he said. "You stay right there."

Cedar sighed and silently thanked whichever politician had decided not to allow Canadian security guards to carry firearms. She jerked her head at Finn. "Let's go." She took off running, the backpack full of blood bags bouncing behind her, Finn on her heels. She waited until they had flown up a flight of stairs and shut themselves into an office before opening the sidh. She could hear Troy pounding up the stairs behind them, shouting into his radio. But by the time he opened the office door, she had already opened the sidh. The last thing she heard before they ran through it was "I know how to find you, Cedar McLeod!"

"Shit!" Cedar said, dropping her blood-filled bag on the floor of their bedroom.

"What?" Finn said. "We got away. It's not like he'll be able to find us."

"No, but he'll be able to find Jane," Cedar said. "He's a friend of her cousin, which is how I met him. And he's enough of an idiot to start harassing her or get her wrapped up in some police investigation . . . all because I wouldn't go out with him. *Ugh*. Where's the

Tír na nÓg witness-protection program when you need it?" She sighed. "We'd better go get them."

A few seconds later they were standing in the living room of Jane's apartment. Felix was sitting on the sofa alone, watching TV with a beer in his hand. He jumped to his feet when he saw them. "What happened?" he asked, rushing over to Cedar. For a moment she was confused, but then she remembered that she was drenched in blood.

"I'm fine," she said quickly. "It's not mine."

"Well, whose is it, then?" he said, stepping back to look at her. "And what did you do to them?"

Before she could answer, Jane emerged from her bedroom, holding a glass of wine, which she promptly dropped. "Oh my god, Cedar! Are you okay?"

"Yes, yes, I'm fine!" she assured her, wondering why they were drinking in separate rooms.

"What's going on?" Jane asked. Hastily, Cedar filled them in on what they'd found out from Helen, their plans to go see Abhartach, and the disastrous run-in at the blood bank.

"Oh, *Troy*," Jane moaned. "What a complete dickhead. God, Ceeds, I'm so sorry my cousin ever introduced the two of you."

"It's no big deal," Cedar said. "But I think you should come with us. Call in sick for a day or two more and let this thing with Troy blow over. He didn't seem too impressed, and I don't want him to take it out on you or send the police to look for me. You can hide out at our place while we track down Abhartach."

"Oh, jeez, I can handle that blockhead," Jane said with a dismissive wave. "I've got loads of vacation days stored up, though. And I'd rather come with you anyway—as long as Abhartach doesn't drain me dry this time, that is."

"You would?" Cedar said, surprised at Jane's laissez-faire attitude toward the whole thing.

"For sure." She grinned. "Adventure is good for the soul, remember?"

Cedar grinned back and hugged her. She stole a glance at Felix, who was watching them warily.

"Okay. Let's head back to Tír na nÓg for now. We're going hiking tomorrow, so pack some clothes. Then let's get out of here before the police show up—or worse, Troy."

꩜

The mood was somber as the four of them sat around the table in the newly restored poppy field in Cedar and Finn's home, their hands clutching steaming mugs of spiced wine. "What if we're too late?" Jane asked. "What if he's dead when we get there?"

"I don't know," Cedar said, staring into the swirling steam rising off her wine. "We don't have a Plan B. But we'll think of one if we have to. I just hope that we *don't* have to."

"What kind of a place do you think this 'Castle of the Blood Visage' is, anyway?" Jane asked, her nose wrinkled. "Doesn't sound all that cheery. I kind of thought the Unseen were all, you know, friendly. Pixies and mermaids and all that jazz. The 'gentle folk.'"

Felix snorted, and Cedar wondered if he was going to point out the damage that Irial had inflicted. But instead he said, "You weren't there for the battle with the Merrow, and you haven't been on the barbed end of a leprechaun's wit. The Irish started calling the Unseen the 'gentle folk' to appease them, so that they'd stop playing pranks on them and cursing their cattle. But that was years ago . . . back when people still believed." His voice sounded sad. "They just keep to themselves now, have for years. But even if they're not all rainbows and lucky charms, they don't deserve this. They deserve a chance."

"Who deserves a chance?" came a small voice from the doorway. Eden was standing there, a book dangling in one hand.

Cedar jumped up. "Eden! I thought you were asleep, honey."

Eden shrugged. "I wanted to see if you were home yet. What were you talking about?"

"Nothing. Let me tuck you back in."

"I heard you mention Abhartach. Is that who you were visiting?"

Cedar sighed. Apparently Eden was not going to let this drop. She wondered how much her daughter had heard. "No. We're going to see Abhartach tomorrow," she answered. "Today we were visiting some other, uh, people."

"Like who? Did you see the Merrow?"

"No, why?" Cedar asked, surprised.

"Just wondering," Eden said with another shrug.

"We're just touching base with some of the other magical creatures who live on Earth. They're called the Unseen," Cedar said, hoping that little bit of information would be enough to satisfy Eden's curiosity without inciting her to come with them. "It's part of Mummy's job." She decided it was time to change the subject. "How was your day? Did you meet Niall?"

"Yeah!" Eden exclaimed, and then proceeded to tell her all about his house and the forest where they'd played and what they'd had for dinner. "We're going to hang out again tomorrow."

"That's great!" Cedar answered. "Now off to bed. We'll be gone again in the morning, but hopefully not for too much longer."

"Okay. Tell Abe I said hi."

❧

Early the next morning, Cedar, Finn, Felix, and Jane appeared on a remote mountainside in MacGillicuddy's Reeks. The clouds above them were lined with a fiery pink as the sun rose in the distance. Most of the mountains were a deep emerald green, but peaks of sheer rock stabbed at the sky on the horizon. In the valley just below them, a mirrorlike lake reflected it all. Cedar had gone skiing in the Rockies a few times, and had seen more spectacular mountain vistas, but these . . . these felt magical, as though she'd gone back in time to the days when the Tuatha Dé Danann called this land home. She wondered if any of her ancestors had stood in this same place and marveled at this same scene.

"So, what's your plan? To hike around and hope we bump into a castle filled with vampires?" Jane asked.

"We could," Finn answered, "but I was thinking it might be faster to fly. There are a lot of unexplored areas in these mountains, and the fortress might very well be invisible to humans. I'll take an eagle form to survey the landscape from the air."

"Or we could start by looking in the areas where the most hikers have gone missing," Jane said. "If there really are vampire-like creatures living around here, they need to get blood from somewhere, right?"

They all turned and stared at her. "What?" she asked. "Don't you guys watch crime shows?"

"It makes sense, I guess," Cedar said. "But how do we find that out?"

"I did some research last night, before we left Halifax," Jane said with a shrug. "It didn't take long. Ireland's missing-persons database is easy to get into. I thought it might be good information to have, just in case." She pulled her tablet out of her backpack, then glanced at Finn. "Not that I don't think your plan is a good one! This might just help narrow down the area you have to fly over."

Finn looked suitably impressed. "Sounds good to me."

Jane pulled up a spreadsheet. "So, there's no guarantee that they're related, but it seems kind of weird that most people who go missing in these parts were hiking in the Beenkeragh area. The online records only go back about twenty years, but of all the missing persons, over three quarters of them were last seen there."

"You're amazing," Felix said, his voice hushed with awe, and Jane blushed.

"I'm just a geek with a computer," she said. "But does that help?"

"Beenkeragh is about three miles from here," Finn said. "You guys head in that direction, and I'll see if I can pinpoint the location of the fortress from the air."

Finn transformed and took flight, and the rest of them started following a narrow path that was more like a goat trail—a tiny, winding gap between the rocks and the brush.

After they'd walked for about half an hour, Finn joined them again. "You're headed the right way," he said. "It's incredible—there's a castle built right into the side of the mountain. It must be invisible to humans or someone would have stumbled across it ages ago. It's huge."

"Unless whoever stumbles across it gets invited to stay for dinner," Jane muttered, following Finn as he led them onto a slightly different path.

Cedar lagged behind a bit so she could have a private word with Felix.

"How's it going?" she asked him. "She seems to be more herself again."

He nodded slowly. "For now," he said. "I think this trip will be good for her, as odd as that sounds. But . . . she's still not over him. She's trying, I can see that, and sometimes it seems like things are back to normal. But we still haven't, you know . . ."

"Ah," Cedar said, then fell silent. She searched for the right words, but he continued before she could find them.

"It's not just that. She'll seem like she's all right, and then she'll say she needs to be alone for a bit, and I'll hear her crying in the other room."

Cedar gave him a sympathetic look. "I'm so sorry. It must be hard on you. But I think it's amazing that you're sticking with her. She'll come around."

"That's what I keep telling myself. How's it going with you guys? I'm guessing it's been a bit of an adjustment, moving to Tír na nÓg and becoming queen in one fell swoop."

"You can say that again," she admitted. "Depends on the day— or the hour. We fight, and then we make up, and then I'm furious at him, and then I can't live without him. It's kind of maddening, to tell you the truth. But I suppose I wouldn't have it any other way."

Felix wrapped an arm around her shoulder and gave her a squeeze. "Well, we both have to believe it's going to work out in the end—and that it's worth the struggle."

"What are you guys talking about?" Jane called back, waiting on the side of the path for them to catch up.

"Just a little history lesson," Felix said smoothly. "Did you know that some people think this castle and the fine folk who live there were the inspiration for Bram Stoker's *Dracula*?"

"I thought that was some Vlad the Impaler guy from Transylvania," Jane said skeptically.

"That's one theory, yes," he said. "But the Irish word for 'bad blood' is pronounced 'droc-ola.' And Stoker's sister-in-law was a MacGillicuddy, so he would have heard the stories of the blood-drinking fairies in these parts."

"How on earth do you know all that?" Jane asked.

"I'm not just a pretty face, my lady," he said with a wink. "No offense, but Halifax got a little boring after twenty years. I read a lot of books."

"Stop talking," Finn said suddenly. They all fell silent and froze in place. Finn slowly circled back to join them. "We're not alone," he whispered. "Stay alert, but try to act natural."

Easier said than done, Cedar thought. She didn't know why they didn't just call out Abhartach's name, but she trusted Finn's instincts. They crept forward, walking in single file. She looked around nervously. She had the distinct feeling they were being watched.

Then she saw it. It was just as Finn had described—a tall stone castle that looked as if it had been carved out of the mountainside. From the sky, it would have looked just like another mountain, and she wondered how Finn had even noticed it. It was awe inspiring, but there was nothing beautiful about it. It was all hard, jagged edges, piercing spires, and an imposing iron gate studded with spikes the size of her forearm. So intent was she on the castle that she didn't notice the dwarves materializing around them until one of them brandished a sword in her face.

"Hey!" Cedar yelled, and before she had time to think, she had raised a circle of fire around herself and her three companions, forcing the dwarves to jump back.

"Bring it down, Your Majesty," Felix muttered in her ear. She lowered her hand and the fire vanished. As soon as the last flames flickered out, Felix started speaking the same strange guttural language he had spoken to Abhartach when they raised him from his grave. There was a volley of words between Felix and the dwarves, all of whom had dark tattoos all over their bodies and were armed with swords, spears, and daggers. But now that her initial surprise had worn off, Cedar noticed how thin and tired they looked. The one brandishing the sword seemed as though he could barely keep it aloft.

"I knew we shouldn't have brought her," Felix said, stepping protectively in front of Jane. "You were right," he said to Finn. "They're sick too. They say they need blood."

"I have blood!" Cedar cried, stepping forward.

"Wait!" Jane said. "You need that blood for Abhartach so he can find the jewels, right? You can't give it to these guys."

Cedar hesitated. "Felix, will you translate for me?" she asked. "Tell them . . . tell them who I am, and that we are here to help them. Tell them that all of the Unseen are sick, and that if we can just see Abhartach, we might be able to find an antidote."

Felix relayed this message to the dwarves, who grunted amongst themselves. His face grew red, and Cedar could see a vein throbbing in his forehead. "What are they saying?" she asked.

"They'll take us to Abhartach, but they want to keep Jane as collateral in case your plan doesn't work."

Cedar stared at him. "Are they insane? We're trying to *help* them!" Her mind whirled. She had to get her friend away—fast—but she couldn't send her back to Halifax in case Troy showed up. "For goodness sake, don't let anyone see you," she said under her breath before she opened a sidh in midair and shoved her friend through it. Without her even having to ask, Finn had moved beside her to close the sidh. The dwarves started shouting all around them.

"Thank you," Felix said. "Where did you send her?"

"Our home in Tír na nÓg," Cedar answered. "She should be safe there." She turned to face the dwarves again, eyes blazing. "Tell them that unless they take us to Abhartach, they are all going to die. The time for pride is over. I can see the sickness in them, and it is the same that is ailing all of the Unseen. Tell them that if Abhartach can help us, the Tuatha Dé Danann and all the Unseen will owe them their gratitude."

Felix relayed her message, and the dwarves started to argue with one another, shouting and grunting and brandishing their weapons. Cedar pulled Felix and Finn in close. "This is taking too long," she muttered. "Let's just go find Abhartach ourselves. He must be inside that castle."

"I wouldn't advise it, Your Majesty," Felix said. "Dwarves are notoriously loyal to their kin. If we offend them, it will be difficult for Abhartach to help us without losing face."

Cedar was preparing a retort when one of the dwarves approached Felix and barked a few short words. "We're in," Felix said. "Let's go—and try to act submissive, if at all possible. We wounded their pride by recognizing their weakness."

They silently approached the fortress, surrounded by dwarves on all sides. As they came near, the iron gate dissolved into smoke. Cedar hurried forward, but was prodded back by a couple of spear-wielding dwarves. She felt a burst of annoyance—between the three of them, she was certain they could take on this rabble of weakened warriors—but she knew Felix was right. They needed Abhartach's help . . . that is, if he was still alive when they got there.

The entrance hall of the fortress was dark and cold, its rough stone walls hung sporadically with low-lit torches. They were ushered up an uneven staircase carved into the back wall, and through a dizzying series of tunnels that took them deep inside the mountain.

"Hey, this is kind of like Felix's house," Cedar said to Finn out of the corner of her mouth, but she fell silent when the dwarf next to her gave her a jab with the hilt of his sword. They walked past a series of heavy wooden doors, and their escorts stopped at the last one. One of them disappeared inside, closing the door firmly behind him. After a few moments, he came out and spoke to Felix.

"We can go in," Felix said, and Cedar and Finn followed him and the dwarf into a small round room. Abhartach was lying under a pile of animal skins on a thick wooden bed, which was the only piece of furniture in the room. He gazed at them fixedly, nodding slowly in greeting. Then he spoke, and Felix translated.

"He says that the Tuatha Dé Danann once again need his help."

"We can help *each other*," Cedar corrected. "Tell him that if we find the jewels, he and his people will be well again."

She stepped back and waited while Felix and Abhartach conversed. Her heart was pounding so loudly she wondered if the sound was luring in the dwarves, but then she remembered that her blood was of no use to them. Still, she felt uneasy. So much for the Unseen being benign creatures. There had been too many "missing" persons on Jane's list for that to be true. At least there would be one silver lining if they failed: MacGillicuddy's Reeks would be a safe place for humans to hike again.

"I've told him everything we know about the jewels. He says he'll do it—if he can. You can give him the blood bags now." Cedar opened her backpack and hauled out the cache of plastic bags, handing one to Abhartach. He ripped a hole in the end with his teeth and started sucking on it hard.

"So they all drink human blood?" Cedar asked as she watched Abhartach empty one bag after another.

"No, or at least they don't all *need* to," Felix answered after relaying the question to Abhartach, who gave his answer between gulps. "Only the mages—the dwarves who can do magic like Abhartach—need blood to enhance their powers. But others believe it gives them greater strength, and can heal illnesses."

Cedar didn't feel all that relieved. "Remind me to do something about that once all this is over," she whispered to Finn.

"Like what? You going to start shipping in bags of blood?" he whispered back.

"Of course not. But if I'm going to help them stay alive, it's on my hands if they eat any more innocent humans."

"You're not responsible for their actions," Finn said.

"Yeah, just their lives," she countered.

"Shhh!" Felix said, and they all fell silent as Abhartach sat up straighter in his bed and closed his eyes. Cedar held her breath. She thought of Logheryman and the old selkie and wondered how many others had died in the past few days. She wanted to shout at Abhartach to hurry up, but she bit her tongue.

The dwarf chieftain started rocking back and forth and moaning in a low, rasping voice. His voice slowly intensified, and soon he was chanting loudly. Then his eyes flew open, but Cedar could only see the whites—his pupils were rolling around in the back of his head.

And then it was over as suddenly as it had begun. Abhartach collapsed back onto the rough pillow of the bed and lay perfectly still, his eyes closed, his arms outstretched. The other dwarf hurried over and pulled the skin covers up over him, glaring at Cedar.

"Is he okay?" she asked Felix, who had also rushed to Abhartach's side. The dwarf's eyelids slowly opened, then closed again. He reached out a tattooed hand and grappled for Felix, who leaned in close enough so that the dwarf's lips were almost brushing his ear. When he straightened up again, the look on his face made Cedar's heart constrict.

"They are nowhere on Ériu," he said. "He says they are either in some other realm . . . or they do not exist."

CHAPTER 11

Eden lay awake in her room until she was sure her parents had left to visit the dwarf. It was time for another lesson, and she had lots to tell Helen—and to ask her. After checking to make sure the coast was clear, she made a sidh into the druid's room. Helen was at her desk, which is where she always was when Eden saw her.

"Hi, Helen!" she said brightly.

Helen looked at her suspiciously. "You're in a good mood. Did you talk to older Eden again?"

"No," Eden answered. "But . . . can you keep a secret?"

Helen laughed, but it was a strangely sad sound. "I've kept secrets my whole life, my dear. What is it?"

Eden sat down on the bed. "Well, I was, um, playing with a new friend, and I know I'm not supposed to, but I kind of made a sidh."

"And how is that a secret? You make one to come here all the time. Everyone knows that's your ability."

"Yeah, but I'm not *supposed* to make them, especially not without a grown-up around." She stuck out her tongue at the thought.

"I see. And where did this sidh lead you?"

"Well, that's the weird part," Eden said. "I was with my new friend Niall. He was teasing me for being born on Ériu, and I wanted to show him that there is magic stuff there too. So I took him to see the Merrow."

"Oh, my child," Helen whispered. "And what did you see?"

"We went to the hut on the rocks near their home, which is where I stayed last time I visited them. But it was different this time, like none of the magic was working. And then one of the Merrow just floated past us and banged into the window. It looked like she was dead. And Niall's dad is a healer, and he said there's this really sick guy in Felix's house who's from Ériu. And he thought maybe they had something to do with each other. No one saw us," she added hastily. "I was really careful."

"Shhh, it's okay," Helen said. "You were right to tell me. I'm not upset—how could I be when the sidhe make it possible for us to have our lessons together?" She smiled kindly at Eden.

"So . . . what does it mean?" Eden asked.

"Part of me wants to just tell you that your mother is looking into it, and it will all work out fine." The lines on Eden's face deepened into a scowl. Helen continued. "But I know how much you would hate that, so that is *not* what I am going to say. You have been through a lot, Eden. And someday, perhaps, *you* will be queen. So it is important for you to know what is going on and why. You will no doubt have to make difficult decisions yourself someday."

Eden felt a burst of pride at Helen's words. Then she listened as Helen told her of an ancient bargain that had been struck with the power of eight magical jewels, a deal that bound the lifeblood of the Unseen to humanity's belief in the magical realm. It seemed like one of the fairy stories she had been fond of back in Ériu—before she had discovered that her own life was a tale of magic and adventure.

"What is my mum going to do?" she asked when Helen finished.

"She believes she can find the jewels," Helen said. "And then she plans to destroy them."

"Why didn't my mum tell me? I bet *I* could find the missing jewels!" Eden exclaimed. "I helped them find the Lia Fáil!"

"I know this isn't what you want to hear, but I believe this one is a task for the queen alone," Helen said.

Eden flared up at once. "You're just like everyone else!" she said, scrambling to her feet. "No one thinks I can do anything! What's the point of having this stupid ability if I'm not allowed to use it?"

"Sit. Down," Helen said, in a voice so steely Eden obeyed at once. "You want to be taken seriously? Stop acting like a child every time you don't get your way."

Eden stared down at the ground, tears filling her eyes. She blinked furiously, trying to keep them from spilling over.

"You will be very powerful one day," Helen told her, her voice softer. "You already are very powerful. But the reason that power is not coming to the fore is because you are not yet ready to wield it. Focus on *becoming ready*, and your power will develop. But you cannot force it or demand it. It has only been a few months since you found out your true identity. Enjoy who you are instead of always wanting to be more. Learn how to focus, how to concentrate. Learn patience, understanding, and compassion. *Then* you will be worthy of the power the universe has seen fit to grant you."

Eden blinked hard again, but she could not stop the tears from coming. She sobbed quietly, feeling so many different things at once and having no idea how to stop them. She felt Helen's arm wrap tentatively around her shoulders, and she leaned into the embrace. Helen felt nothing like her gran, who had been soft and comfortable, like a living, breathing pillow she could nestle down into. In contrast, Helen was thin and bony, and had obviously not hugged many children in her life. But she was the only one still alive who understood her . . . or at least that's how it felt.

After a minute, Eden stopped crying and straightened up.

"Now," Helen said. "Shall we see if we can find your older self in there?"

Eden nodded eagerly. "What should I do?"

"Let's start by sitting up straight. That's right. Now close your eyes."

For the next half hour, Helen led her through a series of exercises to help strengthen her mind. Eden concentrated as hard as she could, and she was thrilled when Helen told her that she was making excellent progress.

"Your mind is very strong, little one," she said.

"I think it's because the older Eden is helping me!"

"Perhaps. Let's see if she'll talk to you. Close your eyes, and try to connect with her deep within your mind."

Eden closed her eyes and thought hard about the last time the older Eden had spoken to her. She tried to remember the sound of her voice, the way it had made her feel. She sat still for what felt like a really long time, until she started to get restless. But just before she opened her eyes in defeat, she felt a stirring deep inside, and then the familiar voice spoke to her.

Hello, little me.

"Hi!" Eden said out loud, still keeping her eyes screwed shut. "I found her! Helen, she's here!"

"That's wonderful, dear, keep talking to her."

"I found the druid lady you told me about. She's teaching me how to do this, just like you said," Eden told her older self.

I knew you could do it. You're very clever. Do you mind if I talk to her?

"Sure! I'll tell her what you're saying."

I'd like to talk to her directly, actually.

"Oh. Um . . . how?"

You just need to give me permission. It will be like you're having a short nap. That's all. Then I'll wake you up when I'm done.

"But I want to hear what you're saying!"

I'll tell you all about it later, I promise. You won't miss a thing.

"Well . . . okay. I guess. Go ahead."

She was right, Eden thought—it *is* like falling asleep. And then there was nothing.

⟲

Helen watched Eden nervously. She had tried to follow the conversation even though she could only hear one end of it, so she wasn't surprised when Eden's eyes flew open, and an older, deeper voice came out of the little girl's mouth.

"Hello, Helen."

"Hello. Is Eden all right? The little one, I mean."

"She's fine, yes. She gave me permission to talk to you through her. You've done good work with her, and quickly too."

"She learns fast. Tell me, how—"

"We don't have a lot of time—though she is perfectly safe, this might wear her out. I've been wanting to speak with you."

"Why me?"

"I need a druid to help me—or my younger self, that is. I want to come out."

"Out?"

"I want to be released from this childish body, and I want to walk in the waking world, not just in Eden's dreams. Can you do that? Can you let me out?"

"But then . . . what will happen to the little one?"

"She will cease to exist in her current form. But remember, she and I are one. She'll be the same person—only older."

"But she'll no longer be a child."

"No. She'll be me."

Helen looked into the brown and gold-flecked eyes that were staring back at her. They didn't look like the eyes of a little girl, and it made her strangely sad. She had only known Eden for a couple of days, but she'd begun to enjoy the child's enthusiasm . . . and trust. The eyes that regarded her now were shrewd and a little wild. And yet, the girl had promised to send her home. Would she be losing that chance if she refused to help?

"I can't do what you've asked of me," she told Eden. "I want to help you—I want to help the *child*—but I don't have the ability to release you. I can teach her how to focus, how to tap into her power, and how to speak to you, but only she can set you free."

There was another long silence, and then Eden spoke, her adult voice sounding strange on her child's tongue. "I feared as much."

"What is there to fear?" Helen asked. "Let her enjoy being a child. You must know that adulthood brings with it many responsibilities—and much grief. Do not rush her into what she does not understand."

"I will wait . . . for now. But I grow more restless each day. Soon, she may have no choice but to accept who she is meant to be."

∽

That afternoon Eden told Niall about the jewels and the Unseen. They were sitting on a thick branch in the woods behind his home, their feet dangling in the air.

"Whoa. That is so cool," Niall said in an appropriately awed voice.

"I told Helen that I really want to help, but she says I need to stay here and concentrate on developing my abilities," Eden complained. She had risked telling Niall about her secret meetings with Helen, and he'd promised not to say anything. She liked having a friend to share her secrets, though she still wasn't ready to tell him about the older Eden. When she had "woken up" from letting her older self talk to Helen, she'd been exhausted. Helen had been cagey about what they'd discussed, and she'd sent Eden back to her room for a nap soon afterward.

"Yeah, my parents say that to me all the time," Niall said. "I mean, not about the jewels and all that, but I'm not allowed to do much more with my ability than run messages for my dad. Some of them are pretty important, though," he added quickly.

A blue butterfly floated past them and landed on the end of the branch. Eden started to move toward it, but as soon as she shifted her weight, it lifted off and started doing loop-the-loops in the air in front of her, as if it were deliberately trying to tease her.

"I wish I could learn how to fly," she said.

Niall laughed. "You can wish all you want, but that's never gonna happen."

Eden scowled at him. "Why not?"

"Because you can only use the abilities you were born with," he said.

"Maybe," Eden shrugged. "But Helen says I'm super powerful, so maybe I'll be able to learn new things too."

"Let me know when that happens," Niall said with a grin. He leaned back against the trunk. "So you gonna go look for them?"

"For what?"

"The jewels, of course! You said you wanted to."

Eden picked at one of her fingernails. "No," she admitted. "I wouldn't know where to look. And . . . well, I don't mind using the sidhe around here in Tír na nÓg or going places with you, but I think I'd be scared to travel all around Ériu on my own."

Eden wondered if he'd call her a sissy, but he nodded and said, "Yeah, you don't want to run into any more dead Merrow or anything."

"What about that guy that your dad is looking after?" Eden asked Niall. "The . . . what'd you call him?"

"The gancanagh," Niall answered. "What about him? He's still really sick."

"Maybe we should go visit him," Eden said.

He narrowed his eyes at her. "No way. We'll get caught."

"No, we won't," she said. "Felix is still away, and your dad is back at the house with your mum. I can make the sidh, and we'll look through it to see if anyone is around before we go through. I've only been in Felix's living room, but you'll know how to find the sickroom from there, right?"

"I don't know about this," Niall said, but Eden had already jumped down from the tree, landing on the ground like a cat on her hands and the balls of her feet. Niall had been teaching her how to do it, and she had picked the ability up quickly. "What are you going to say to him?" he asked.

Eden shrugged. "I dunno. We can cheer him up. Maybe we can ask him what a gancanagh is. Besides, if I'm queen someday I'll need to know about all these things."

Niall gave her a skeptical look. "You know you're probably not going to be queen for like a million years, right?"

Eden made a face at him. "I'll still need to know," she said. "You coming or not?"

Niall jumped down from the tree. "Okay. But we'd better not get caught."

"We won't," Eden assured him. She opened a sidh and peered through the shimmering patch of air into Felix's living room. She was pretty sure he was gone, but if he caught them, she could always say they had just come to visit. The room was empty. She grabbed Niall's hand and pulled him through.

"See? No one's here," she whispered.

"You don't know that," he said, looking around nervously.

"It's just Felix's house—I've been here bunches of times. You have too! You said you help your dad all the time! There's nothing to worry about."

"I'm not worried," he said defensively. "*I* just don't get any special treatment when I break the rules."

Eden wrinkled her nose. "I don't, either."

"Yeah, right," he muttered, but he led the way into the twisting maze of hallways and doors until he stopped in front of one. "This is it," he whispered. They pressed their ears against the door, listening.

"I don't think anyone's in there," Eden said. She put her hand on the latch and turned it. The room was empty, except for a bed and a long table and a set of cabinets against the wall. Her mother would have called it modern. Eden would call it boring. But the man on the bed . . . *he* was not boring. He looked like he'd once been incredibly handsome, but now he was more like a skeleton with skin stretched over it. Eden tiptoed over to his bedside, all nervousness gone.

Hello, who do we have here?

The voice in Eden's head made her jump. It was as if older Eden had suddenly thrust herself at the forefront of Eden's consciousness. Eden looked down at the man again. Clearly the older Eden found him *very* interesting.

"Hi," she said.

The man opened his eyes, which were as black as ink, and blinked a few times. He seemed to be having trouble focusing on her. "Hello," he said at last, and his voice came out all thin and raspy. "Who are you?"

Eden cocked her head, waiting to see if older Eden would say something else, but she didn't. "I'm Eden," she answered. "This is Niall. What's your name?"

"Irial," he croaked. "Why . . . ?"

"We came to visit you," Eden said. "You probably don't get a lot of visitors."

One of Irial's cheeks lifted slightly, as if he was trying to smile. "You're right," he said.

Niall was still glancing nervously at the door, but Eden was transfixed. Irial's forehead was shiny with sweat, and there was a strand of curly black hair stuck in it. She reached out to brush it off his forehead, but he flinched away.

"I wasn't going to hurt you," she said, withdrawing her hand.

"I'm sorry," he said. "It's just . . . a habit. Most people can't touch me."

"Why not?" she asked.

"I'm a . . . gancanagh," he said.

"What's that?"

He seemed to be searching for the right words—or maybe just the energy to speak. "Women—human women—fall in love with me very easily."

"Really?" Eden asked, fascinated. "Just by touching you?" Niall made a face, which she thought was rather juvenile.

Irial nodded stiffly.

"I know why you're sick," Eden said.

He raised his eyebrows. "Indeed?" He made a garbled sort of sound that she thought was maybe a laugh. "Then you know more than I do."

"They haven't told you? You made a deal that you would be safe as long as the humans believed in you," she explained. "But now they don't, so you're going to die."

"I don't remember making any such deal," Irial said. His voice was starting to fade even more, so Eden had to lean in close to hear him.

"It was a long time ago, and it wasn't just you—it was all of the Unseen. But don't worry: my mum is going to save you," Eden said.

"And your mother is . . . ?"

"The queen," Eden said. "She's going to find and destroy the magic jewels that made the spell. Then you'll get better."

"Ah, yes. Your mother is very brave. And very kind."

"She is," Eden agreed. Then she asked, "Why do they call you the Unseen? I can see you just fine. Is it only humans who can't see you?"

Irial started to shake his head, but then winced in pain. "Oh, they can see us well enough if we choose to show ourselves to them. No, it's because in the great dealings of the gods we have been left to our own devices. The Danann, in particular, prefer to pretend we do not exist. Until now, that is. That's why your mother is so special."

"Not all of us are like that! My dad told me that while he was on Ériu, it was his job to find all of the other magical creatures and make friends with them."

A faint smile passed over Irial's features. "Ah, yes, I heard there was a rogue Danann making the rounds a few years ago. Didn't have the pleasure of meeting him myself, though. You, your father, and your mother seem to care more than most. Not that it matters. Soon, we'll all be dead."

"No, you won't," Eden said stubbornly. "My mother is going to save you. And if she can't, I will."

CHAPTER 12

Cedar stared between Abhartach's insensate form and Felix, not registering at first what the dwarf had told them. She had been so certain this plan would work. Then she swiveled on her heel and faced Finn. "The druid lied to us. I *knew* she couldn't be trusted!"

"We don't know that for sure," he said. "Maybe they were stolen by one of us—maybe Abhartach can't find them because they're in Tír na nÓg."

"Or maybe Helen thought she'd send us on a wild goose chase, looking for magic jewels that don't exist. Can he try again?" she asked Felix. "What if I bring him more blood?"

Felix shook his head. "He says he gave it everything he has, that he does not have the strength to look again. But Cedar, I have to agree with Finn. Helen *may* have made the whole thing up . . . but it's just as possible that they were removed from Ériu sometime in the last thousand years—either by the person who stole them or someone else, maybe even one of our people."

"I think we should go see Brighid," Finn said. "She helped us find the Lia Fáil against crazy odds; maybe she can help us now."

"She helped us find the Lia Fáil by sending us to Abhartach," Cedar pointed out. "But you're right—she might know something we don't. We'll go to Brighid's. And if she can't help, Helen's going to answer to me."

146

∾

Cedar opened the sidh to the front gate of Brighid's island home. She'd half expected it wouldn't work; the last time they'd tried to visit Brighid without an invitation, they hadn't been able to open the sidh onto her property. But the Elder goddess had either lowered the security or was expecting their arrival. It was late evening in Thailand. The horizon was a deep purple, and a white moon hung in the sky, just brushing the top of the mountains that rose from the ocean like silent sentinels. Cedar pressed the silver button and the gate slid down silently. When they entered the front hall, it was not their friend who met them, but Vanessa, one of her human attendants.

"We've come to see Brighid," Cedar said.

"Yes," Vanessa said. "She will see you." She led them to the balcony overlooking the ocean.

Brighid was sitting in a wicker chair lined with a flowered cushion, her back to them as she stared out over the ocean, watching the moon rise. A deep blue shawl was draped over her shoulders. She did not turn, though she must have heard them arrive.

"Brighid?" Cedar said. Slowly, the goddess turned her head, and Cedar could not keep a shout of surprise from escaping her lips. Brighid's once flawless skin was now an emetic shade of gray, like porridge left out on the counter too long. Her prominent cheekbones were still there, but the skin was pulled so tightly around them that it gave her a skeletal appearance. Her eyes were sunken and rimmed with black. Her lips, once full of color, were so pale they could barely be distinguished from the rest of her face. Her normally lustrous hair hung lank around her shoulders. Her dull eyes passed over them, but then she turned back to the ocean without a word. Cedar rushed to her side and took one of her hands in her own. It was like holding a butterfly—she worried she might crush it if she held on too tight.

Felix had rushed to Brighid's other side. He looked completely bewildered by the state of her. "How is this possible?" he whispered. "What's happened to you?"

There was a long silence, and then Brighid's lips parted. When she spoke, it was in a paper-thin whisper, a marked contrast from her usually strong and confident voice.

"My time . . . is over," Brighid said, her eyes never leaving the horizon.

"No," Felix said fiercely. "There must be some explanation. This is impossible. *We don't get sick.*"

Finn looked utterly lost. Cedar reached out a hand and drew him over to her. He sat down next to her at Brighid's feet, looking up at his friend imploringly. "Brid, please, tell us what has happened. Tell us how we can help you."

A faint smile flickered over Brighid's wasted face, and she stretched out a bony hand to cup Finn's cheek. "You must let me go, Fionnbharr. There is nothing that can be done for me. For any of them."

"Any of them?" Cedar repeated softly. "Do you mean the Unseen? We've just been to see Abhartach—he's sick too. So are all of them, from what we can tell. Is this the same thing? But the rest of the Danann aren't sick. It doesn't make sense."

"I should have been the first to die," Brighid whispered. "Leave me. I will be gone soon . . . but not soon enough."

Cedar and the others exchanged startled glances. "Brighid, this isn't *you* talking," she said. "Let us help you. Tell us what we can do and we'll do it!" Normally, Cedar would have expected a sharp retort—or a peal of laughter. But instead Brighid stayed silent.

"Of course," Felix breathed, understanding dawning across his face.

"What?" Cedar asked.

"She was the one who made the deal," he answered. "Didn't you?" He looked at Brighid, but she didn't seem to hear him. He stood up, and Cedar and Finn pushed themselves to their feet too. "It makes sense," he continued. "Let's assume that Helen's story about the Unseen is true, and that the jewels exist. None of the Unseen has the power to wield such a spell. And where did the jewels come from in the first place? *Brighid* cast the spell, so she is bound to it, just as the Unseen are."

"Is that true?" Cedar asked Brighid. "Why didn't you tell us? Does that mean you know where the jewels are?"

Brighid's shoulders slumped, and Finn lunged forward to catch her before she fell out of her chair. "It is true," she whispered. "And the jewels are gone. I was a fool. I deserve my fate." Her eyes closed, and she slumped forward. Felix lifted her into his arms and gently laid her down on one of the balcony's lounge chairs.

"Is she . . . ?" Cedar asked in alarm.

"No," he answered. "She's only sleeping. But she is very weak."

"This can't happen," Cedar said, starting to pace the balcony. "There has to be another way." Then the solution came to her in a rush of adrenaline. She felt dizzy with the shock of it. Of course. There *was* another way.

"Cedar?" Finn asked, his eyes wary. "I recognize that look. What are you thinking?"

"We've been assuming that the only way to help the Unseen is to break their bond with the humans. But we can't do that because the jewels are lost. What we *can* do is convince the humans to believe in magic again, by showing them real proof. Once enough of them believe in magic, the spell should kick in again, and the Unseen will get better."

For a moment, Felix and Finn were both perfectly still. Then they both spoke at the same time: "No."

"What do you mean, no? If we don't do anything, the Unseen are all going to die. Including Brighid," Cedar said, her voice rising.

"I know it probably seems like an obvious solution to you, Cedar, but hear me out," Felix said. "It's true that the humans used to know about us, but that was a very, very long time ago. If they found out there were magical beings out there who never grew old, who could grant their every wish, they would stop at nothing in their efforts to access that power."

"So what do you suggest? That we just let the Unseen die? I can't stand by while that happens. I won't. I'm the only one who needs to make a scene—I won't expose the rest of us. They don't even need to know that Tír na nÓg exists."

"And if you're captured?" Finn asked darkly.

"Then I'll escape through the sidhe."

"Even if you're unconscious?" he asked. "And let's say you're right— you know you can't close the sidhe. You could be followed. If you came back to Tír na nÓg, you might lead their armies straight to us."

"Well, then, I wouldn't use the sidhe," Cedar said stubbornly. "But once I explain what I am, and show them what I can do, they'll *have* to believe in magic. I'm living proof."

"You can't . . ." Finn's voice broke. "Cedar, you don't know what they'll do to you. You wanted to leave Ériu in the first place because you were afraid of the tests they'd run on Eden if they found out about her."

"Yes, because she's a *child*."

"There must be another way!" he said. "We don't know for sure that the jewels aren't still here. Maybe the illness clouded Abhartach's ability—maybe he was wrong! We need to keep looking!"

"Finn, look at Brighid," Cedar said, waving her arm toward their friend. "We don't have time. This plan will work. I know you're worried about me, but I can do this without getting hurt."

"You don't know that!" he exploded. "Let's take a second to think about human history! It's a pattern that happens over and over again—the humans find someone they think is a god, and at first they worship him. Or her. But then they start blaming that god for everything that goes wrong, demanding more than he or she is able to give. And then they decide that god is to blame for *all* of their problems, and all of a sudden he or she is public enemy number one."

"Finn, you're exaggerating. It doesn't have to be that way."

"It *is* that way! Look at Jesus, for Christ's sake! Look what happened to him! Joan of Arc! Rasputin! There are dozens of examples!"

"It's not going to come to that. I won't be there for long enough," she said quietly. "And even if it did, in the absolute worst-case scenario, don't you think some things are worth dying for? Isn't my single life worth the lives of all the Unseen?"

Finn's eyes were burning into hers. "Not to me," he said. "Not to Eden."

Cedar turned away, unable to hold his gaze any longer. Then she opened a sidh to her bedroom in Tír na nÓg.

"What are you doing?" he asked.

"I'm going to get Jane," Cedar said. "She must be wondering what's happened to us. I'll be right back." She disappeared through the sidh before he could stop her, and was relieved when he didn't follow. She *did* want to make sure Jane was okay, but for the most part she just wanted a few quiet moments to think. Could she really go through with this plan? Would it work? Would she be putting her people in jeopardy? Herself?

"Jane?" she called out. "It's okay; it's just me." She jogged around the pond and through the field of poppies, calling her friend's name. There was no answer.

Is nothing simple? she thought as she pushed open the door leading to the willow-lined courtyard. She expected to see Jane chatting with Riona on one of the benches, but the room was totally empty.

Now she was starting to worry. "Where, oh where have you gone, my friend?" she muttered under her breath. Then she stopped in her tracks and smacked herself on the forehead. How could she have been so stupid? She immediately made a sidh leading to Felix's house. "Jane?" she yelled. She ran through the rooms, trying to remember where Felix had stashed Irial. She was so intent on her search that she bowled into the red-haired little boy who had brought her the message at Eden's birthday party.

"Niall!" she shouted as he picked himself up off the floor and prepared to take off.

"What?" he yelled, but then he recognized her and his face turned red. "Oh! I'm sorry. Your Majesty, I didn't—" He cut off in midsentence and looked wildly around, as if searching for someone else.

"It's okay, I didn't mean to scare you," she said. "Is there a woman here? A human woman?"

"A human? No," he said, his eyes round.

"Where is Irial?" she asked. "And what are you doing here?"

He glanced away. "I was helping my dad. He's just, uh, taking a break, so he's not here right now." He led her through the maze of rooms and hallways until he pushed open the door to one of the rooms.

"Can you wait here, please? I won't be long," she said, leaving him in the hallway and closing the door behind her. Irial looked worse than ever, but he managed to open his eyes and fix them on Cedar.

"Did she come here?" she asked.

"Who?" he croaked.

"Jane. The human," Cedar said. She cursed herself as her heart rate picked up at the sight of him.

"No," he answered.

"We're doing everything we can," she assured him, wondering how long he'd been alone.

"Have you figured out what's causing the illness?" he asked. Cedar glanced toward the door, then sat down gingerly on the edge of his bed.

"It's a curse. It was placed on the Unseen a long time ago, when you were being hunted. So long as humans believed in the world of magic, you would be protected from your enemies. But if they stopped believing, you would die."

Irial's eyes were wide. "She was right, then."

"Who was right?"

"Oh . . . uh, one of the old selkies told me a story like that, long ago. I didn't really believe her at the time. Is there anything that can be done?"

Cedar looked down at her hands. "There were these jewels that were involved in the making of the spell. If we could destroy them, it would break the bond, and you would get better. That was our plan. But . . . they're gone. We can't find them. So . . . there's no other choice. There's only one way to make the humans believe."

Irial was still staring at her as though he wasn't quite following. "How?" he asked.

"I'm going to show them who I am. What I can do," she said. "Once they see my abilities, they'll *have* to believe. It's the only way."

Slowly, Irial drew out his arm from under the blankets. He reached out a thin, pale hand to Cedar, his palm open.

"It's okay," he said when she shrunk back. "I can't hurt you."

She placed her hand in his, and a thrill of warmth ran through her veins.

"You would do that . . . for us?" he asked.

"Yes," she answered.

"Then you are the greatest queen the Tuatha Dé Danann have ever known," he whispered.

"Thank you, but I'm not so sure about that," she said. She forced herself to stand up. She had already lost too much time. "My friend Jane is wandering around somewhere in Tír na nÓg. I have to find her before I go."

Irial nodded. "Will she be okay?"

"She's getting there. It's not your fault. You can't help how you were born."

Irial didn't say anything, but he was still staring at her as she left the room. Niall was waiting for her in the hallway, hopping from one foot to the other.

"I need to ask you a favor," Cedar said. "Stay here until your father comes back. Don't let anyone in except him. *Especially* not any humans. Okay?"

The boy looked slightly bewildered, but nodded sharply.

"Jane, Jane, Jane, what are you up to?" Cedar muttered as she wound her way to the entrance of Felix's house and stepped out into the evening air. And then she saw her—a slight figure wearing an oversized hooded cloak, walking straight toward her. Throwing her hands into the air, Cedar raced to intercept her.

"What the hell, Jane? I told you to stay put! If anyone sees you . . ."

Jane shrugged. "I didn't know when you'd come back to get me. I was just going for a walk."

"I know exactly where you were going," Cedar retorted angrily. "You were going to see Irial."

Jane glared at her. "So what if I was?" she said. "It's not what you think. I just wanted to see him again. Then I'd know for sure that I was over him."

"You *can't* see him," Cedar said. "*Ever.* You don't Facebook-stalk a succubus. Don't you want to patch things up with Felix? *He's* the one you have *real* feelings for. But if you don't start making an effort, you're going to lose him."

Jane stared at the ground and pulled at the cloak, cinching the hood around her head. "I think . . . I think maybe it's too late," she said, her voice so low that Cedar had to lean in to hear her. "I don't see how he could want me back after . . . after what I did."

"Oh, *Jane*," Cedar said, not sure whether to hug her or throttle her. "He *does* want you back. He knows it wasn't your fault. He just wants to go back to normal—or whatever normal is for you guys. You have to trust him."

Cedar pulled her inside Felix's house, and through the still-open sidh that led back to her home.

"So what happened with the vampire-zombie-dwarf?" Jane asked once they were back in the willow-lined courtyard. "Did he lead you to the jewels?"

Cedar quickly brought her up to speed.

"I dunno," Jane said when Cedar finished. "Are you sure? I have to agree with Finn and Felix. It sounds awfully risky."

"It probably is," Cedar admitted. "I'll have to be really, really careful, and I'll need to pretend there's just one of me, like I'm the last of the fairies or something. But hopefully that will be enough. We're running out of time, and I really think it will work. But I want to talk to Eden first. I don't know how long it will take or how many humans I'll have to convince before the Unseen start getting better. Can I trust you to stay here for a few minutes? Don't even think about going back to Felix's house."

Jane rolled her eyes, but nodded. Cedar went into Eden's room and looked up. She could see Eden sitting on a branch, her nose stuck in a book. She climbed her way to the top and sat down beside her.

"Mum!" Eden leaned over and wrapped her arms around Cedar. "You're back! How was Abhartach? Did you tell him I said hi? Is he sick too?"

Cedar drew back and looked at her. "What do you mean, *too*?"

Eden froze. "Oh, I just heard something about the Unseen being sick. Is he?"

Cedar frowned. Word about Irial must have gotten around. But she had intended on telling Eden what was going on, anyway. If Cedar was really going to go through with her plan, Eden deserved to know why.

"Well, yes. Abhartach and the rest of the Unseen are sick. It's a long story, but it's because humans have stopped believing in them."

"Like Peter Pan," Eden said, nodding wisely.

"Kind of, yes. So we have to help the humans believe in magic again. That's what I came back to tell you. I'm going to show them what I can do, and hopefully that will convince them."

"But you always told me that we should *never* show them what we can do," Eden said.

"Normally, yes," Cedar said. "But in this case it's the only way to save our friends. Remember Brighid? She's sick too."

"But what if . . . what if they lock you up in a zoo? Or do experiments on you?" Eden asked.

"They won't," Cedar said. "I'll be really careful. There's nothing to worry about."

"I'm coming with you," Eden said. Her little face was intense. She looked far older than her seven years.

"Absolutely not."

"You just said there was nothing to worry about!" Eden cried.

"There isn't. It's just that . . . you've been through so much lately. And we don't know what will happen."

"So? *You've* been through a lot too. I want to help."

Cedar wrapped her arms around her daughter and pulled her close. "I know you want to help, baby, but this is something for the grown-ups, okay?"

Eden squirmed away and glared at her.

"Eden, listen to me," Cedar said. "It's not that I don't think you could help. I do. I know that you are strong and brave and I'm really proud of you. But someone has to stay here in Tír na nÓg, right? They need your help *here*."

Eden huffed. "How can I help here? No one lets me do anything."

"You'll be the only person here who can open the sidhe, in case someone else needs to come to Earth," she pointed out.

Eden was silent for a moment. "Fine," she finally said. "I guess."

"I'll be back as soon as I can," Cedar assured her. "And I'll make sure to take my starstone so you can keep me up to date on what's going on back here."

Eden nodded, but her eyes were still uncertain.

Cedar took a deep breath. "Daddy will be back soon. He'll come say good night in a bit. I'll see you soon, my heart."

She jogged down the staircase carved into the tree trunk, afraid to look back, afraid of what she might see in Eden's eyes. She had heard everyone's objections . . . but the more she thought about it, the more convinced she was that she was doing the right thing—the *only* thing. She thought of Logheryman's body lying at the bottom of the grave she had dug for him, of how sunken and defeated Brighid—the most alive person she had ever known—now seemed. She wondered if *this* was why the Lia Fáil had chosen her, to save the Unseen from extinction.

When she reached the courtyard, she discovered she was not alone.

Gathered around the waterfall in the center of the room was her entire Council—Rohan, Gorman, Anya, Nevan, Maran, and Amras—plus Riona, Seisyll, Sam, and Murdoch. Jane was hovering in the back. Finn stood in front of them all.

"You wouldn't listen to reason," Finn said. "I had no choice."

Cedar's insides twisted. She could see with her eyes what was happening . . . but her heart wouldn't believe it. He wouldn't do this to her. Not Finn. "What is this?" she asked.

"Finn told us what you're planning to do," Riona said. "You can't, Cedar."

He would.

"Did he also tell you that all of the Unseen will die if I don't?" Cedar said, once she had found her voice. She could feel her cheeks burning, and she clenched her fists to keep the fire inside. "Did he tell you that *Brighid* will die?"

"I told them everything," Finn said. "But this is not a road we can go down. Abhartach might have been wrong. We should keep looking for the jewels. We'll start near Kells and go from there. We'll seek out all of the Unseen. One of them might know something. You don't have to do this."

"You've been very admirable, Cedar," Riona said, her voice low and soothing. "No one will accuse you of not trying. But this isn't your fight."

"It *is* our fight!" Cedar said, looking around the circle for some sign of support. "We have the chance to save their lives! Why *wouldn't* we take it?"

"You don't know for sure your plan would even work," Rohan said. "At the first sign of your powers, the humans might sweep you away."

"And what if you lead them back here?" Gorman said. "Forgive me for saying so, Your Majesty, but your first duty is to your *own* people, not the Unseen."

Cedar shook her head, refusing to believe what she was hearing. "Do none of you agree with me? You all think we should just let them keep dying one by one while we look for jewels that may no longer exist?"

"You're so new to this world, Cedar," Nevan said. "But the reason the Tuatha Dé Danann have lasted so long is that we didn't get involved in the conflicts of others. And above all, we do not reveal ourselves to humans."

"I'm not saying we should do nothing," Finn interjected. "I want to help the Unseen too. But I don't think we've exhausted all our options yet."

"If you do this, your actions could have devastating consequences for all of your people," Murdoch growled. "Do you really want to cause a war with Ériu? Humans have always feared any beings that are different from them, and rest assured, if they find out about us, they *will* want to destroy us. You know better than anyone what they're capable of, and how dangerous their weapons are. If they find a way into Tír na nÓg and attack us, I do not think we could withstand them. Many lives would be lost on both sides."

Cedar sank down onto one of the benches beneath the willow trees. It didn't have to be that way—not if she was careful. She could hear Maeve's voice in her head, the voice from her dream. *If you had just listened to me, you would be living a normal, peaceful life. We all would. But you've always had to do things your way.* Is that what this was? Was she just doing things her own way again? Was she just supposed to ignore what was happening to the Unseen so they could all live a normal, peaceful life? She looked around at the faces of her friends, family, and advisers, all of them fixed on her. Some looked sympathetic; others looked worried. Some were threatening. No one spoke. They were united against her.

She stood up and took a deep breath. "I'm going to go back to see Brighid," she said. Out of the corner of her eye she could see several of them exchanging glances. Perhaps they had expected her to yell some more.

"So you agree—you will not reveal yourself to the humans?" Gorman asked.

"No," she said matter-of-factly. "I'm going to make sure she's still alive, and then I'm going to do whatever it takes to keep her that way."

Several voices broke out at once, renewing their arguments.

"That's enough!" she roared, and the room fell silent. She stood perfectly still. "The Lia Fáil chose me. I know that some of my people think that it made a mistake, that I shouldn't be queen. Maybe they're right; maybe I'm *not* fit to be a ruler. But I believe that turning our backs on those who are dying would be far worse—for them *and* for us—than taking the risk to help them. Are we really the kind of people who would turn away from the suffering of others? Are we not better than that? If not, consider this my abdication."

Without another word she turned her back on them and returned through the air to Brighid's balcony. She could hear Finn coming through behind her, but she ignored him. Maeve had been right. She was on her own now.

"How is she?" she asked Felix. Brighid's eyes were closed, but Cedar could see the shallow rise and fall of her chest.

"Still very weak," Felix said. "What's going on?"

"She's still bent on this mad plan of proving that we exist," Finn said from behind her. Jane had followed him through the sidh. She moved to Felix's side, but stopped about two feet away from him.

"But—" Felix said.

"Just . . . leave her alone," Finn said. His voice sounded wooden, and he stayed several steps behind her, his eyes on Brighid.

"Where will you go?" Jane asked in a small voice.

Cedar didn't know how to answer. She hadn't thought this part of the plan through yet. "I'm not sure," she said. "CNN? The BBC?"

She looked down at Brighid's wasted body again. If she was going to go through with her plan, this was the time. She closed her eyes and imagined the local TV station in Halifax—she'd start small. If she tried to transport herself into one of the large networks, she'd probably get jumped by security before she had time to do anything. She spared a glance at Finn, his face a mirror of her own misery. He was looking at her imploringly, but he didn't speak. She forced herself to look away. She had to do this now, before she lost her nerve. "I'll be back soon," she whispered. Then she stepped toward the sidh.

"*Stop.*"

Cedar froze midstep at the sound of Brighid's frail yet forceful voice. She was trying to pull herself up into a sitting position. "Close it," she said to Finn, who snapped Cedar's sidh shut at once, his eyes wide and full of hope.

"You must not do this," she said, her sunken eyes trained on Cedar. "Fionnbharr is right—it would be madness. It would mean the end of all of you. There is . . . perhaps another way."

They all stared at her, waiting.

"It is a very slim chance," she continued. "But you have a knack for achieving the impossible . . . I know where the jewels are."

CHAPTER 13

Eden could always tell when she was dreaming. Sometimes she dreamed of home—being back in school with her friends, going to the park with Gran, playing in her old bedroom. Those dreams made her sad, and she tried to forget about them. Other times she dreamed of Nuala, and in those ones she was running, always running, through grassy fields and over rough rocks that scraped her hands and knees when she fell. Once, she had a lovely dream in which she was queen of Tír na nÓg; she wore a sparkling silver crown and a ruffled yellow dress and ate cream puffs and custard and all her favorite foods. But the dreams she liked best were the ones in which she went to visit the Elders— thanks to her conversation with Nevan, now she knew that's who they were. She'd had these dreams ever since she could remember, back before she and Mum and Dad had even come to live in Tír na nÓg. Of all her dreams, they felt the most real. She knew that the Elders were far removed from her, off in the Four Cities, and that her conversations with them were imaginary, but she looked forward to them all the same.

That was the kind of dream she was having now. She was running down a skinny path between tall white trees, their green leaves high above her. She felt light of body and heart, as if she were floating, being drawn along by some invisible force. And then she saw them—a dozen or so tall, richly dressed men and women, waiting for her, just as they always were.

"Eden!" one of them cried, a woman with skin so pale Eden could see the blue veins beneath it. But her lips were a deep, dark crimson, and her black eyes were rimmed with red, almost like she'd been crying. But Eden had met her before, and she knew this was not unusual.

"Hello, Morrigan," Eden said pleasantly. "Where are the crows today?"

"Hunting," the Morrigan answered, "but they will return."

"How are you, child?" boomed Manannan mac Lir, thumping her on the back.

Eden thought for a moment. It took her a while to remember what had been on her mind before she fell asleep. "I'm worried," she admitted. "I'm glad you're here—or that I'm here." She never knew exactly where "here" was in these dreams.

"Worried?" the Morrigan asked. Her cloak was as black as coal, and it was long enough for the fabric to puddle onto the grass beneath their feet. "What's the matter? Don't you enjoy Tír na nÓg?"

"Oh, I do, very much!" Eden said. "It's amazing. It's just . . . I'm worried about my mum. She's gone to show herself to the people on Earth, I mean, Ériu."

The chatter that had been bubbling in the background fell instantly silent. All the Elders were looking at her, and those who had not yet greeted her gathered in close.

"Whatever do you mean, child?" asked Teamhair. "Surely you are mistaken. Your mother is queen of the Tuatha Dé Danann. She would never be that foolish."

Eden hesitated, not sure of how to respond. "Well, she said she had to make the humans believe in magic again to save the Unseen."

There was a heartbeat of shocked silence; then one of the Elders cursed and said, "Brighid!"

"My mum says *she's* sick too."

Teamhair let out a long, slow breath. "Brighid got herself into this mess. And now she risks exposing all the Tuatha Dé Danann to save her pride."

Eden was confused—obviously there was more going on here than what her mother had told her about. But before she could ask questions, the Dagda knelt down before her, and took hold of both of her hands. She had always liked the Dagda. From her lessons with Nevan, she had learned that he was the oldest of all the Elders—and the most important. But to her, he had always felt more like a grandfather than anything else. She looked into his warm blue eyes and relaxed. Whatever was happening, the Dagda would be able to fix it.

"Eden, my dear," he said. "You must convince your mother to not go through with this plan."

"Why?" Eden asked. "She said she would be safe."

The Dagda shook his head. "It is not as safe as she thinks," he said. "And if she does this, it would threaten all of our kind."

Eden's eyes grew wide. "Why?" she asked again.

"Our days of peacefully coexisting with the humans are long over," he said. "They have changed, almost unrecognizably so. Their technology is greater than we ever imagined they would achieve."

"You're scaring the child," Teamhair said with a sharp look at the Dagda.

"She needs to know what is at stake. You know she is more than just a child," he replied, his eyes still focused on Eden. "I know your mother thinks she is doing what is best, but you must stop her. She thinks she will inspire them to believe in the world of magic once again. But she cannot turn back the hands of time. They will be impressed with her abilities, yes. But they will not worship her. They will enslave her and, if given the opportunity, all the Tuatha Dé Danann. You are the only one who can stop this from happening."

Eden pulled back from him, waiting for one of the others to contradict him, to tell her that it wasn't that bad, that her mother would be safe. But none of them spoke; they just watched her silently. "How can I stop her?" she whispered.

"Find her. Tell her that *you* can find the jewels."

"I . . . I can?"

"Yes, my child. You, and you alone, have the power to end this."

Eden stared at them, wanting to believe them, but she didn't see how it could be true.

Finally, the Morrigan spoke.

"Go, child. Do not linger here among the dead."

Eden turned and started running, and then sat up straight in her own bed, screaming.

❦

At Brighid's words, Finn fell to his knees beside her chair and clasped her hand to his lips. Cedar could hear him whispering, "Thank you, thank you."

She felt a strange collision of relief and disbelief. "You know where they are? Where?"

"I am the only one who knows what really happened," Brighid said. "When I die, it will be up to you to fix the mess I've made. I'm sorry."

Cedar pulled a chair close to Brighid's other side and sat down. "You're not going to die," she said through gritted teeth. "Not if I have anything to say about it. Don't give up hope. You have to *believe.*" Finn continued to hold Brighid's hand while Felix and Jane gathered in close, wide-eyed.

Brighid laughed, which quickly led to a coughing fit. When she recovered, she said, "My misguided belief is what created this disaster in the first place. But I will tell you the truth, while I still can.

"You know that the Tuatha Dé Danann were defeated by the Milesians and banished to Tír na nÓg. But there were many other magical beings in the world besides us. They had no part in the war against the Milesians, so they stayed on Ériu. They kept to themselves, for the most part, which is how they got the name 'the Unseen.' When I decided to settle on Ériu many years later, I found most of them quite charming—and those that weren't charming were certainly interesting, which was just as good.

"And then Christianity arrived. At first, it seemed as though things would stay more or less the same. The monks were respectful of the old ways, and many of them even wrote down tales and legends about our people. I, myself, decided to play the part of an abbess for a while so that I could learn about this new religion from the inside. It was fascinating in many ways. But then . . . something changed. A new group of abbots started to gain power. They feared the old ways and tried to turn the people against them. They started to twist our stories, making all of them point toward *their* god. They turned the sacred wells that had been built by my sisters into 'holy wells' to honor their saints. They called us demons. And they vowed to crush any vestiges of magic that were left in the land. It was a crusade—a genocide. The Unseen drew further into the dark, but these men of the church were relentless in their mission to find and kill them.

"I had many friends among the Unseen, so I started hearing the terrible stories about what was happening to them. Pixie forests were being torn down. The Merrow and the selkies were being caught in nets and put to the sword. Even the dwarves were being hunted mercilessly."

Brighid closed her eyes again, drawing in a deep, shuddering breath. Finn smoothed the hair off her forehead with his hand. "It would be easier if . . . ," she murmured.

"What is it?" Cedar asked. "What can we do?"

"I need . . . a druid," Brighid whispered. "Is there . . . a druid you can bring to me?"

Cedar and the others exchanged long glances. "I'll go get her," she said.

She disappeared through a sidh that brought her directly to Helen's quarters. Helen was, as always, at her desk.

"I need you to come with me," Cedar said, indicating the sidh that still sparkled in the middle of the room.

"To where?" Helen asked, showing no sign of moving.

"To see Brighid."

Without another word, Helen swept past Cedar, moving through the sidh. When Cedar followed her through it, she was already at Brighid's side.

"She's unconscious," Felix said. "But before she went under, she said that the druid can connect the two of you, giving you access to her memories."

"Like Liam did with Eden and me?" Cedar asked. She wasn't thrilled about the prospect of entering another dream sleep. Last time, Nuala had almost killed her.

"And like Maeve did with Eden and Nuala," Felix reminded her.

"Can you do it?" Cedar asked Helen.

"Yes," the druid replied brusquely.

"I'll help you," Felix said, and Cedar nodded. She would feel better drinking the potion if she knew Felix had helped make it. Brighid's attendant Vanessa appeared at once, and led the two of them back into the house. Jane sat down next to Brighid and smoothed the blanket wrapped around her legs.

"Cedar?" Finn had come up behind her. "Can we . . . talk for a moment?"

She shook her head. "There's nothing to talk about. You betrayed me. I can't believe you rallied the others against me like that. I would never do that to you."

"I didn't betray you," he said. "I'm trying to *save* you."

Cedar didn't answer.

"If this doesn't work," he continued, "if whatever Brighid shows you is wrong, or we still can't get the jewels . . . I'll come with you."

She was sure she had misheard him. "What?"

"I'll come with you. We'll do it together."

Cedar stared at him. "You just brought the whole Council, along with everyone I know and respect, against me to convince me to not go through with my idea. Now you're saying you'll just go along with it? What am I missing here?"

"I don't *want* you to reveal who you are. I still think it's too dangerous. And yes, I tried everything I could to get you to change your mind. But if that's not going to happen, I'm going to come with you. I'm not going to let you do it alone. If I'm with you, we can open *and* close the sidhe—it's the only thing that makes sense. And with my shape-shifting ability, it will be much easier to convince the humans that magic is real."

Cedar heard his words, but they weren't sinking in.

"But why?" she asked.

At this, Finn actually smiled. "Don't you get it?" he said. "I don't want the Unseen to die any more than you do. But if I have to choose between them and you, I'm going to choose you. Every time. Maybe it *is* your job to save the world. But it's *my* job to save *you*, to do everything I can to keep you from getting hurt. So if you go, I'm coming with you."

Cedar tried to think of a response, but her mind seemed to be moving too slowly. Instead she put her hands on either side of his face and kissed him hard. "We will talk about this—*all* of this— later. But for now . . . thank you."

Just then Helen and Felix returned. Helen was carrying a tray with two steaming mugs. "Drink this," she said, handing a mug to Cedar while Jane propped Brighid up and Felix gently spooned some of the liquid into her mouth.

"How will she be able to communicate with me if she's unconscious?" Cedar asked, gulping down the hot liquid as fast as she could.

"Brighid has a very powerful consciousness," Helen assured her. "I'm sure she's just waiting for you in there."

"Wait," Finn said. "What happens if Brighid dies while Cedar is in her head?"

"That, I do not know," she said. "But the more time you spend debating this, the better the chances that she *will* die."

Cedar stretched out on another lounge chair and wrapped Brighid's hand tightly in her own. With her other hand, she threw back the rest of the tea. She gave Finn one last lingering look, then closed her eyes.

CHAPTER 14

When Cedar opened her eyes again, she was standing inside a long wooden hall filled with people. She looked around nervously, but no one took any notice of her. Two long rectangular tables arranged like a T, heavily laden with trays of bread and meats, filled most of the space. A small group of musicians stood in a corner, playing what Cedar took to be flutes and fiddles, along with some instruments she didn't recognize.

The hall was dark, and Cedar had to breathe through her mouth to avoid the pungent smells of animals and people who obviously did not have access to modern plumbing. She didn't know exactly where or when this memory of Brighid's took place, but she had a feeling it was from a very, very long time ago. Her eyes scanned the crowd, which consisted of mostly men, with a scattering of a few women and children. Then she saw Brighid, sitting near the end of the table, engaged in animated conversation with the man next to her. Brighid was tall and regal once more, her long black hair done up in a complicated plait that wrapped around her head. Cedar edged closer and waved, but Brighid did not seem to notice her standing there.

She wasn't sure what to expect. She had been able to interact with Eden and Nuala in the last dreamscape she'd crashed. But this was different. She wasn't inside a dream—she was inside one of Brighid's memories. Cedar waved her hands right in front of her friend's face, but she betrayed no sign of recognition. Then the door at the end of the hall burst open, and a messenger rushed inside. He spoke rapidly to the man at the far end of the table, all the while looking and gesturing at Brighid. She stood, nodded to her host, and then followed the messenger outside.

Cedar followed too—relieved to get out into the fresh air. Another man was waiting there. He was short and balding, dressed in a rough brown cloak.

"Eoghan! What brings you here?" Brighid cried. "Why ever did you not come inside?"

The man called Eoghan looked pointedly at the messenger, who hastily left them.

"I cannot stand the niceties of court, as you well know," he said. "The king is still aggrieved that I refused to enter his service."

"You cannot fault him for wanting the most famed druid in Ireland at his disposal," Brighid pointed out. She started to walk away from the hall, and Eoghan and Cedar hurried to keep pace with her. "But tell me, what has happened now? Is it the Unseen? I'm assuming that's why you have come."

"I'm afraid so. When we spoke last, I thought perhaps it was an anomaly, that just a few of the abbots wished to do our friends harm. But my son—" He paused, his face stiffening. "My son has converted, and is in the service of the new bishop, the one who was sent from Rome. He still has *some* honor, however. He warned me that they are quite serious about finding—and destroying—all the Unseen. The campaign has begun in earnest."

"Why waste their energy?" Brighid said, picking up her pace even more. "The Unseen are no threat to them."

"They see anything that is not of their god as a threat, including druids such as myself. They wish to banish any signs of magic," Eoghan said.

"Then they are fools. Do they think the people of this land will abandon the truths that are right before them? The kings of Ireland go hunting with the Tuatha Dé Danann. The Merrow guide the fishermen when the ocean is rough. The selkies marry humans and bear children with them. How does this church think it will convince the people that what they have seen with their own eyes is not real? It is absurd."

"The church is rich and powerful," the druid said. "We do not know what they are capable of. If they succeed in killing all of the Unseen, the humans will forget they existed within a few short generations."

Brighid stopped suddenly, and Cedar almost ran into her. "You believe we have reached that point? Are the Unseen in that much danger?"

"I am afraid so," he said. "We must act now if we are to save them."

Brighid stayed still, but looked out over the hilly countryside. Cedar thought the scenery looked vaguely familiar, and then realized why. "Tara," she breathed. But this was not the Tara she had visited to find the Lia Fáil, where there were only shadows and fragments of a grand past. A massive ring fort crowned the hilltop, and barns and smaller shelters dotted the perimeter. Cedar craned her neck to see if the Mound of Hostages, where she had found the Lia Fáil, had been created yet, but it was not visible from where she stood. She snapped back to attention when Eoghan spoke again.

"Brighid," he said softly. "You are the most powerful being in Ireland—and the only one who cares about the Unseen. The other gods exist only for their own pleasure. You, of all the Danann, have the will and the power to protect those who are vulnerable."

"I cannot go against the church," Brighid said, still staring out at the countryside. It was a perfectly clear day, and Cedar could see white-tipped mountains in the distance. "The Dagda has forbidden it. He says Ireland must take its own course, with or without us."

"But surely there is something you can do," Eoghan pleaded. "Some spell of protection. Perhaps Tír na nÓg could offer them refuge."

Brighid nodded. "I thought of that as well, but the others have refused. They say the Unseen belong here on Ériu."

"Then what?" Eoghan asked in a small voice. "Will the Tuatha Dé Danann just leave them here to be slaughtered?"

Brighid turned slowly to face him. "No. Not this Danann at least. I will give them what protection I can . . . but I need some time to think. I will call for you when I am ready."

The druid bowed low. "I knew you could be counted on," he said. Then he turned and walked over the nearest ridge, disappearing from sight.

Cedar stood and watched Brighid for several long minutes. The Elder goddess seemed frozen in place, her gaze fixed on some spot on the distant horizon. Then the world around them started to swirl in a blur of green and blue, and Cedar closed her eyes to keep her head from swimming as she was shuttled into a new memory.

❧

When she opened them again, she was standing on the edge of a small clearing in the woods. The sky above her was dark, illuminated by neither stars nor moonlight. A fire burned in the center of the clearing, but there was no wood. The flames licked at the ground without spreading. Gathered around the fire was a group of people—at least, *some* of them looked like people; others were something else entirely. She recognized a dwarf, his skin covered in the same dark tattoos she'd seen on Abhartach and the other dwarves at Dun Dreach Fhola. The Merrow, too, were represented, as Cedar could tell from the long multicolored hair that flowed down the back of one of the women sitting in the circle. She was speaking in a low, anxious tone to a woman with jet-black hair, whom Cedar guessed to be a selkie. Beside them stood two horses, one dark and one white, engaged in their own conversation. Cedar assumed they were a púka and maybe a kelpie, but she wasn't sure which was which. Next was a gaunt young man who sat slightly apart from the others, staring into the flames, ignoring the seductive glances of the scantily clad woman sitting beside him. And a creature no bigger than Cedar's hand flitted around the fire, propelled by delicate golden wings. It was a meeting of the Unseen.

"Welcome, friends," Brighid said, emerging from the woods. Sound erupted from all around the fire, as each member of the Unseen started asking Brighid questions, demanding to know what the Tuatha Dé Danann were going to do to help them.

"Half of my people have been caught, and I don't know what's become of them," wailed the Merrow woman.

"They're setting traps for us, traps we cannot avoid," the leprechaun said in his high-pitched voice. "I can't even work in my own backyard anymore."

"They burned my sister alive," whispered the leannán sí, who had been making eyes at the leprechaun. On and on the reports went, and Cedar listened with mounting horror. Brighid finally raised her hand. Silence fell once more.

"The Tuatha Dé Danann do not care about your plight," she said, her voice laced with bitterness. "But I do. Alone, I cannot act against these men who seek to destroy you and your kind. And there is no refuge for you in Tír na nÓg."

"Then what are we to do?" cried the pixie, hovering in the air in front of Brighid's face. The goddess held out her hand, and the pixie landed on her palm, folding her arms.

"I have devised a spell that will protect all the Unseen from harm," Brighid said. An excited murmur broke out around the circle. "You will be hidden from those who wish to harm you. You may still show yourselves to other humans, if you wish, but those who look for you with murder in their hearts will not be able to find you."

"And what is the cost of such a spell?" the white horse asked in a deep, slow voice. The animated chatter of the others stopped at once.

"There *is* a cost," Brighid said, nodding in the horse's direction. "But not an insurmountable one." Slowly, she withdrew a silk cloth from her pocket and unwrapped it. She lifted it up to show eight blue jewels. In the firelight, they looked as if they were alive, the colors dancing and shifting inside them. "These jewels come from the Four Cities, the homeland of my people," she said. "They were once used in the swearing of oaths, but their power is hardly just symbolic. Once we cast the spell, the stones will hold the essence of the agreement made by each of you."

"And what *is* this agreement?" the white horse said, tossing his mane.

"Over all my long years, there is one truth I have come to count on," Brighid said. "There is nothing so powerful—for good or for evil—as belief. The men who persecute you believe they are doing the right thing by snuffing out that which they deem unnatural. But *they* are the anomaly, not you. This spell harnesses the power of the humans' belief in us, in magic, in the world they cannot see unless we choose to show it to them. As long as the humans believe, you will be protected from harm."

"And if they stop believing?" asked the raven-haired selkie.

"It will not come to that. To be human *is* to believe," Brighid said, her head held high. "But should the unthinkable happen, or should humanity itself be on the verge of extinction, the bond can be severed by destroying the jewels that bind the agreement. I will ensure that the jewels are kept safe, should this ever come to pass."

The black horse snorted and pawed at the ground. "How do we know this will work?" he asked, his voice dripping with suspicion. "You said the Tuatha Dé Danann will not help us. I find it hard to believe they approve of this plan."

"The Tuatha Dé Danann do not know of it," Brighid said stiffly. "You are right. They would not approve."

The horse snorted again. "You're asking us to tie our existence to the faith of humans," he said. "How do we know this isn't just some other way of eradicating us?"

"Because I am taking the same risk you are. Once you have each sworn on a jewel, *I* will swear by all eight. Your fate will be mine."

The black horse lowered his head. One by one, the beings around the circle nodded their acceptance too. "There is still a risk," the Merrow representative said. "But it is one I will gladly take on behalf of my kind if it means we will be shielded from those who would see us destroyed."

Brighid nodded. "Then each of you must take one of the jewels, and I will cast the spell." The Unseen each accepted a jewel. Some of them held it up close, gazing into its depths as though mesmerized by what lay within.

This is it, Cedar thought. If only she could stop this moment from happening, but what would have happened instead? The Unseen would still have been wiped out. She watched as Brighid paced around the woodless fire as if in a trance, chanting strange words and raising her arms to the sky. In unison, as though by some secret signal, the Unseen started to chant with her, clutching the jewels, which had begun to glow with some inner light. Cedar felt goose bumps dance across her skin. What was happening here was so much more powerful, so much more ancient than anything she had ever known. She felt ashamed of her people for abandoning the Unseen to their fate, and proud of Brighid, whom she had once mistakenly thought of as one of the most self-absorbed creatures in existence. Brighid was the only one who had stood up for these ancient beings, and now she was paying the price with her life.

Brighid raised her arms once more, and the jewels flew into her outstretched hands. The Unseen were silent as the goddess continued to chant, and then a ball of light rose out of the cluster of jewels, floating high in the sky before exploding like fireworks over those gathered in the clearing. Brighid sank to her knees, and the fire in the center went out.

"It is done," Cedar heard her say into the darkness.

∞

When the darkness lifted, Cedar's vision was assaulted by blue. She almost took a step forward, but then she looked down and froze. She was standing on the edge of a cliff. Waves crashed into the rocks below her, and the ocean stretched out as far as she could see, blending in with the hazy azure sky at the horizon. Then she noticed someone standing next to her. Brighid's long hair flowed out behind her like the sails of a great ship. She was dressed in a long white gown that floated gently around her, defying the strong winds that whipped and tangled Cedar's hair.

Brighid turned and started to walk inland. Silently, Cedar followed, looking around for some clue as to where—and when—they were. As they crested a small hill, Cedar could see a group of men building a structure out of wood. They seemed to be in the center of a small island—Cedar could see glimpses of blue on the horizon in all directions. Brighid continued toward the men, and Cedar hurried to keep up. None of the men seemed to notice Brighid, until one man on the edge of the building site glanced up in their direction and jumped back with a shout.

"What is it, Colum?" one of the others shouted. The man named Colum stared at Brighid, who stood quite still in front of him, and then gave an uneasy glance back at the others. It was obvious that they noticed nothing out of the ordinary—certainly not a regal woman dressed all in white. Colum turned his gaze back to Brighid.

"I have come from the Lord," she said. Immediately, Colum dropped to his knees.

"He's having another vision, like the one that brought him here to Iona," Cedar heard one of the other men mutter, and they all pulled back a respectful distance.

"What do you want with me?" Colum asked.

Brighid smiled and helped him to his feet. "You will do great things for your Lord," she told him. "Your exile from your native land will not be in vain. But the Lord asks a favor of you."

"Anything," he said, unable to look Brighid in the face. Cedar listened, enraptured.

"You have heard my name," she said. "Brighid of Kildare, they call me. The Lord has seen fit to send me to give you this task."

"Brighid of the holy fire," he whispered, falling to his knees once more.

Brighid let him stay there, and opened her hand. Eight blue jewels lay glittering in her palm. As Cedar watched, their colors glistened and shifted like the waves of the ocean. Colum couldn't keep his eyes off them.

"You will build a holy fortress here," she said. "You must keep these jewels and protect them at all costs." She snapped her hand shut and tucked the jewels away in a pouch at her waist.

"Of . . . of course," he stuttered. "But . . . why me?"

"Ireland is changing, and you are at the center of that change. Where there is power, there is safety. And I've been watching you, Colum Cille. You have a strong heart."

"Are you a spirit?" he asked.

"Something like that. The importance of these jewels cannot be overstated. You must protect them with your life, and see that others do the same, throughout the generations. Do you understand?"

"Yes," he said, nodding. "But if I knew what they were, I would be better able to protect them."

"You need only know that the Lord commands it."

Colum bowed even lower, so that his forehead almost touched the ground.

"I will not leave them with you now," Brighid continued. "But later today a servant of mine named Eoghan, and one of his brothers, will arrive wishing to enter your service and join your community. You will accept them without question into your company. They will have the jewels with them, and they will guard them. When they die, others will come to take their place. They will know little of your religion, but you will teach them. Be kind. They are not to be harmed by you or your enemies."

Colum ducked his head. "It will be as you say."

"If word gets out that you have eight holy gemstones here in your community, you will be more vulnerable to attack," she pointed out. "The Lord wishes you to speak of this to no one, save those who will succeed you, so that they, too, can carry out his holy commands."

Colum nodded vigorously. Brighid rested her smooth white hand on top of his head.

"The Lord gives you his blessing," she said softly. "Now go and do great things, Colum Cille."

Once again, the world around Cedar started to swirl, the colors of the countryside blending together in a haze. She could no longer see Colum or Brighid, which worried her. For a moment she thought Brighid might have died, and that she'd become trapped in her friend's fading consciousness. But then her vision cleared, and a new scene appeared before her . . . but not one she had been expecting.

She was in a white-walled home with large open windows. Outside, Cedar could see a lush vineyard under a blazing sun. The room she was in was sparsely decorated, with a few vases and urns clustered in a corner, and flowers hanging from vines that crept across the ceiling. In the center of the room was a large, low bed. Reclining on this bed were Brighid and a very handsome man with thick red hair and a neatly trimmed beard. They were lying naked in each other's arms, the sunlight bouncing off their sweat-soaked skin, and Cedar automatically looked away. But then Brighid spoke, and Cedar snapped to attention.

"Thor, my love, this might be one of the longest romances I've ever had," Brighid purred, trailing a finger along his red beard.

Cedar's mouth dropped open. *Thor?* Her knowledge of Norse mythology was limited to the Marvel universe, but if anyone were to have the god of thunder as her lover, it would be Brighid. She crept closer to the bed so that she wouldn't miss a word.

He grinned at her and kissed the top of her head. "For me as well," he said. "I only wish I had found you sooner. I fear I had some competition among your human admirers," he added with a wink.

Brighid laughed. "As much as I love my humans, most of them can't do what you just did." She stretched languorously and gave a satisfied sigh.

"Why *do* you love them so much?" Thor asked. "Why choose to live here, when you could be in Tír na nÓg?"

"I could ask you the same thing. Why do you choose to live in Asgard? Don't you find it rather tedious, living century after century with the immortals, where everyone can do anything? Dull, dull, dull. Ériu, on the other hand, is *fascinating*. To watch these people deal with grief, loss, sickness, hunger, day after day . . . it's positively inspiring. There's so much more *life* here."

Thor seemed to consider this. "But . . . they're so weak, these humans," he said.

"I beg to differ. *We* are the weak ones, because we very rarely face a challenge we cannot easily overcome. Look at you," she said, running her hands along his sculpted arms. "You were born into a royal family, with extraordinary strength and skill and a magic hammer that can destroy anything it touches. I do not mean to belittle your achievements, but you did not become who you are through years of toiling in the fields and battling to protect your wife and children from harm and starvation. They are stronger than we will ever be, I'm afraid."

"But doesn't it bother you that these humans you love so much worship a new god?" he asked.

"The Irish, you mean?"

Thor nodded. "Don't you feel . . . spurned?"

Brighid laughed. "I *never* feel spurned, darling, though if you were to leave me for a milkmaid I might change my mind. It honestly doesn't bother me at all. Besides, I think the Irish have a bit of a god complex themselves. We are not so much their gods as their heroes, their champions, their legends. We are their history, their identity. People never stop believing in such things, even if they move on to other so-called gods."

Thor looked thoroughly bewildered. "You don't thirst for revenge on this new god who has taken over?"

Brighid pulled him down for a long, slow kiss. Releasing him, she said, "Revenge has its place. But not in this matter. The humans have not turned away from us; they have merely added another god to their repertoire. The Tuatha Dé Danann and all the other magical beings of Ériu will always be a part of them. I have never been more certain of anything."

Thor looked so nonplussed that Brighid laughed again. "I'm a lover, not a warrior," she said. "But there really is no need for revenge. And as far as I know, the rest of the Danann are happy in Tír na nÓg. Aren't you happy in Asgard? You could always come settle down here with me, you know."

"Asgard is perfect," Thor said stonily. "And it will never be taken from us. But this god they call Christ is encroaching on our lands here on Earth, and our people in the North. Every day, more of them turn from us and declare their allegiance to him. Some remain faithful—they wear my emblem to proclaim that they will not turn. But their numbers are dwindling. And so we must look to other lands that can be conquered, other peoples to subdue, other followers to be gained."

Brighid eyed him sharply. "That sounds like Odin talking, not you. The raids on Ireland by the Northmen—is that *your* doing?"

Thor reached down and lifted the covers to his shoulders. Brighid tugged them down to his waist again, her own naked body still sprawled on top of the sheets. "My father believes that if we conquer new lands, the people will worship him, as is his due. Forgive me for saying so, but he saw the weakness of the Tuatha Dé Danann in Ireland. It seemed as though they were willing to just hand over their land and followers to the upstart god without a fight. It was an opportunity he could not pass up."

"I see. So he saw a land in transition and decided to capitalize on the chaos?"

"Something like that," he muttered.

"Hmm. And how has that worked out so far?" Brighid asked, one eyebrow delicately raised.

Thor glowered. "You know perfectly well. Many of my Northmen have converted to the new religion of the Irish. Now they are bringing it home to our lands, where it is taking root."

"Odin must be furious," Brighid remarked calmly.

"He wishes to destroy this new god. But . . ." Thor looked around furtively, as if ensuring that Odin's ravens were not perched on the windowsills. "My father does not have the strength he once did. I have counseled him against an outright war, and for once he seems to be taking my advice. I think he realizes this might be a battle we cannot win."

"Well, you are wiser than he is," Brighid said, making absentminded circles with her fingers across Thor's smooth chest. "You cannot force people to follow you, no matter how many battles you win. The humans are not fools—at least, most of them are not. Nor are they slaves, though I'm sure your father would disagree with me there. But they have a profound capacity for belief. I would stake everything on it. In fact, I have."

"What do you mean?" Thor asked.

Brighid paused, staring up at him through her dark eyelashes. "You'll be the only one I've told, you know. Besides my druid, that is."

"You know you can trust me with anything," Thor said.

Cedar listened as Brighid told Thor about the eight jewels and the spell she had cast over the Unseen, though she left out the fact that she, too, was bound by this spell. She told him how she had hidden the jewels with the monk Colum Cille, who was now renowned as the creator of the Book of Kells and the greatest of

Ireland's men of the cloth. Cedar wanted to scream at Brighid to stop talking, but she knew this conversation had already happened. By now, she had also figured out what the consequences would be.

"These jewels . . . they have the power to control belief?" Thor asked, his brow furrowed.

Brighid narrowed her eyes. "That is not what I said, so don't get any ideas," she said, her voice suddenly serious. "I told you: belief cannot be forced. You would do well to take that message to your father."

Thor nodded slowly. "My father . . . he has not been himself lately. He is consumed by the need to keep his followers—or gain new ones. It is his obsession."

"Well, my dear, perhaps sooner or later he will come to see that there are more pleasant obsessions to be had," Brighid said, stretching out on the bed again and drawing him toward her.

Thor leaned into her, and Cedar was relieved when the room started to swirl around her in a blend of whites and yellows.

◌

When the world settled again, Cedar found herself in a musty wooden barn with dirt floors and the reek of animals. It was completely dark except for the light of a torch being held by a small man cowering in one of the corners. The light shook, creating strange shadows on the walls of the barn. Cedar looked around for Brighid; this was her memory, so she had to be there. Then she realized why the man was cowering—Brighid was emerging from the shadows directly across from him, and her countenance was terrifying.

"For your sake, I hope I misunderstood your message," she said in a voice that was dark and low and deadly.

The man in the corner cowered even more, and Cedar wondered if his torch would set the barn on fire. When he spoke, his voice came out in a squeak. "I am but the messenger, O Mighty One," he said. "Cleos, who was in charge of the jewels, is dead."

Brighid towered over the man. Her fury was almost palpable, yet Cedar could tell she was trying to keep it contained. "Tell me," she demanded.

"They were in the cover of the Great Book of Colum Cille," the man began, his voice trembling on every word. "It was the safest place for them—that book is protected day and night."

"Colum Cille," Brighid repeated. "Is he still alive?"

The man looked confused. "Of course not," he answered. "That is, he died many hundreds of years ago."

"The Order of Druids assured me they would be kept safe!" Brighid raged. "They were to never be left alone!"

"They weren't, O Mighty One," the man pleaded. "Cleos was with them nearly all the time, and when he had to attend to other duties, I would take over. There have always been two druids with the jewels, just as you commanded."

Brighid's voice was dripping with venom. "Then how did you manage to lose them? Was it the Northmen? Your skills should be enough to ward off any attack."

"It was no man who attacked him," the druid said. "We found Cleos still alive in the rubble of the church. Before he died, he told me the book had been taken from him by a red-haired . . . god. We found the book, but the cover—and the jewels—are gone."

Brighid froze in place, her eyes still fixed on the quavering man in the corner. Cedar watched as the truth impaled her friend like a stake. All the anger she had been directing at the druids now turned inward—and toward the red-haired lover with whom she had shared her secret. She closed her eyes, and Cedar felt a deep ache in her stomach. She, too, knew the searing pain of betrayal.

"What should we do?" the druid asked.

"Speak of this to no one," Brighid said; then she stalked back into the shadows and disappeared. Cedar stood confused for a moment, wondering why she was still there, until the light the druid was holding started to spin around her. When she opened her eyes, she immediately recognized where she was.

They were back in the Hall in Tír na nÓg, but it was larger and grander than the one where she now held court. It was night, and the marble pillars shimmered like starlight. Between them were pillars of white fire that gave off light but no heat. Something akin to a firefly flew around Cedar's legs. But her attention was quickly drawn to those sitting in the center of the courtyard. There were eight men and women, but they were more resplendent than anyone Cedar had ever seen, even the other Danann she knew. Then she realized: these must be the Elders. She had heard many of their names as she tried to learn the history of her people, but she had no idea which one was which. She knew Brighid, who was standing in the center of the circle, was also an Elder, but she seemed smaller in both stature and countenance than these other beings. Perhaps it was because Cedar had always seen her in human surroundings or because she now regarded her as a friend, not a goddess. It was as if the Elders emitted raw power just by existing. Brighid was wearing a simple white toga with a gold clasp at the corner. The Elders, on the other hand, were dressed in rich, intricately embroidered robes and gossamer gowns as delicate as butterfly wings.

They sat calmly, serene expressions on their faces, regarding the maelstrom before them. Brighid paced angrily inside the circle, her agitation channeled into every movement.

"We *must* get the jewels back from Asgard!" she said, spit flying from her mouth. "They were stolen from us!"

"They were stolen from *Ériu*, where *you* left them, in the care of *humans*," one of the Elders pointed out, his calmness a stark contrast to Brighid's fury.

Brighid stopped pacing for a moment and glared at him. "I left them in the care of my most trusted druid and his successors," she retorted. "I hid them as best I could."

"Obviously, it was not well enough. Nevertheless, this is hardly an issue we can go to war against Odin about. Most of us didn't even know about the existence of these jewels until today. You cannot choose to act alone and then expect the rest of us to pay for your mistakes, Brighid."

"This isn't about me living on Ériu," she snapped. "If Odin destroys those jewels, the enemies of the Unseen will be able to track them down and exterminate them. They must be under our control! We don't know what he plans to do with them! I'm not asking you to wage war on Asgard—I'm just asking for permission to go there myself and bring them back."

"In the state you're in, Odin would certainly interpret your visit as an act of aggression," pointed out another Elder.

"What is the matter with you all?" Brighid raged, waving her hands wildly in the air. "Don't you care about what happens to the Unseen? They are our allies . . . our friends!"

"They made this decision," said one of the Elders as she rose to her feet. "As did you. If you had come to us for counsel, we would have advised you against this foolish plan. What possessed you to bind these beings to humanity in the first place?"

"It was the only way. You would not let me raise arms against the new church, and you also refused to let the Unseen flee to the safety of Tír na nÓg. It is *your* inaction that is to blame!"

"We all must fend for ourselves at some point or another. It is no different for the Unseen. They did not rise to our aid when the Milesians attacked us."

"Is that what this is? Revenge?"

"Of course not," another Elder snapped. "But we cannot be held responsible for the fate of every creature in every realm. Besides, it appears they do not need us—they have you. But I must say, to bind one's existence to the faithfulness of humans is an act of madness. You cannot possibly trust the humans so much."

"You do not know them like I do," Brighid replied, her shoulders back, her chin thrust forward. "You do not hear their stories, their songs, their poems. So long as humans exist, the Unseen will be safe."

Some of the Elders exchanged dubious glances. Clearly, they did not share Brighid's confidence. But one of them approached her and wrapped an arm around her shoulders, as if to offer her comfort—or lead her away. "Then there's nothing to worry about, is there?" the woman said. "What does it matter if the jewels are in Asgard or here or on Ériu?"

"It *does* matter!" Brighid retorted, shrugging off the woman's arm. "Odin is crazed over the loss of his followers—if he destroys the jewels, the bond will be broken. The church is growing in strength, and they have lost none of their zeal for wiping out those who follow the old ways. If the bond is broken now, the Unseen will be destroyed. The jewels need to be kept *safe*."

"I'm sure if he went to the trouble of stealing them, he won't be in any hurry to destroy them," interrupted another Elder. Some of them were looking at Brighid with sympathy, but others were exchanging amused glances, as if her melodramatics were not new to them. "But I am curious. How did he come to know of the existence of these jewels in the first place, hmm?"

Brighid's shame and rage were almost tangible, even through the memory. "He has his ways of knowing things, just as we have ours."

"There is no cause for us to anger Odin," said the first Elder who had spoken. "We do not need to wage war over the fate of the Unseen. I forbid you from going to Asgard, Brighid. Though you have chosen to live on Ériu, you are still one of the Tuatha Dé Danann, and I am still your High King."

Brighid's voluptuous mouth was a thin white line. After a moment of stony silence, she gave him a terse nod.

CHAPTER 15

Cedar awoke with a start. She was still clutching Brighid's hand. The sky was a clear blue, and Cedar squinted in the bright sunlight.

"Are you okay?" Finn asked at once. Felix elbowed him out of the way and placed his hand on Cedar's head.

"She's fine," he said after a moment. Then he gently untangled her hand from Brighid's.

"Is she still alive?" Cedar asked. Felix nodded.

"What did she tell you?" Jane asked.

"She took me inside her memories—several of them. I saw why the spell was set, how it was cast, and I watched as she entrusted the jewels with a monk named Colum. I think he was—"

"Colum Cille," Helen said eagerly. "You might know him as Saint Columba. The greatest of Ireland's saints. It was he who began work on the Book of Kells. You saw him?"

Cedar nodded. "Yes. We were on Iona, I think, and they were just starting to build something—a church, maybe. She left a druid there to watch over the jewels."

Helen's gaze was envious. "I have studied the Book of Kells my entire adult life. To witness the founding of the great monastery at Iona . . ."

"What happened then?" Jane prompted. "Did you find out who took the jewels?"

"This is going to sound really odd," Cedar said.

"Odder than everything else we've gone through?" Jane asked.

Cedar had to smile. "You're right. I guess it's on par. Brighid had a lover." She stopped, wondering how much stranger her world could get. "Thor," she finished. The rest of them exchanged glances, and she wondered if they were doubting her. "Like, from the movies. She told him about the jewels. He stole them and took them to his father in Asgard."

"*Thor?*" Jane asked, her mouth gaping open. "*Asgard?* Are you serious?"

Cedar nodded. "I know it sounds crazy, but—"

"But no crazier than Tír na nÓg and stones that roar and portals in space," Jane finished for her. "I get it. But holy jeez. Is every superhero movie I've ever seen real?"

"Hardly," Felix answered. "The Thor from the comic books is a very, very loose interpretation of the actual Thor from Norse mythology. He's the only one of the Avengers who exists in real life."

Jane looked at him curiously. "You know who the Avengers are?"

He shrugged modestly. "I'm more of a Batman guy, myself." At this, Jane actually giggled, but then she turned bright red and stared down at her Doc Martens.

"Brighid tried to get permission from the Elders to go to Asgard and get the jewels back, but they refused," Cedar continued. "They basically told her that she and the Unseen had made this bed and now they had to lie in it."

Felix rubbed the back of his neck. "That sounds like them, all right."

"You saw the Elders?" Finn asked.

"I'm assuming that's who they were. This all seemed to happen a really, really long time ago. That memory was definitely in Tír na nÓg, though; we were in the Hall."

"I actually remember that day," Felix said. "I wasn't in the Hall, but everyone was talking about some scene that happened between Brighid and the others. She didn't come back to Tír na nÓg very often after that."

"Why wouldn't they let her go to Asgard?" Jane asked.

"They thought it would start a war between the two worlds—Asgard and Tír na nÓg," Cedar said. "And they said that if Brighid was so sure that the humans would continue to believe, it didn't matter where the jewels were, as long as Odin didn't destroy them." She grimaced at the irony. "And now that's exactly what we're trying to do."

"Did she tell you how to get there?" Felix asked quietly.

Cedar felt unsettled by the tone of his voice. "No," she said. "Is it . . . hard?"

"It's impossible," he answered. "Asgard used to be connected to this world, just as Tír na nÓg was connected to it by the sidhe. The bridge was called Bifrost. But it's been closed for centuries."

"How did it get closed? Can we reopen it?" Cedar asked.

Felix shrugged. "No one knows. But I'm assuming it was done on Odin's end. Maybe he wanted to sever all ties with humanity. It's hard to say with Odin. He's temperamental, to say the least. But I don't think it's something we can easily reopen . . . It's based on the magic of their world, not ours."

Cedar stood and started pacing around the balcony. She could feel the eyes of the others on her, but she ignored them. Brighid had told her there was another way, and then she'd shared these memories with her. Why would she have done that if it weren't possible to get to Asgard? *You have a knack for achieving the impossible*, Brighid had told her. But how? What did she need to do?

"Have you been to Asgard?" she asked Felix. "Do you know what it looks like?"

Felix shook his head. "No," he said. "I thought of that, but I don't know if the sidhe would work, anyway."

"Why not?" she asked.

"The sidhe are meant for traveling from Tír na nÓg to Ériu, or within either world . . . just as Bifrost was intended for travel between Asgard and here. I don't know if travel between the two Otherworlds is possible."

"But haven't any of the Tuatha Dé Danann been there? Didn't you have meetings with the other gods or something?"

"It might have happened, but I was never privy to such knowledge. I'm pretty sure none of the other gods has been to Tír na nÓg. I think that if such meetings happened, they would have been here on Ériu. Neutral ground."

Cedar considered this. Even if Brighid was right and there *was* another way, she was running out of time. Soon all of the Unseen would be gone, and there would be no one to save. "Listen," she said to the others. "We don't know how to get to Asgard, and we're running out of time. I think we should stick to my first plan—proving that magic is real. By the time we figure out how to get to Asgard—if it's even possible—most of the Unseen could be dead. We have to act *now*."

"Try," Finn said quietly.

"Try what?"

"Try to open a sidh to Asgard."

She stared at him. "You know I can't. I don't know what it looks like."

"Maybe you don't need to."

"Of course I do—we've already tried to get places I can't see, and it doesn't work."

"Why don't you just try, Ceeds?" Jane asked, standing beside Finn. "Eden used to need a door, and now she doesn't, right? So maybe if you try hard enough, you won't need to know what it looks like."

Cedar closed her eyes, took a long, deep breath, and tried to calm the disquiet inside. She imagined that she was alone, back in her poppy field under a gentle morning sky, about to practice a new skill. She repeated the name over and over again in her head: *Asgard, Asgard, Asgard.* She tried to imagine what it would look like, even tried to remember how it had appeared in the movie she'd watched with Jane. But she could not picture even that clearly. She concentrated on the warm center of power she felt right beneath her rib cage and placed her hand on it. Then, without opening her eyes, she made a motion with her hand, imagining a door opening in the air in front of her, imagining the eight jewels lying on the other side.

When she opened her eyes, there was nothing there. Her eyebrows knit together, and she fought the ridiculous lump that was growing in her throat. "See?" she said, her voice breaking. "There's no other choice."

"Eden can do it," said Helen, who had been silent throughout their exchange.

"What?"

"Eden can open the sidh to Asgard. I am almost certain of it."

Cedar narrowed her eyes at the druid. "Why would you say that? How do you even know about Eden?"

"I've heard the guards talking about her," Helen said. "*And* I have the Sight. I've seen her in my visions. And it is my belief that her powers far outstrip your own, if you'll forgive me for saying so. If she were to try, I think she would succeed."

"It's worth a shot," Finn said. "It would take less than a minute for her to try, so we won't be wasting too much time. If it doesn't work . . . then I'll do as I promised."

Cedar wanted to object. She didn't want Eden to get wrapped up in this. What if Eden failed, and then blamed herself for

Brighid's death? But if she *didn't* fail . . . well, maybe they should give her a chance.

Wordlessly, she made a sidh back to Tír na nÓg and stepped through it, leaving the others to follow her into the outer common room of her home.

"Where's Jane?" she asked as Finn, Felix, and Helen emerged from the sidh.

"She said she'd stay with Brighid," Felix said, his face soft. "She didn't want her to be alone if . . ."

"I'm glad," Cedar said. "Someone should be with her. Stay here. I'll go get Eden." She stepped into the inner courtyard, shoving willow branches out of her way as she rushed toward Eden's room and opened the door. She tilted her head up and called, "Eden!" There was no answer. It was still morning in Tír na nÓg, but Eden should have been up by now. When she reached the top of the tree, though, her daughter was nowhere to be found. Cedar picked up the glittering starstone that hung from a knot in the tree next to Eden's bed. She raced back down the stairs and into the courtyard, then knocked on Rohan and Riona's door. After a few minutes, Riona appeared, looking at Cedar with surprise.

"There you are!" she said. "Rohan!" she cried over her shoulder. "She's here!"

"What has happened?" Rohan said, looming behind his wife. "What have you done?"

Cedar drew back, stung. "I just need Eden," she said. "Do you know where she is?"

"She went to Niall's," Riona said. "Is Finn here? He said he would bring you back."

"Nice," Cedar muttered. "He's in the front room. We have a druid with us, so I didn't want to bring them inside."

"A druid? Why—"

"I don't have time to explain," Cedar said. She held up Eden's starstone. "She didn't take this with her. Can you tell me how to find Niall's house? I need to get her. We're just . . . trying something different."

Several minutes later, Riona and Cedar were knocking on Atty's front door. Finn and the others had stayed behind in case Eden came back early.

Atty looked surprised to see them when she opened the door. "Riona! Queen Cedar! What an unexpected pleasure. What can I do for you?"

"We're here to get Eden," Riona said. "She came here this morning to play with Niall."

Atty looked taken aback. "I've been here all morning, and I haven't seen her."

"How did she get here?" Cedar asked, turning toward Riona.

"She made a sidh. I saw her go through it. It brought her right outside of this house. She waved to me to show me that she'd arrived and that Niall was home, and then she closed it."

"Well, I haven't seen Niall all morning, either," Atty said. "I assumed that he was playing out in the forest, like he usually does in the mornings. But it's strange that he wouldn't tell me Eden was coming over."

Cedar's stomach started to feel uneasy, but she pushed the feeling away. Just some miscommunication, was all. Eden and Niall had gone off to play and forgotten to tell his mother where they were going. "I'll go look for them," she said.

"They usually don't go far," Atty said, pulling on a cloak and joining them outside. The three women walked through the forest, calling for their children. After several minutes, it was clear that Eden and Niall were nowhere within earshot.

Cold hands reached in and wrapped themselves around Cedar's heart. She told herself to breathe, that it was impossible for this to happen again.

"Cedar?" Riona was looking at her with concern. Cedar realized she was clutching her stomach.

"I'm sorry, I—" She sat down hard on the nearest log, her head swimming, her breath coming in quick, shallow gasps. The next thing she registered, Riona was kneeling beside her, murmuring something comforting into her ear. Cedar tried to pull herself together. This was no time for panic. She need to be cool, collected . . . *regal.* She had to find Eden and get to Asgard. She stood up and waited for the wobbling in her legs to subside. Then she took a deep, cleansing breath and made a sidh back home. When she stepped through it, Riona and Atty on her heels, Felix and Finn rushed over. She waved them off.

"We can't find her. She went to visit Niall this morning, but we can't find either of them. Her starstone was still in her room so we can't use it to get a hold of her. Let's split up. Finn, go to your brother's and see if they're at his place. Felix, do you think they might have gone to your house? I saw Niall there once. Probably best to check." She opened sidhe for both of them, and they set out at once.

"I'll get Nevan," Rohan said. "Eden's mind is closed to her, but she might be able to contact Niall telepathically."

"Good idea," Cedar said.

"I can look for her as well," Helen said. She had been standing behind the others, half concealed by the shadows in the corner of the room. "But I'll need someplace quiet. I'll go back to my room."

Cedar hesitated, but then nodded. While she couldn't think why Helen would want to go back to her cell, she didn't have time to worry about it.

"I'll escort you on my way to Nevan's," Rohan said, and the two of them left.

Cedar went back to Eden's bedroom, on the extreme off-chance her daughter had left a note or some sort of clue. But there was nothing. If she had planned on being gone long, surely she would have taken the starstone. She could feel the cold edges of panic creep in again, but she pushed them aside. A child who could travel through portals at will was unlikely to stay in one place for long. She sat down on Eden's bed and picked up the latest book her daughter had been reading: *Harry Potter and the Goblet of Fire*. They had read the first three books in the series together, but Cedar hadn't had time to read this one with her. *This is the last time*, Cedar said to her daughter silently. *This is the last time I'll involve you in something like this, I promise. You deserve a childhood.*

She sat for several minutes, half-expecting to see a patch of shimmering air appear before her, followed by Eden and Niall. She thought about Brighid and wondered if she was still alive. What if they couldn't find Eden and they weren't able to open the sidh to Asgard? There was no way Cedar could put Plan B into action without knowing that her daughter was safe first. Her thoughts were interrupted by Finn's voice down at the bottom of the tree. "Is there any sign of her?" he hollered. Cedar leaned over and peered at him through the branches.

"No. So she wasn't at Dermot's?"

"No," he answered. "They haven't seen her. Felix is back too; they're not at his place."

"What about Nevan?" Cedar asked as she ran down the stairs.

"They're just getting back now," Finn answered. Together they headed to the common room. Rohan had just entered, Nevan with him. "Did you find them?"

Nevan bit her lip as she came up to Cedar. "Your Majesty . . . Cedar . . . I don't think they're here. I think they've left Tír na nÓg."

"You didn't have to come, you know," Eden said. She and Niall were standing in the hallway of her old apartment building in Halifax. Eden knew Jane still lived in the building, but she didn't know which apartment was hers. She was missing her morning lesson with Helen, but this was more important.

"Why'd you come and tell me you were going here if you didn't want me to come with you?" Niall asked, staring in wonder at the fluorescent lights and the carpeted floors. "I think it's awesome. No one gets to come to Ériu anymore!"

"We're not here for fun," Eden reminded him. "We have to find my mum before she tells people who she is."

"Why didn't you just use your starstone?" Niall asked.

"I tried that, but it didn't work. She didn't pick up."

"Pick up?"

"You know, answer it."

"Maybe she just wasn't wearing it or something," Niall suggested.

"It doesn't matter," Eden said. "I can find her this way."

"So you're just gonna knock on every door?"

"If I have to." Eden took a deep breath and knocked on the door in front of her. After a few seconds a man opened it. He was wearing a white tank top and black track pants, and he looked like he hadn't shaved in a few days. His belly hung out a little from the bottom of his tank top. Eden wrinkled her nose as the smell of stale beer wafted into the hallway.

"Yeah?" he said.

"Do you know where Jane lives?" Eden asked boldly.

The man stared blankly at the two children standing in his doorway. "Where are your parents?" he asked, squinting at them.

"They're visiting their friend Jane," Eden said. "We're trying to find them. We just don't know which apartment she lives in. She has tattoos and crazy hair and stuff."

"Don't know her," the man said gruffly. "What's her name again?"

"Jane," Eden repeated. "I . . . don't know her last name."

"How come you kids are out here by yourselves?"

"Never mind," Eden said, backing away. "We'll find them." She started to walk down the hallway toward the next door.

"That man is still watching you," Niall whispered as he followed her. Eden knocked on the next door, but there was no answer. She glanced back over her shoulder, where the man with the big belly was leaning out into the hallway, his eyes fixed on them.

"Why don't you come in here, and I'll call them for you?" he yelled down the hall.

"They don't have cell phones," Eden answered, grabbing Niall's hand and continuing down the hall. There was no answer at the next door, either. "Everyone must be at work," she muttered.

"Hey!" the man called again. He had come out of his doorway and started walking toward them. "I've got some snacks. I'll help you find this Jane person."

Eden remembered her mother's stern warnings about *never* going anywhere with someone she didn't know. She shuddered, remembering what had happened the last time she'd broken that rule.

"No, thanks," she said, and started to run toward the stairwell. She heard footsteps behind her—heavy ones that did not belong to Niall—and smelled a sickening waft of body odor and stale beer. The man grabbed her arm.

"I'm not going to hurt you," he growled. "Just come quietly."

"Help!" Eden yelled to Niall, who grabbed the man's arm and tried to wrench it away. But the man was much stronger, and the three of them wrestled in the hallway . . . until suddenly, they weren't in the hallway anymore. They were on the floor of Eden's favorite bookstore. "Help!" she screamed again, and the man started, immediately releasing her and backing away.

"Hey!" A store employee in a blue vest rushed toward them. Eden's attacker stared wildly around, and then took off running out of the store. The employee chased him, yelling something into his headset, while another employee ran up to Eden and Niall, who were both wide-eyed and breathing heavily.

"Are you okay?" she said. "Where are your parents?"

"They're . . . um . . . shopping next door," Eden improvised, giving Niall an alarmed glance. He was walking in circles, taking in the shelves of books and toys and the brightly colored displays with a look of wonder on his face.

"What *is* this place?" he asked, his mouth hanging open.

The employee gave him a strange look. "Why don't you kids come with me? We'll find your parents for you. Who was that man who grabbed you? Did you know him?"

Eden shook her head. "No, he just . . . appeared out of nowhere."

"We'll have to call the police," the woman told her as she led them to the front of the store.

"What's that?" Niall asked, but Eden shot him a silencing look.

"We don't want the police to come!" she whispered into his ear. "And stop acting like such a weirdo! We need to be alone so we can use the sidhe to get out of here!" She turned back to the lady who was tugging them along. "Excuse me? I have to use the bathroom," she said. She nudged Niall with her elbow.

"Uh, me too," he said.

The lady looked at them in concern. "Of course. I'll take you there," she said, leading them off to the side, to a small hallway with two doors. "I'll wait right here," she said.

Niall started to follow Eden into the women's bathroom, but she shoved him out. "Not this one! You're supposed to go in *that* one . . . I'll be right there." She whispered the last part.

Once inside a stall, Eden closed her eyes and tried to remember the one time she'd walked into the men's room by mistake. It had been humiliating at the time, but now she was glad it had happened. A few seconds later, she was standing next to Niall, who was examining one of the hand dryers with interest. He waved his hand in front of it and jumped back when a loud blast of hot air shot out.

"C'mon," she said, tugging on his sleeve.

"Where are we going?" he asked.

"We need to get away from these humans—they think we're just lost kids," she said. "My mum said that Brighid was sick too, and that she was trying to save her. I'll bet Brighid can tell me where she is."

"*Brighid?* Like . . . the Elder who went to live with the humans? You *know* her?" Niall asked.

"Of course," Eden said smugly. "I've been to her house before. It's really cool. C'mon." She laughed at the look on Niall's face. "There's nothing to be scared of. She's super nice!"

"What if she tells our parents where we are?" he asked.

"I don't think she talks to the other Tuatha Dé Danann much," Eden said. "Except for my mum and dad and Felix. Don't worry; I'll ask her not to tell." Without waiting for him to respond, Eden made a sidh leading into the expansive entrance hall of Brighid's house. After closing it behind them, she turned to look at Niall. "Nice place, eh?"

Niall nodded, his eyes wide. "Are you sure we're allowed in here?" he asked, his voice echoing off the glass walls.

"How else are we going to find her?" Eden said. She raised her voice and called, "Hello? Is anyone there?"

She heard running, and then Vanessa, the woman who'd helped them in the spa pools, appeared around a corner. She stared down at the two children. "How did you get in here?" she asked, her voice stern.

"We're looking for Brighid," Eden said, confused by the unfriendly welcome. "Well, we're looking for my mum, Queen Cedar."

"Your mother is not here, and Brighid is unwell. You should go home," Vanessa said.

"Please," Eden said. "We just need to find my mum. She's making a big mistake, and the other Elders sent me to stop her. I just need to know where she is."

Vanessa continued to glare at her. "The other Elders sent you?" she asked.

Eden nodded.

"You must not do anything to upset Brighid," Vanessa said, sweeping out of the room. Eden and Niall followed her onto the balcony, both of them keeping silent. The first person they saw was the last person Eden had expected.

"Eden? What the hell are you doing here?" Jane asked.

"I'm looking for my mum!" Eden said, rushing forward.

Jane looked thoroughly bewildered. "She's not here—she went looking for you!" She bent down so that her gaze met Eden's. "Didn't she find you?"

"I . . . ," Eden faltered, glancing first at Niall, then back at Jane. "I haven't seen her since yesterday. She told me what she was going to do." She saw the look of alarm that spread across Jane's face. She was about to ask what was wrong, but then she caught sight of Brighid.

"Oh no! What happened?" Eden cried, rushing to the Elder's side.

Brighid was lying down, swathed in blankets, her lank hair fanned out across the pillow behind her. At the sound of Eden's voice, she opened her eyes. "My child," she whispered. "Whatever are you doing here?" She struggled to lift a hand from under her blankets, and ran a thin finger along Eden's cheek.

"My mum told me you were sick," Eden said, staring unabashedly at Brighid's sunken features. "But you look *really* sick." She couldn't believe this wasted person lying in front of her was the same as the vibrant, elegant lady who had given them such lovely things and helped save them from Liam's druids. She felt more afraid staring down at Brighid's gray skin and pale lips than she had at any time with Nuala. Suddenly none of this felt like an adventure or a game anymore. She started to cry. "Are you dying?"

"Yes," Brighid said. "I am."

"My mum is trying to save you," Eden said, all of a sudden unsure about her mission.

"So she is," Brighid said. "She is trying to save me and all of the Unseen."

"But . . . I had a dream," Eden said. "The Elders were in it. They told me I had to stop her. But if I stop her, you'll die."

"Stop her from doing what?" Brighid asked.

"From telling everyone who she is and what she can do," Eden said. "The Elders said the humans would capture her. They said that she didn't have to do it. They told me I could find the jewels. That's why we came to find her."

"As Jane told you, your mother is not here," Brighid said. "But her plans have changed. She does not need to reveal herself. They were right. She does need you, child. You must help her open a sidh to Asgard. Go back to Tír na nÓg—your mother went to look for you."

"She's in Tír na nÓg?" Eden asked. "But I tried to reach her through the starstone, and it didn't work."

Jane spoke up, her face aghast. "She was asleep—it was when she was in Brighid's memories. I saw the stone glow, but I forgot to mention it." She swore, then covered her mouth. "She's going to kill me."

"So she's back home?" Eden asked.

"Yes, and you'd better get back there quick," Jane said. "Everyone in Tír na nÓg is probably looking for you."

Eden and Niall shared an alarmed look. "We're gonna catch it," he said.

"We were just trying to help," Eden said, but she knew they'd be in trouble. She wished she hadn't dragged Niall along with her.

"Go now, child," Brighid whispered.

"What about you?" Eden asked.

"I am not long for this world," Brighid said. "Perhaps you will see me in your dreams someday."

At this Eden started to cry again, but Niall reached out and put his arm around her. "C'mon," he said. "You heard what she said . . . They need you. Let's go."

Reluctantly, Eden moved away from Brighid and opened a sidh back to her room in Tír na nÓg. She cast one last glance behind her before stepping through the sidh, but Brighid had already closed her eyes.

CHAPTER 16

Why would she have left?" Finn said. "I mean, she must have *left*—no one else can open the sidhe. Unless someone forced her."

"I don't think so," Cedar said in a strained voice. "She wanted to help. I told her she couldn't, that she had to stay here. But she knew about the Unseen, and I told her about what I was planning to do."

"So you think she's gone to Ériu? To do what?" Felix asked.

"Here I am," came a small voice from behind them.

"Eden!" Cedar cried, flinging her arms around her daughter and pulling her in for a tight hug. "Where did you go? Why did you leave?" She could feel herself trembling as she held Eden even closer. Finn came up behind her and wrapped his arms around both of them.

"Ow," Eden said, but she didn't try to get away. Cedar pulled back a little so she could look at her daughter. Niall was standing behind her, avoiding his mother's eyes.

"Where were you?" Finn repeated.

Eden looked at the floor. "I'm sorry," she said. "I know I shouldn't have gone, but I was just trying to help. I had a dream about the Elders, and they told me I had to stop you. They said I could help you find the jewels instead—that I was the only one. But then I saw Brighid, and she's really sick, Mum! We have to help her."

206

Eden's eyes were full of fear, and Cedar felt her anger dissipating in an instant.

"The Elders spoke to you?" Finn asked, looking around at the others in the room.

"I meant to tell you," Nevan said. "She mentioned her dreams to me the other day, but I wasn't sure what to say because I didn't know what it meant. She recognized the pictures we have of the Elders; she picked them out right away from a book we were studying."

The room was quiet as all of those gathered there looked at Eden with something akin to awe.

"What does it mean?" Riona asked. No one answered.

"Am I in trouble?" Eden asked.

"No, my heart," Cedar said. "We'll talk about it more later. But you just can't do things like this—*no matter what.* I know you want to help, but it's too dangerous, and we don't even know exactly what we're dealing with here. I'm so glad you're okay. Did anyone see you?"

Eden nodded sheepishly. "I went back to our old building because I know Jane still lives there, and I thought you might be with her. But then this man from down the hall started chasing us. He grabbed me, so I made a sidh to the bookstore to get away, but he came with us, and then the guy from the store chased him, and we pretended we had to go to the bathroom so we could make another sidh to Brighid's house."

Cedar tried to keep her voice steady as all the possible scenarios ransacked her newfound calm. "See? *This* is why you can't make any sidhe without a grown-up. That man could have really hurt you."

"I know," Eden said. "I'm sorry."

"It's okay," Cedar said. "You're safe now. Did you see Jane at Brighid's?"

"Yes, and she told me I had to come back here. She said you were looking for me."

"I was. I was really worried about you; we all were. But the Elders were right; we need your help. Remember how I told you that the Unseen are all sick because the humans have stopped believing in them?"

Eden nodded. "That's why you were going to prove that magic is real."

"There might be another way," Cedar said. "Brighid used these magic jewels to make the spell that binds the Unseen to the humans. If we can find the jewels and destroy them, everyone will be okay."

"But the jewels are missing," Eden said. "No one can find them."

"Wait, who told you that?" Cedar said, frowning.

"Um . . ." Eden stalled.

"I didn't tell you about the jewels," Cedar said. "Who have you been talking to?"

"It was the Elders, in my dream," Eden whispered.

"Right," Cedar said. "Did they tell you where they are?" Eden shook her head. "We need you to try to make a sidh. Brighid told us that the jewels are in a faraway place called Asgard. It's another magical kingdom like Tír na nÓg, except—"

"I know what Asgard is, Mum," Eden interrupted.

"You . . . you do?" Cedar asked.

"Yeah, it's where Thor and Odin live."

"How do you know about them?"

"My friends Cole and Berkley used to play Avengers at recess," Eden explained. "I was always Black Widow." She made a faux martial arts stance, and Cedar had to smile.

"Well, this is different," Cedar said. "This is the *real* Asgard, and I'm pretty sure you don't know what it looks like."

"I can try!" Eden said eagerly. "I've been working on focusing my power! I bet I can do it!"

"Wait," Rohan said. "You can't just march into Asgard without an invitation from Odin. He'll take it as an act of aggression."

"It *is* an act of aggression!" Cedar exclaimed. "He stole something from us, and we're going to get it back."

"So you want to start a war with Asgard now?" Rohan asked. "Can you come up with a plan that doesn't involve bringing us to the brink of disaster?"

"I'm not trying to start a war with anyone," Cedar said. "I'm trying to save lives. We control the sidhe. Odin can't reach us."

"Odin does whatever he damn well pleases," Rohan said. "You don't know what you're getting us into. We need to consult the Council, and then consider how to best approach him."

"Damn the Council!" Cedar said. "I said it before—doing nothing is not an option. We don't have time for a meeting. So if you want to go get them, go ahead and do it. But hopefully we'll be in Asgard by the time you get back."

Rohan looked mutinous, but he kept his peace. Cedar turned back to Eden. "I've already tried to do it myself, and it didn't work. Let's see what happens when you try."

She watched as her daughter squeezed her eyes closed. No one else in the room moved or even breathed. The silence was as unnerving as it was absolute. Then Eden finally opened her eyes, and looked in pained disappointment at the regular air in front of her.

"I can do it!" she said. "Let me try again."

"What if the two of you tried it together?" Finn suggested.

Cedar grabbed Eden's hand and held it tight in her own. "Okay, on the count of three. One, two, three." She closed her eyes and concentrated with all her might. *Asgard, Asgard, Asgard.* But there was still nothing; she could tell it hadn't worked even before she opened her eyes.

"What more can we do?" Cedar asked.

"Mum?" Eden tugged at her hand, and Cedar bent down to listen. "I think . . ." Eden looked around hesitantly. "I think I know who can help us."

"Who?"

"Don't be mad," Eden said. "But I've been taking secret lessons on using my powers from Helen, the druid lady."

"*What?*" Cedar said. Images of Liam flashed into her mind. *I was right*, she thought. *Helen pretended to help us, but it was just a way to get to my daughter.* She threw out her arm and opened a sidh to Helen's room, ready to storm in and drag the druid out by her throat. But Finn put his hand on her arm.

"I'll get her," he said, and stepped through the sidh before Cedar could argue.

"It's not her fault, Mum. I asked her to help me."

"How did you meet her? What was she teaching you?" Cedar asked. Riona and Nevan looked stricken. They were the ones who spent the most time with Eden when her parents were not around, and they clearly felt guilty for not having noticed what was going on.

"Cedar, I had no idea. She must have opened the sidhe from her room," Riona said.

"It's fine," Cedar said through gritted teeth, though it was far from fine. She didn't blame the others—who knew better than she did how easily Eden could escape out from under a caregiver's nose? "Eden, answer my question."

Haltingly, Eden told them about the older Eden inside her, and how she had told her to find Helen.

"Helen didn't tell me to do anything bad," Eden said in a pleading voice. "She just taught me how to focus, how to connect with the older Eden. We were just starting."

Finn returned through the sidh with Helen. The druid's expression was stoic, but Cedar thought she could sense a flicker of fear behind her eyes. *And you should feel that way*, she thought.

"You lied to me," Cedar said.

"I can help you," Helen said in return.

"I don't need your help."

"What you *need* is to get to Asgard. I can help Eden open the sidh. The child needed guidance! That's all I gave her!"

"I'm her mother! You should never have talked to her without my permission!" Cedar said.

She felt Finn's hand on her arm again, but she shrugged it off.

"How can you help?" he asked Helen. Cedar glared at him. What was he thinking?

"Did she tell you about how her older self lives inside her?" Helen asked. Finn nodded. "I can try to bring that part of her to the fore. She will have the power that's needed to open the sidh to Asgard."

"What do you mean, 'bring that part of her to the fore'?" Cedar asked. "How could that possibly work? She's only ever been that Eden in her dreams."

"This might be our only chance," Finn said.

"Finn, it's too dangerous!" she retorted. "Do you really want a druid messing with Eden's mind again after what happened last time?"

"She's given us no reason not to trust her," Finn said. "I think she's really trying to help."

"No," Cedar said. "I won't allow it. Eden has been through too much already."

"I can do it, Mum!" Eden said. "I know I can!" Without warning, she dropped down into a cross-legged position on the floor and closed her eyes.

"Eden, stop! What are you doing?" Cedar shouted, but Eden was either ignoring her, or couldn't hear her. Cedar stared at her daughter, and for a moment it was as though she was looking at a stranger. Eden was a naturally fidgety child; Cedar had hardly seen her sit still for more than a second. But now, she was as still as the furniture in the room, solid and unmoving. Her face was devoid of expression, and Cedar had to look closely to make sure she was still breathing. But as Eden sat there motionless, Cedar could hear something emanating from her. Her Lýra, the musical signature that helped distinguish the Tuatha Dé Danann from humans, grew louder, stronger, and clearer. Cedar was so used to it that she usually didn't even hear it anymore, but it was as if someone had turned up the volume. And then Eden opened her mouth to speak, but when she did, it wasn't her seven-year-old self.

"Hello, Mother," she said in the deeper, grown-up voice that Cedar remembered from the dream-share.

"What is this?" she said, rounding on Helen. "What did you do to her?"

"She's doing this herself," Helen said.

"It's okay, Mum," came Eden's deep voice again. "I'm okay—the little me, that is. She's fine."

"How are you doing this?" Cedar asked. "I thought . . . I thought it was only a dream."

Eden laughed. "It's more than a dream, I'm afraid. But if I'm not mistaken, we don't have much time. I can help you. I can open the sidh to Asgard, but not like this."

"What do you mean?" Cedar asked.

"I need to come out."

"What?"

"In order to use my power in the waking world, I need to *be* in the waking world."

"No." Cedar got down on her knees in front of Eden. She was afraid to touch her, afraid that she might somehow hurt her if she brought her out of this trance . . . or whatever it was. "Eden?" she said, getting as close as she dared. "Listen to me; you need to come back. You are a little girl, and you are going to stay that way for a long time, do you understand? You don't need to grow up yet."

Eden laughed again. "Mum. My childhood ended the day I opened that first door. *You* are the one who doesn't understand. You can't keep me here forever—or even much longer. Let me be who I'm meant to be." At this, Eden's eyes flew open, but she looked past Cedar, straight into the eyes of the druid standing behind her.

"Free me."

"No!" Cedar yelled, and before anyone else could react, she raised a wall of fire, separating her and Eden from the druid. She heard someone scream, and she saw figures moving on the other side of the flames. Then something burst through the wall. It was a phoenix, its feathers the bright red-orange of the fire it had just passed through, but she only saw it for an instant before Finn was standing beside her.

"Help me get her out of here!" Cedar yelled, but when she turned to pick Eden up off the floor, her daughter was no longer there. Then the flames were snuffed out as suddenly as they'd been created, leaving only a charred line in the room and a thick cloud of smoke in the air. Cedar stared around wildly, wondering who had extinguished them. "Eden!" she yelled. Then she saw her. Materializing from the smoke was the same Eden she'd seen in the dream-share, the one who had saved her from Nuala. Only this time she was real, in the flesh, and walking toward her. She had her daughter's fine features—her olive skin, her large brown eyes flecked with gold. Her hair was darker, and it tumbled in waves down her back. She was slightly taller than Cedar, and was wearing a black gossamer gown that wrapped around her body like the smoke from which she was emerging.

"That's better."

"Change her back!" Cedar demanded, rounding on Helen, who took a step away from her.

"She didn't do this, Mum," Eden said, smoothly stepping between them. "I did. All Helen did was give me the confidence I needed."

Cedar was breathing heavily. Everyone else in the room was as still as Eden had been moments before. Cedar looked at the adult woman in front of her and could feel part of her heart breaking. "Please," she said, looking into the familiar-yet-strange brown eyes. "Go back to being a child. This isn't right."

Eden put a hand on Cedar's shoulder and drew so close that their faces were almost touching. "I'm still your daughter," she said. "Eden isn't gone; I'm right here in front of you."

Finn stepped forward, his face ashen and his eyes wide as he approached his daughter.

"Hey, Dad," she said, giving him a shy smile.

"You're beautiful," he said.

"I look like you," she said, smiling bigger this time. Then she clapped her hands twice and said in a commanding voice, "I know you're probably all freaking out right now, but that can wait. We have a sidh to open, and there's no time to lose. Let's try it again." She closed her eyes and lifted her arms in front of her, the black dress swirling around her legs as it caught in the sudden wind. The others backed away from her, giving her space. But Cedar moved closer, unable to take her eyes off the woman-child before her. Without warning, Eden's hand shot out and grabbed Cedar's, holding it in a viselike grip. Cedar felt a shock as more power than she had ever experienced jolted through her arm. She heard Eden's voice say,

"Together, Mum!" She hesitated, and then she, too, closed her eyes and tried to draw from the deep well of power at the center of her being. She could feel it coursing through her, and the arm that was not holding Eden rose up in the air. She heard a voice inside her head, but she could not tell if it was her own.

Let go.

She felt a release of energy, a blossoming even greater than when she'd stood on the Lia Fáil for the first time. She gripped Eden's hand tightly as the power flowed between and through them. Then she felt Eden's hand slacken, and she opened her eyes.

It was more of a gate than a door. It was higher and wider than any sidh she'd ever created. It seemed more solid and corporeal too; two twisting stanchions that curved and joined at the top. There was too much light emanating from between the posts for her to see through to the other side—a bright swirl of purples and pinks, like oil skimming the top of a puddle.

"You did it," Finn breathed, coming up behind them.

Cedar let go of Eden's hand, staring between her daughter and the sidh in wonder. Then she looked at Finn. "Let's go."

"I'll come too," Felix said, stepping forward.

"No," Cedar said. "It should just be the two of us—Finn and me. That way, he can't possibly think we mean to do him harm."

"You're assuming he'll just hand the jewels over," Felix pointed out.

"I'm hoping," she said.

"You're going to need my help," Eden said matter-of-factly.

"Eden, you already have helped us. I know . . . I know you're not a child anymore—not right now, at least. But this doesn't have to involve you. Leave this to us, and then we'll deal with"—Cedar waved her hands in Eden's direction—"with whatever this is."

Eden looked intently at her. "I'm not going back, Mother. I'll never be that child again."

Cedar flinched as though Eden had slapped her. "We'll see about that," she said. "For now, stay here."

"And how are you going to get back? Or were you planning on just leaving this sidh open so that Odin can send his army through it to take over Tír na nÓg? I'm sure he'd jump at the chance."

"She's right, and we don't have time for the two of you to argue about it," Finn said. "I don't even know if I can close this kind of sidh. Without her we might *have* to leave it open. We can end this now, Cedar." He held out his hand to Eden. She took it, but her eyes were still locked on her mother. Cedar stared back, her jaw set. And then Eden turned her head and took a half step away.

"Wait," Cedar said. She seized Eden's other hand, and the three of them walked through the sidh together, leaving the others to stare after them in awe.

CHAPTER 17

When they emerged on the other side, there was no question that it had worked. The world they were now in was remarkably different from their own. Gone were the trees and meadows and gentle hills of Tír na nÓg. The land around them seemed carved entirely out of stone, great slabs of rock rising up on all sides. Thick clouds obscured the sky, but Cedar could make out jagged mountains looming around them. A few scraggly trees were trying to eke out an existence here and there on the cliffs and ledges, but to Cedar's eyes it seemed to be a futile attempt. How could anything grow in this land of cold, hard gray?

She was still holding Eden's hand, and all three of them were craning their necks skyward. They were standing at the base of a great arched gate that was hundreds of feet tall, the top concealed in the clouds. On either side stood column after column, curving into the distance as far as Cedar could see, forming a massive and impenetrable wall. Each column was of a different design, and some protruded from the wall while others were slightly recessed, with towers jutting into the sky, black windows making gaping holes in the wall. A chill ran up her spine, and she tightened her grip on Eden's hand.

"Amazing," Eden whispered.

"Are the Norse gods . . . giants?" Cedar asked as they took a few tentative steps forward. "Everything just seems so . . . huge." In

Brighid's memory, Thor had seemed no larger than the average Tuatha Dé Danann male.

"I don't think so," Finn said. "But I suppose we'll find out soon enough."

They reached the base of the gate and started to pass beneath it. It was eerily silent. The only sound was the soft fall of their footsteps on the cobblestone passageway. A single raven circled overhead before disappearing into a puff of cloud and then reemerging. The clouds grew thicker and lower as they passed between the walls, which were as deep as a city block. They still held hands as they slowly moved forward.

When the clouds suddenly lifted, a man stood before them. He had red hair that fell past his shoulders and a red beard with a single braid down its center. Dressed in polished armor, he gripped a large stone hammer in his hand. Cedar recognized him at once.

"Thor," she said, letting go of Eden's hand and stepping forward.

Thor stared at her, his expression fierce but curious. He did not relax his grip on the hammer.

"You are Tuatha Dé Danann," he said, the hint of a question in his voice.

"Yes," Cedar said. "I am Queen Cedar. This is Finn—Fionnbharr—and Eden, our daughter."

Thor swept his eyes over Cedar's companions, his gaze lingering on Eden for a moment that felt far too long. Cedar and Finn were still wearing their human clothes, whereas Eden was wrapped in the gossamer gown. "How did you come here?" he demanded.

"Through a portal from Tír na nÓg," Cedar said, gesturing to the open sidh on the other side of the gate. Thor narrowed his eyes, and then stalked past them toward the sidh. "Close it," Cedar whispered to Eden, and just as Thor reached the sidh, it snapped shut, leaving only empty air where there had once been a gateway between worlds. Thor turned around slowly, his eyes dark.

"You have something of ours," Cedar said with as much authority as she could muster. "We would like it back." When he did not answer, she added, "Brighid sends her regards."

Cedar heard the unmistakable rumble of thunder from somewhere above them.

"You speak of the jewels," Thor said slowly. Cedar waited, hoping to draw out more information from him, to determine if he would be a friend or foe to them on their quest. "I expected you sooner."

"My predecessors did not wish to anger your father," Cedar said. "Nor do I. But we have no choice—we had to come. We only want the jewels, and then we will leave."

"Did she send you?" Thor asked. "The Brighid I knew would have come herself."

"Brighid is dying," Cedar said bluntly. "We need the jewels to save her life."

Her statement had exactly the effect she'd been hoping for. He gripped his hammer tightly in both hands, his body suddenly tense and coiled.

"*Dying?* How is that possible?"

"You *know* how it's possible," she told him, her gaze unflinching. "She showed me her memories. I saw the two of you together. She told you about how the Unseen were protected by the jewels. Well, the humans have turned from their belief in magic, and so the Unseen—and Brighid—must die. She didn't tell you that part—that her fate was tied with theirs."

He stared at Cedar for a long, disbelieving moment, and then his shoulders slumped and his hammer hung loose at his side again. She felt almost sorry for him. He really hadn't known it would come to this. He looked down at the stone passageway beneath their feet. "I told her it was folly. But she was *so* certain. Even *I* believed her, in the end." His voice was low and quiet, as though his own memories were tugging at him.

"And then you betrayed her, and stole the jewels for your father."

"It is something I have regretted for many lifetimes of men."

"You can make up for that now. Give us back the jewels, and you'll save her life."

"What will you do with them?"

"Destroy them," Cedar said. "It will break the bond between Brighid and the Unseen and the humans."

She could see the conflict on his face. His mouth was a thin, hard line, and one of his eyebrows was twitching. His hands were clenched at his side, one of them still gripping the great hammer.

"It is not a decision I can make," he said at last. "But I will take you to my father. Have you no finer clothes?"

Cedar wanted to kick herself for not thinking to change. How could she present herself as the queen of a great race on par with Odin and his kin when she was dressed like a human college student? "No," she answered. "We are still in disguise from a trip to Ériu, and we had no opportunity to change. I hope Odin does not take offense."

"It is hard to say what will give him offense these days," Thor muttered, but then he seemed to check himself. "My father is a proud man. We had better find you something suitable for an audience with him, if you do not object."

He led them the rest of the way under the gate and up a long, winding pathway of large cobblestones. The sound of his boots echoed against the stone walls and buildings that rose up around them.

"Where is everyone?" Cedar asked.

"There are not many left," Thor answered without elaborating. In the distance Cedar could see a long hall, so long she could not see where it ended. The roof looked like polished gold, and the walls were all silver. She could make out large doors along the side, but no windows.

"Is that Valhalla?" Finn asked with wonder.

"Yes," Thor grunted. "The perpetual circus of fools."

They stayed silent for the rest of the journey, until Thor took them through a door at the bottom of a large round tower. A spiral staircase rose above them, hugging the stone walls. Thor rang the cord of a heavy brass bell, and a few seconds later an old woman with a long gray braid emerged from a side door. Her pale eyes grew round at the sight of them. She was followed by a young girl, to whom Thor spoke quietly. The girl bowed before leaving the room by the same door through which they had entered.

"Give these two the finest garments you have," Thor told the old woman, gesturing toward Cedar and Finn. "Something that has not yet been worn in front of my father." He glanced at Eden. "She's fine. She can wait down here with me."

"She'll come with us," Cedar said. "And I know she doesn't look it right now, but she's only seven years old, so you keep your eyes off her, do you understand me?"

Thor looked taken aback, and Cedar wasn't sure if it was because he wasn't used to being addressed in such a manner or if he was shocked—and disappointed—to learn of Eden's true age.

"Seven? But how . . . ?"

"I'm not seven anymore," Eden said, a hint of steel in her voice. She was looking at Thor in a decidedly grown-up manner. "I'll be fine. Really."

Cedar grabbed Eden's arm and pulled her to one side, though there was scant room for privacy in the small chamber. "You *are* seven, whether you look it or not. We let you come with us, but that doesn't mean you get to do whatever you want. I'm your queen, and more important, I'm your mother. You don't argue with me in front of"—she struggled for the right word—"foreign gods. Is that clear?"

Eden exhaled slowly. "Yes, Mum. I apologize."

"Looks like family dynamics are the same everywhere," Thor said, smirking. "Perhaps we should all go up together." He headed up the spiral staircase, followed by the old woman. Cedar hesitated, wondering if they were being led into a trap. She gave Finn an inquiring glance, but he shrugged, so she followed Thor and the woman after glancing behind to make sure Eden was coming too.

The room they entered was much larger than the one at the bottom of the stairs. It was still round, but as large as the common room in Cedar and Finn's home. Bolts of fabric in a myriad of brilliant colors and textures hung from the walls, along with reams of lace and gold and silver thread. An ornately carved wooden chest stood between two tall, narrow windows, curved to perfectly fit the wall. Dresses and robes as fine as any Cedar had ever seen hung on the marble mannequins that stood throughout the room.

Eden's eyes lit up, and she started walking between the mannequins, admiring their garments. The old woman grabbed Cedar's arms and raised them, and then stood back, looking at her with a critical eye. "Something new, I think. My lord?"

Thor smiled. "You are the queen in this chamber. I will leave the clothing of our guests up to you."

"I should have thought of this before," Cedar muttered to Finn as the woman bustled around them, examining them from every angle.

"You had a lot on your mind," he answered. "Personally, I prefer you in blue jeans."

"Tell me, how has Brighid been . . . before the illness, that is?" Thor said as he watched the woman work.

Cedar wasn't sure how much to tell him. But if she could renew his interest in Brighid, he would be much more likely to help them.

"She's saved a lot of lives recently," she said. "She helped avert a war between Tír na nÓg and Earth. And she helped us find Eden when she had been kidnapped earlier this year."

"And does she still love humans over her own kind?"

"It depends on which of 'her own kind' you're talking about, I think," Cedar said, lifting her arms again so that the old woman could spin gold fabric around her torso. "Brighid is, as you know, a wonderful, infuriating mass of contradictions." She smiled as she thought of her friend. "One minute you think she's the most self-absorbed person you ever met, only concerned with her own pleasure. The next, you find out that she would sacrifice everything, even her own life, to protect those she loves—or those who simply need her help. I think she's an amazingly sensitive, caring person. And to be honest, I think that a lot of the confidence she shows is bravado. It's a mask." She paused for a breath before looking Thor directly in the eye and continuing. "You have no idea how deeply you hurt her."

He didn't answer, but walked over to the other side of the room and stared out of one of the small windows. Eden was leaning against the sill of the other window. She looked tired.

"Are you okay, Eden?" Cedar asked.

"Yes, of course. This is incredible," she said, gazing out of the window.

"What do you see?" Cedar asked, trying to smooth over their confrontation—and give Thor time to think about what she had said.

"Mountains," she answered. "It looks like it goes on forever. Is there anything in this world besides stone?" She looked inquiringly at Thor.

"There is beauty in every world," he said, still staring out the window. "If you know where to find it."

Eden squinted out at the landscape, as though looking for those patches of beauty. Cedar watched her silently. Who was this tall, confident, powerful young woman, and what had happened to her inquisitive, feisty little girl? Eden had said she couldn't go back to being the way she was before, but did she mean that she couldn't . . . or wouldn't?

The old woman stepped back, and Cedar looked down. She was wearing a gown of gold, with a long bell sleeve that fell to her knees on the left side. A winglike ornamentation curved over her left shoulder, joining with the bodice at the breast. Her right arm and shoulder were bare. In a few solid tugs, the woman had smoothed Cedar's long black hair and tied it up with a clasp of pearls.

"Worth the detour," Finn said, giving her an admiring look. He, too, was dressed in gold, in a long robe decorated with fine red leather. Over at the window, Eden gave a low wolf whistle, and Thor nodded in appreciation at the old woman, who bowed and left the room.

"Much better," Thor said approvingly. "You look most wonderful, Your Majesty. I have sent a message to my father, and he is expecting us."

Cedar, Finn, and Eden followed Thor down the stairs and across a large square courtyard to the entrance of another tower, this one many times larger and higher than the one where they'd just been outfitted for their audience with Odin. Every post and beam seemed to be carved with intricate knots and designs. Cedar noticed that the designs were similar to those found on the Hall in Tír na nÓg. *We are not so different*, she thought.

"Welcome to Hlidskjalf, the seat of my father," Thor said, pausing outside the door.

The great stone door swung open to admit them, and Cedar tried to calm herself as they passed through it. Thor had seemed reasonable; but from all indications, they could not expect the same from Odin. She took a deep breath as they walked into the throne room.

She had expected more of the gray stone that seemed to be the defining feature of Asgard. Here in this great hall, the floor and the walls were indeed stone, but hanging from above were the branches of a huge tree, larger than any Cedar had seen on Earth or in Tír na nÓg. Green and gold leaves spilled from the branches and swayed softly in the air above them.

"Yggdrasil," she heard Finn say softly beside her, and not for the first time she wished she had paid more attention to the stories he had told her back in Halifax. "The world tree."

Cedar didn't know what a world tree was, and though she thought it was beautiful, her attention was fixed on the man sitting on a tall golden throne at the end of the room. He was older than she'd expected. She had assumed that all of these gods remained at their peak, like the Tuatha Dé Danann, but this man's hair was white, and his shoulders were slumped forward. Resting on each shoulder was a black raven. He only had one eye, which was narrowed at them. Where his other eye used to be was a simple black patch. A long spear rested across his knees.

"So the deceivers have come at last," he croaked as they approached the throne. Thor went to stand at his father's side. "Leave us," Odin said, and the guards and attendants in the room immediately filtered out of the door.

"We come in peace," Cedar said, feeling vaguely ridiculous that she'd just used that phrase in real life. "We bring greetings from all of the Tuatha Dé Danann, and wish only to reclaim that which is rightfully ours. We are in a time of great need."

Odin started to laugh, but it sounded more like he was choking. "Great need?" he sputtered. "Ah, yes, we are all in great need these days." Then his face returned to stone. "Let's dispense with the diplomatic niceties, shall we? The jewels will stay here, and if you hope to leave this hall alive, you will tell me how they work."

Cedar bristled at the threat, but took a deep breath and tried again. She wanted to keep this exchange peaceful if at all possible. "I will gladly tell you how they work. The jewels are from our homeland, the Four Cities," she said, trying to keep her voice level. "They are used in the binding of agreements. They were most recently used to bind the fate of many beings, including one of our own kind, to humanity's belief in that which is beyond them. But as you must know, humanity no longer believes in such things, at least not enough to sustain the strength of the spell. In order to save these beings, we must destroy the jewels and break the bond. That is the only purpose of the jewels."

Surely he could see that he had nothing to gain from keeping them . . .

"A fine story," Odin said slowly. "A fine lie. One I have heard before. My son Thor came to me with the same tale. He was deceived by one of your kind, the one who enjoys slumming with the mortals. Though he told me about the jewels, he was too enamored with this woman to guess at their true power. A jewel that can control belief is a powerful treasure indeed."

"What Thor told you is the truth!" Cedar insisted. "I don't know what you think they will do for you, but it won't work!"

"It will work if you tell me *how* it works," Odin said, his voice booming through the hall.

"I *did* tell you," Cedar insisted. "You can choose to not believe me, but it doesn't change the truth! These jewels won't help you reclaim your human followers, if that's what you're hoping. That time is over—for all of us."

"Liar!" Odin stood up, his spear slamming against the floor and causing the whole building to tremble. "I have heard tell of the wonders of the Tuatha Dé Danann. Your presence still lingers in the minds and hearts of the mortals on Midgard, while our followers

have proven themselves faithless maggots. The Danann whore knew this, and she deceived my son."

Cedar was burning with anger at his insults, but she was also beginning to think that he was quite mad. How could she make a bitter, insane god see reason? "Brighid told your son the truth," she said again, her voice firm. "You are very powerful. If the jewels could help you, you would have discovered their secret centuries ago. That's because *there is no secret*. They can't help you, but they can help us. Please, people we care about are dying."

Odin sat down hard on his throne. "I care not whether your people live or die. It is their own fault for making such a foolish agreement, if that is indeed what happened."

"Why does it even matter to you if the humans don't believe anymore?" Cedar exclaimed. "It doesn't take away any of your power. It doesn't change who *you* are."

Odin rose again from his throne. Slowly, step by step, he descended the few short stairs, until he was standing directly in front of her. Everything in his countenance spoke of disdain. He was only inches away from her face, and her stomach clenched. She could sense Finn and Eden behind her, not moving, the tension in the room coiling, readying for the explosion. Odin's one eye was icy blue, the white shot through with red veins. It traveled up and down Cedar, and she suppressed a shudder. The skin on his face was paper thin, almost translucent. She could see the veins and capillaries spreading out in all direction like a spiderweb beneath the skin. The ravens lifted up off his shoulders with several loud squawks and started circling above.

"What is a god without followers?" he said, his eye still roaming over her body. "Nothing. Just a human in a borrowed dress."

Cedar heard a growl from behind her, and turned around to shoot Eden a silencing look. But when she locked eyes with her daughter, she promptly forgot about Odin's insult. Eden's olive skin was ashen, and her face shone with a fine shimmer of sweat. Was she that afraid of the Norse god? The younger Eden would have been terrified; perhaps the transformation was not as complete as she had been led to believe. Finn must have noticed as well, for he wrapped his arm around Eden's waist. Cedar turned back to Odin, determined to get this over with and get back to Tír na nÓg.

"If you wanted the humans to believe in you so badly, why did you withdraw from them? You don't need the jewels—you can just show them who you are."

Odin looked at her shrewdly through his one good eye. "An excellent suggestion. Perhaps I shall pay Midgard another visit. It has been too long." The corner of his mouth lifted up, wrinkling his cheek. "Though I wonder if you would approve of the manner of my arrival. Bifrost has been closed. But my son tells me *you* can create portals between the worlds."

Cedar thought fast, trying to remember what she had heard about Bifrost, the bridge between Asgard and Midgard. Felix had said that it was closed. His assumption was that Odin had done it . . . but now she wasn't so sure. All Odin wanted was for people to worship him, so if he could have gone to Earth before now, he would have.

Odin laughed again. "It seems you are a little behind, *Your Majesty*. I would like nothing more than to pay a last visit to Midgard. But Bifrost was destroyed before I had the chance. Now, however, there is someone in my throne room who can travel between worlds at will. It is a gift I did not even think to ask for."

Cedar felt herself grow cold all over as she realized what he was saying. Odin didn't want worship. He wanted revenge.

"Cedar," Finn whispered urgently from behind her. Eden was leaning heavily on him, her face an alarming shade of white.

Cedar immediately put a hand on her daughter's forehead. It was ice cold. Eden blinked back at Cedar, her eyes afraid and confused, childish once again. She wasn't scared of Odin—she was sick.

Thor hastened to Finn's side. "What is wrong with her? Is it the curse?" He no longer looked like a warrior god standing guard at his father's side, but like an ordinary man, helpless in the face of something he could not change. His eyes beseeched Cedar, even as she, too, looked at her daughter in dismay.

"Nothing is wrong with her!" Odin snapped. "It is a ruse, a distraction. And no one told you to leave your post." Thor lingered for a moment, and then returned to the dais, his face once again as hard as the walls behind him.

"Maybe it was the transformation," Cedar said to Finn. "Her body can't handle it. Hang in there, my heart," she whispered into her daughter's ear, stroking her arm.

She swiveled back around and faced Odin with a newfound fervor. "We must leave at once. Give us the jewels before it is too late. This is your last warning."

Odin seemed unmoved by Eden's sudden illness, and Cedar's threat appeared to amuse him. "Create a portal to Midgard for me, and I will give you the jewels." He held up a hand, and the two ravens that had been circling overhead flew down to land on his shoulders again. Four black beady eyes and one blue one stared unblinking at her.

"The only sidh I will ever open for you is one to Hell," Cedar snarled, not flinching away from his gaze. Without warning, the ravens flew from Odin's shoulders toward her face, their talons outstretched. She automatically lifted her hands to protect herself and felt searing pain as they ripped into her flesh. In an instant, Finn was in the air as a massive eagle and charged the ravens, who left Cedar and soared toward the high ceiling, Finn in pursuit. But they were unnaturally swift, and they darted and clawed at him as they led him in chase. Cedar brought her bloodied hands down from her face and summoned fire into her palms. She turned to direct the flames at Odin, but he was no longer there. And neither was Eden.

CHAPTER 18

O din!" Cedar bellowed, staring around wildly.

"You had your chance," came a voice from the golden throne. Odin had returned to his perch, but now Eden was lying limply across his lap. A silver dagger was resting between her breasts, the hilt clenched in his hand. Thor was still standing beside the throne, his knuckles white around the grip of the hammer, his eyes flickering between Eden and his father.

Odin's voice was completely devoid of emotion. "I told you that if you opened the portal I would give you the jewels. It seems that my offer was not enough for you. So I have a new proposal. Open the portal, and I will give you your daughter's life."

Eden's eyes flickered open, and Cedar saw her lips move. "Don't do it," she mouthed.

Cedar walked slowly toward the throne, her hands down at her sides, her fire extinguished. "We have done nothing to you. You would kill my only child, starting a war between our people, just to get revenge on a race that no longer worships you?"

Odin moved the dagger to Eden's neck.

"You are not a god," Cedar continued, her voice shaking with anger. "You are nothing but a pathetic old man."

She stopped walking when Odin pressed the dagger into Eden's skin, and a thin line of red appeared at her throat. "Stop," Cedar whispered. "She's just a child. She has nothing to do with this."

"She has everything to do with this," he answered. "Open the portal, or she dies."

"I can't," Cedar said, but then threw her arms forward desperately as he moved to plunge the dagger into Eden's neck. "I mean it! I can't open the portal without her. I'm not strong enough. It's the only reason she's here with us. *She* opened it."

Odin relaxed the hand that held the dagger, but did not release Eden. "She's just a child, and yet more powerful than the queen of the Tuatha Dé Danann? Do you expect me to believe that?"

"Yes," Cedar said, stumbling forward. "Eden is—or will be—much stronger than I am. I couldn't open the sidh—the portal—between Tír na nÓg and Asgard without her help. If you harm her, you will never reach Midgard."

"And your male companion? I suppose you'll tell me next that you need him too?" he said.

Cedar was about to say yes, that she needed him more than anything, but she didn't get a chance. A great black serpent, its head larger than Odin's throne, reared up from behind the king. A single black feather drifted to the ground beside it. Odin jumped up and grabbed his spear, and Eden slid off his lap onto the stone floor. Thor yelled, "Jörmungandr!" and swung his hammer at the snake's head, but it darted away at the last second. Cedar ran to Eden and pulled her off the dais, hiding her behind a stone pillar in the corner.

"Eden," she whispered, her hands on her daughter's face. The wound at her neck was not deep; Odin had barely scratched the skin. Eden tried to look at Cedar, but her eyes were unfocused. Her skin was like wax, and she didn't even seem to have the energy to raise her own head.

Cedar pulled Eden into her arms and whispered, "It's okay, baby, we're going to get you home." She leaned her against the pillar and ran back into the hall, where Finn, as the great snake, was still doing battle with Odin and Thor. Thor had wedged himself between the snake and his father, as if he was trying to protect him.

Cedar threw out her hands, and a wall of flame rushed toward Odin. Thor pulled his father away at the last second, and started to wind up his hammer, preparing to throw it at Cedar.

"How dare you bring Jörmungandr against us!" Thor bellowed.

"I don't know what you're taking about!" Cedar yelled back, opening a sidh to the other side of the room. "Finn's a shape-shifter!" She stepped through the sidh, which put her behind Odin and Thor. Odin threw his spear at Finn, striking him in the tail. The Finn-serpent let out a hiss of pain, and Odin rushed toward him with a war cry.

"You have to stop this!" Cedar said, stepping into another sidh that brought her directly to Thor's side. "Thousands of innocent people will die if you don't!"

Thor didn't attack her, but he looked away, staring at Odin and the great serpent. "My father—"

"Is your *father*," Cedar said. "He's not you. *You* are the one with a choice here. You can redeem yourself, save Brighid, and prevent a new war between our people."

Thor's body was rigid, but his eyes were dark, as if a storm raged behind them. "I did not ask for this," he said. "I did not want this. But I have no choice—you must see that."

"You do have a choice," she said. "And you just made it." With that, she turned and ran straight toward Odin and Finn, hands blazing with fire. If Thor would not end this, she would—no matter what it took. She threw everything she had at Odin as he darted and dodged around the snake's coils, trying to avoid the fangs that were as long as his spear. But he was faster than both of them.

Odin dodged her flames and took both of her wrists in his grasp. She screamed in pain and tried to wrench free, but his grip was like molten lead. His other hand was squeezing her throat. Thor had taken up his father's battle with Finn, preventing the serpent from coming to her rescue. Cedar tried to focus her fire, tried to fight back, but her vision was starting to blur and she could only concentrate on trying to suck in enough air.

"You think you have what it takes to rule?" Odin said, pulling her face close to his. "I have ruled this kingdom since before the Tuatha Dé Danann first set eyes on Midgard. There is too much human in you—I can smell it, like a rotting corpse. You're no queen. You don't have the stomach to rule a great race, to do whatever it takes. That is why *I* am still here, and why *you* have come crawling to me." He dropped Cedar to the ground and she gasped for breath, her throat burning.

"You call yourself a king?" she rasped. "No one believes in you; no one follows you. And your own son hates you. You have nothing left, and you know it."

He turned away and retreated several paces. For a moment, she thought that she had gotten through to him. But then she saw the spear hurtling toward her. She tried to lunge out of the way, knowing it was futile, but then she heard a great clang of metal, and the spear was knocked to the floor beside her. Thor's hammer flew back through the air to its master.

"The Danann were once our allies, Father," Thor said. "Do we really want to start a war with Midgard *and* Tír na nÓg? Can we even survive such a war, with so few of us left? I beg you to consider what you are doing!"

Odin rounded on Thor, his face twisted in fury. His spear was still lying on the floor, and Cedar took her chance. She dove for it and hurled it at Odin's back. It did not miss its target. It plunged deep between his shoulder blades, and he fell forward at his son's feet.

"No!" Thor roared. His hammer fell from his grip, landing with a discordant clang on the stone floor. He dropped to his father's side and turned him over. Odin's eyes were open and unseeing. Cedar tensed, ready for another attack. But Thor did not stand; he just stared down at his father's still face, as though he could not believe the enormity of what had happened. "Father, no," he whispered. "No, this is not what I intended."

"It had to be done. He would have destroyed us all," Cedar said, but she knew her words would mean little to the son of the man she had just killed. She could feel Finn come up behind her, but she kept her eyes on Thor. She did not regret her actions, but the look of grief on Thor's face was heartbreaking. She wished this could have ended another way.

When Thor spoke, his voice was so spectral she had to strain to hear him. "I had a choice. I made it." His next words surprised her. "The jewels are in the seat of the throne. Take what you came for." Then he picked up his father's body, cradling it like a child, and headed toward a door that was set in a crevice in the stone wall.

"Wait," Cedar called after him. He stopped. "You did the right thing. You saved a lot of lives. I am sorry it had to end this way. But the alternative—"

"I know," he said. "My father's time ended long ago. He does not belong in this world any longer."

"Come with us," she said on a sudden impulse. "There is no need for you to be trapped here any longer."

For a moment she thought he was considering her offer. But then he shook his head and said, "No. I must lead my people now— what is left of us. Tell Brighid I am sorry. And . . . tell her I never stopped caring for her. She has been the only beauty in my bleak life." Then he was gone.

"Cedar—the jewels," Finn said urgently. He was back in his usual form, and he'd retrieved Eden from behind the pillar. She was unconscious, and he cradled her close to his chest. His leg was stained red with blood, but his jaw was set.

Cedar ran up the steps to the golden throne. She pulled at its seat, but it wouldn't budge. "I can't open it!" she yelled. Finn gently laid Eden back down and limped forward to join her, but not even their combined efforts made it budge.

"Stand back," Cedar said at last, and Finn hoisted Eden into his arms again and retreated several paces. Cedar closed her eyes to channel her power, and for a moment she feared she would once again lose control of the fire. Distressing images started to flicker before her mind's eye—Eden lying limp across Odin's lap, a trail of blood across her throat; Thor's hollow eyes as he cradled the body of his father; Brighid's wasted form shrouded in a blanket.

She forced her eyes open.

"Not this time," she said. She set her hands on the throne and focused all of her anger, all of her fear, all of her determination to save the people she loved—and those she didn't even know—into her hands. She could feel the power flowing through her veins like lava. White flames erupted around the throne, and the gold started to glow red, bubbling and running into a molten stream that dripped onto the stones below. Cedar could feel the heat, but it did not burn her. She stayed where she was, hands pressed against the throne, until all the metal melted away, leaving only a puddle of gold that ran down the steps, hardening as it cooled.

Lying in the center of the puddle were the eight blue jewels she had seen in Brighid's memories. Rather than picking them up, Cedar focused her flames on the jewels, hoping the heat would destroy them. But when she withdrew her hands, they remained unblemished.

"We'll bring them back to Tír na nÓg," Finn said, coming up behind her. His face was pale, and his leg was still gushing blood. Cedar nodded, scooping up the jewels and tucking them inside her gold dress. She started to think of Tír na nÓg, readying herself to try and form the sidh on her own. But before she got very far, she glanced down at the floor where Odin had fallen. Thor's hammer was still there.

"Wait," she said to Finn, running down the steps toward the hammer. She set the jewels on the floor, and then wrapped both hands around the grip. When she lifted it above her head, the sound of thunder rumbled in the sky above them. Then she brought the hammer down with all her force. When she lifted it again, a deep fissure had appeared in the stone floor, and around it was a fine misting of blue dust. She swept up the dust and placed it in her pocket before walking back to the dais and placing the hammer on top of what was left of the golden throne. "Thank you," she whispered. She realized that Thor would never have left the hammer behind accidentally, even when faced with the death of his father. It had been his final gift to the woman he had once—and maybe still—loved.

"Cedar, we have to get Eden to Felix—quickly!" Finn said. As he said this, they could hear shouting from outside the tower. Their welcome was over. "Can you do it without her?"

"Yes," Cedar said, and as she said it, she knew it was true. "It's just going home."

☙

Cedar opened the sidh back into the common room, where they had left the others. It had been easy, just as she'd known it would be. The room erupted into chaos as soon as they came through.

Riona and Rohan descended on them at once, but Cedar ignored them, scanning the room for the person they needed most. "Felix!" she bellowed. "Felix, help us!" And then he was there, taking Eden from Finn's arms, and the room fell silent around them.

"What happened to her?" he said, laying his hand on her forehead.

"I don't know," Cedar whispered. The fact that they had found and destroyed the jewels didn't seem to matter anymore, not if Eden's life had been the price. "I think it was maybe the transformation—she just grew weaker and weaker."

Felix sank to his knees, still holding Eden. Finn wrapped his arms around Cedar, and she felt Riona's hand on her shoulder.

"Felix, tell me, what can I do?" she pleaded. "Can I get something from your healing rooms? Can I connect with her somehow? What will help her?"

"I think you're right," he said. "I think the power needed to maintain the transformation is sucking the life out of her. But . . . it might be too late. She might not have enough power to change back."

Cedar heard his words, but refused to believe them. *There is always hope*, she had told the druid, when they thought the jewels were lost for good.

The druid.

"Where's Helen?" she cried.

"I'm here, Your Majesty," Helen said, stepping out from behind Nevan and Atty. Her face was full of sorrow—and fear.

"Can you help her? She said you were teaching her how to access her power. Can you undo the transformation?"

Helen looked hesitantly at the limp girl in Felix's arms. "I'll try."

She knelt down next to Eden and cupped the girl's face in her hands. She spoke softly into Eden's ear, a strange, humming language that Cedar didn't understand. She placed her hands on Eden's chest as her voice rose, filling the room. Then she stopped, and looked back at Cedar.

"The little one is still inside. But she needs her mother. Come, tell her you are waiting for her."

Cedar knelt beside them, and Felix shifted Eden into her arms. She could feel the hot tears rolling down her face, stinging the raw marks Odin's ravens had left on her cheeks. Eden's head was lying against Cedar's shoulder, and Cedar buried her face in her daughter's hair, her eyes squeezed shut to try to stem the tears. "Come home, baby. Come back, and be my little girl again."

There was a wave of power, like a burst of energy passing through them. She felt the change take place in her arms, but she was afraid to open her eyes in case she was wrong. Then she heard the voice of her little girl. "Mummy?"

Cedar's eyes flew open, and there was Eden—small, beautiful, and wonderfully alive—gazing up at her with wide brown eyes. Cedar held her close and started to cry in earnest, finally free to give in to the magnitude of what had just happened. But she smiled through her tears as she felt Finn's arms wrap around them both. He was weeping and laughing too, and then Felix was clapping him on the back and shouting, "She's okay!" and Nevan was so happy they could all hear her cheering inside their heads, and Niall was scrambling over them trying to get to Eden, and it was pure, glorious pandemonium.

Finally they all managed to stand, and Cedar turned to Helen, one arm around Eden. "Thank you," she said.

Helen smiled, her gaze still on Eden. "You have a very special girl there, Your Majesty."

"We found the jewels," Cedar said, suddenly remembering. "We destroyed them." There was another round of cheering, and Cedar gave them an abbreviated version of what had happened in Asgard. "So I used the hammer to destroy them," she finished, pulling a handful of sparkling blue dust out of her pocket. They all crowded around to see it. "I don't know if it has any further use or not, but I thought I would bring it home just in case." She looked at Felix. "Did it work? Has the curse been broken?"

"I've been here the whole time, waiting for you," Felix said. "Let's find out. Would you mind?"

Cedar nodded and opened a sidh into Felix's home. Everyone in the room started to crowd toward it, until Felix held up his hand. "Let's not startle him to death," he said. Cedar gave Eden another squeeze before following Felix through the sidh. They jogged down the hall to Irial's room and pushed open the door.

He was gone.

Cedar and Felix exchanged startled glances, and then Felix ran over to the bed and stared down at the empty sheets. "What the . . . where did he go?"

"It's a good sign!" Cedar said. "He couldn't have gone anywhere if he was still sick. He could barely move!"

Together, they ran through Felix's halls of healing, shouting Irial's name. There was no answer. Felix seemed worried, but Cedar was too elated by Eden's recovery to be unduly concerned. They destroyed the jewels; it *must* have worked. "We'll find him. We only just broke the curse, so he can't have gone far." They went outside and started walking around Felix's home, looking for any sign of the wandering gancanagh.

They found him standing on the banks of the river, staring into the water as it rushed past. He was dressed in the simple robe they had given him, his hands outstretched in the wind. "Irial!" Cedar called. He turned, and she let out an involuntary gasp. He had been breathtakingly handsome even while near death. Now his cheeks were flushed with health and his eyes shone with new life; he was the most gorgeous thing she'd ever seen. Without thinking, she ran to him and flung her arms around his neck. "It worked!" she shouted, hugging him tightly. He seemed startled by the sudden show of affection, but then his body relaxed and he returned the embrace. She pulled back, grinning. "You gave us a bit of a fright, running off like that! How are you feeling?"

"I feel . . . wonderful," he said, as though he could not quite believe it himself. "How did you . . . ?"

"We found the jewels after all," Cedar said. "They were in Asgard. It's a long story, and you'll hear it all later. But I'm so glad you're okay."

Felix was staring at Irial as though he, too, could not quite believe the transformation. "If you don't mind, I'd like to examine you one last time, just so I can document the change. It won't take long."

Irial nodded, but his face was somber. "Toirdhealbhach—Felix—I just need to say again how sorry I am about what happened with Jane. And . . . you know it wasn't the first time I allowed a human woman to touch me, even after I knew what I was. You gave me the chance to do the right thing all those years ago, but I haven't always done it. This brush with death . . . well, I've had a lot to think about. It won't happen again. I guarantee it. I want to live freely, and I want the same for . . . for women like Jane. There will be no more entrapment, not from me."

Cedar watched as the muscles in Felix's face twitched. But then he closed the gap between him and Irial and embraced the gancanagh, pounding him on the back before stepping back. "You're going to do just fine," he said. "You might not believe so yet, but the world is lucky to have you in it."

"Why don't you two head back to your place, Felix, and you can check Irial over one last time. I need to go see Brighid. She must already know that we succeeded, but I want to tell her about what happened with Thor. I think there might still be a chance for them."

"I'm sure Jane will be glad to see you as well," Felix said. "Ask her if she'll come back with you. We're long overdue for an honest talk."

They returned to Felix's house, and Cedar stepped back through the sidh to her own place, where Finn, Eden, Helen, and the others were still gathered, listening to Finn tell the story of their time in Asgard from his perspective. They all looked up at her expectantly as she entered.

"He's fine," she told them, unable to keep the smile from spreading across her face. "He's in perfect health." She took hold of Finn and Eden's hands. "We did it." Then she told them about her plan to go see Brighid and bring Jane back here—and Brighid, too, if she wanted to come. "I'll be right back," she said to Eden with a wink.

She opened the sidh into the entrance hall of Brighid's home, and after giving her one last wave, Finn closed the sidh behind her.

"Hello?" she called, expecting Vanessa to show up out of nowhere like she usually did. But her voice only echoed in the cavernous hall, which was darker than normal. "Hello?" she called again. "Vanessa? Jane? Brighid?" She walked down the hallway and swept around the corner, where she saw a faint light flickering from behind the glass doors that led to the balcony. She slid open the door and stepped out. Jane was standing against the railing, watching the sun rise behind the great mountains that rose up out of the ocean. "Jane?" Cedar said softly, feeling a dreadful certainty descend upon her. Something horrible had happened here.

Jane turned around. Her eyes were red and her skin was blotchy. Black mascara streaks were smudged down both her cheeks. She shook her head sadly, and then her chin crumpled. "I'm so sorry, Cedar."

"*No*," Cedar whispered, running over to the lounge chair where they had left Brighid. It was empty. The blankets that had covered her were folded neatly at the foot of the lounge, as was the simple black dress she had been wearing.

"What happened? Where is she?" Cedar stared at Jane in confusion, refusing to believe what her eyes—and the hollow feeling in the pit of her stomach—were telling her.

"She fell asleep after we sent Eden back to Tír na nÓg," Jane said. "And . . . she didn't wake up. I sat next to her the whole time, holding her hand. I had my fingers on her wrist, so I could feel her pulse. But then it . . . stopped. And a few seconds later she just disappeared. There was this white wispy thing that kind of hovered here for a minute, and then that was gone too."

Cedar sank down onto the foot of the lounge, too shocked to cry. "I was too late," she whispered. The sun had now crested and was flooding the balcony with light. It was a new day, a new world. Brighid had been part of this world for hundreds of years, and now she was gone. The people and creatures of Ériu had suffered a great loss, even if they did not realize it.

"Ceeds, what happened?" Jane asked. "Did Eden find you? Where is everyone?"

"It worked," Cedar said, still staring at the empty space where Brighid should have been. Haltingly, she told Jane everything. But her triumph was now tainted by the knowledge that it hadn't been enough.

"You did your best," Jane said. "You never gave up. You did more than anyone else would have. And you saved a lot of lives."

"I know," Cedar said. "But this was the life I wanted to save the most."

CHAPTER 19

Jane said good-bye to Cedar just inside the doorway of Felix's home. Cedar had offered to come with her to tell Felix the terrible news, but Jane could tell that all her friend wanted to do was to be with her family. Besides, sitting vigil at Brighid's bedside had given Jane a lot to think about. She needed to see Felix—alone.

She walked through the silent halls of his home. She could have called out his name, but she wanted to take her time. She trailed her fingers along the walls, wondering what it would be like to live here, to belong to this magical world. She knew she could never be one of them, but maybe she could become a part of their lives one day, not just through Felix's furtive visits to her apartment, but here in Tír na nÓg, out in the open. It had happened before, she knew. She had been reading the old stories, and one in particular had struck a chord. Niamh, the daughter of the High King of the Tuatha Dé Danann, had fallen in love with Oisín, one of the mortal sons of Fionn mac Cumhaill, and she'd brought him back to Tír na nÓg to rule with her. Niamh and Oisín's story had a tragic ending: Oisín had longed to return to Earth to see his father and brothers, so Niamh had let him go, with a warning not to step off his white horse. When he arrived back in Ireland, no one but the oldest townsfolk had even heard of the great Fionn mac Cumhaill. He and his followers had died over three hundred years ago. While he was trying to help some men load a boulder into a cart, Oisín slipped off his horse. As soon as he touched the ground, he became an ancient old man. He never saw his love again. *We could be different*, Jane thought. *I could stay here forever . . . We could write our own story . . .*

She heard his voice coming from one of the healing rooms and stopped outside the door. She couldn't make out what he was saying, but then someone else spoke, and she recognized that person's voice at once. Irial. Her heart sped up and she cursed it. But in a way, she was glad Irial was still here. She needed to see them both. She needed to be certain.

She pushed open the door without knocking. Irial was sitting shirtless on the edge of the bed, laughing at something Felix had just said. Felix's back was to her, but she could see he was holding a crystal vial of what had to be Irial's blood. Then Irial saw her, and the impact was immediate. He leapt off the bed, clutching a white sheet to his chest, and retreated to the farthest corner of the room before Felix even had the chance to turn around. When he did, his eyes lit up. "Jane!"

She stood frozen in the doorway, staring at the two men who had held her heart. But this time, it felt like she was seeing them both clearly for the first time. The attraction to Irial was still undeniable; she could feel the tug of her body toward him. But she no longer felt compelled to obey it. She looked at him curiously. How had she once believed herself in love with this stranger? She turned her back to him to face Felix, who was watching her cautiously.

"Are you okay?" he asked.

"Yes," she said, and before he had a chance to say anything else, she grabbed Felix's shirt collar and pulled him toward her. Irial cleared his throat, but she ignored him, lost in the embrace of the one man she had truly loved.

"I'll just . . . go, then," Irial said, and out of the corner of her eye she saw him tiptoe out of the room, a brilliant smile on his face.

Felix was whispering her name. "Jane, Jane, Jane. You came back to me."

She kissed him again, and then pulled back so that she could look at his face. "Did you really doubt that I would?"

"I hoped, I truly hoped," he said. "But . . . I was never quite sure. I thought that maybe once you had the taste of another . . ."

"It was a drug. A toxin. Nothing more."

"You don't want to go back to him?"

"No. I don't care if I ever see him again. But even if I had to see him every day, it wouldn't change how I feel about you. You are the one I want to be with. Forever." She clapped a hand to her mouth, suddenly aware of just how serious things had become. "I mean . . ." she stammered.

He gently took her hand from her lips and kissed it. "I want that too."

Forever. She wanted that so badly, but . . .

"Felix, listen, before we start making promises we can't keep, you have to remember . . . I'm human."

"Delightfully so," he agreed.

She shook her head. "You don't understand what I mean. I'm going to keep getting older, while you stay"—she waved her hands at him—"perfect."

"'Perfect' and 'young' often have little to do with each other, if that's what you mean," he said. "But if it makes you feel better, I'll let you in on a little secret. Ever heard of the story of Niamh and Oisín?"

"Yes," Jane said, "Exactly. But—"

"Stories change a lot over the years. This particular one contains both truths and falsehoods. Oisín stayed here for hundreds of years without aging a day, even though he was human. He did go back to Ériu—"

"I know," she said miserably. "And then he became old and died."

"Yes," Felix said, tilting her chin up so that she couldn't avoid his eyes. "But it didn't happen all at once like the story said. Oisín left Niamh. He never meant to come back. He started aging once he returned to his homeland, but he lived for many, many years before dying peacefully as an old man."

"But . . . why?"

"Niamh couldn't bring herself to believe that he was never coming back, that he had left her of his own free will. She believed what she wanted to believe: that he didn't return because he accidentally touched the earth and aged three hundred years in an instant. Her version of the story took root, and it's the one that's still being told to children in Ireland today."

"So if I stay here with you, I'll stop aging," Jane said.

"And if you ever choose to leave, you'll be as beautiful as you are today, no matter what world you choose to live in."

"What about Cedar? Will she really make an exception to the rules just for us?"

"I think we'll be able to convince her. Besides, we don't need to decide right away. I'm happy to stay in Halifax for a while, or just on weekends, or whatever you like. I just thought you might like to know that 'forever' is an option, if you want it."

"'Forever' sounds very nice," Jane said. "But for now, I'm happy with 'today.'" She sighed, knowing that what she was about to say would dampen his newfound happiness. "I need to tell you about Brighid . . ."

⟪

Irial wandered slowly around Tír na nÓg for what felt like hours, neither knowing nor caring where he was going. It was dark out, and a thrill ran through him as he looked up at the stars, so distant and yet so startlingly bright above him. The air held just a hint of chill, but it was not at all unpleasant. He had spent many bitterly cold nights alone and unsheltered, trying to stay away from humans while still keeping warm and nourished. And now, here he was, a guest of the Tuatha Dé Danann in the Otherworld. Logheryman had been right; the queen had done the impossible. She had risked everything and—in doing so—saved them all. Irial had spent most of his life being shunned or merely tolerated; he had never before encountered such a genuine, generous person. But then he thought of Syrna and wondered if she was still alive. She, too, had offered him understanding.

"Irial?"

A woman's voice brought him out of his reverie. He looked up and realized that he was nearing the entrance of a great white building with tall, twisting spires. Queen Cedar was walking toward him. "What are you doing here? Is everything okay?"

Irial hastily bowed. "Yes, Your Majesty. I was just taking a stroll to give Toirdh—that is, Felix and Jane some time together. They were, uh, making up." As the queen grew closer, he could see that her eyes were red, as though she had been crying. "Oh no," he whispered. "Your friend?"

"She didn't make it."

"I'm . . . so sorry," he said, not sure what else to say. He felt a sudden stab of guilt, that he should be alive when others among the Unseen had not survived.

"Thank you," Cedar said. "I was going to wait until morning, but since you're here, there's something I wanted to talk to you about."

"Anything."

"Someone needs to go to the Unseen and explain what has happened. They've all been impacted by this. Many of them have lost people they love, and they deserve to know why. They shouldn't have to live in fear that it will happen again. You know where to find them, and they'll trust you—you're one of them. Perhaps together we can start building some bridges between the Unseen and the Tuatha Dé Danann."

Irial ran his hand through his dark curls, considering. What else did he have to do? He knew firsthand the misconceptions the Unseen had about the Tuatha Dé Danann. What better way to repay the queen than to make sure the Unseen knew they owed their lives to her? "I'd be honored," he said.

"Thank you," she said. "I'll probably join you on some of these excursions, but I have a feeling you may want to visit the selkies alone?" A hint of a smile played at the corner of her lips.

"How did you—"

"She was quite worried about you," Cedar said. "And I think she'll be very happy to see you again."

ৎৎ

After saying good-bye to Irial, Cedar proceeded into the Hall and down the stairs that led to the dungeons.

Before running into the gancanagh, she had been sitting by Eden's bed, watching her sleep. She had tried sleeping herself, but the thought of the empty lounge chair on Brighid's balcony had kept her awake. She dreaded breaking the news to Eden in the morning. She and Finn had held each other and cried, until he, too, fell asleep. But there was no rest for Cedar—not yet. She couldn't stop thinking about Thor, either—wondering what he was doing now, how he was coping with his father's death.

"That's not going to be us," she had whispered to Eden. "You and I will be a team. I promise." She thought about Odin's last words to her. *You're no queen. You don't have the stomach to rule a great race, to do whatever it takes.*

He was wrong, she had thought. *We are—and will continue to be—a great race, and I can rule. There's just one thing I need to fix.* She knew what she had to do, and headed for the dungeons under the Hall.

The guards jerked to attention when they saw her—they had hardly been expecting her; it was almost midnight. She smiled at them and made her way to Helen's door. One of the guards moved to open it for her, but she held up her hand. "Unlock it, but do not open it," she said. After he stepped back, she knocked softly on the door. There was silence for a moment, and then the door handle slowly turned, and the door opened.

Helen stood inside, watching her warily.

"I know it's late. I'm sorry," Cedar said. "May I . . . come in?"

"Of course," Helen said, stepping aside so that Cedar could enter. She motioned toward the one chair in the room, the one behind the desk.

"Oh, no, thank you," Cedar said. "I'm fine standing."

Helen sat in the chair and folded her hands on the desk.

Cedar took a long breath, and then said, "Listen, I know I already thanked you for helping bring Eden back, but I also wanted to say that I'm sorry. I'm sorry I didn't trust you. I have not treated you very well."

Helen waited.

"So . . . you and the other druids are free to go. I'll open a sidh to wherever you want. You're also welcome to stay, if you'd rather. I realize . . . that I've been acting rather foolishly. No, worse than that. I couldn't see past my own anger, my own prejudice. But I have a chance to change all that. I want to put this animosity between our two peoples behind us. We lived in harmony once, and there is no reason why we cannot do it again."

"That is quite a change of heart," Helen said. "Can I ask what brought this on?"

"We're all in this together," Cedar said. "Unseen, druids, Tuatha Dé Danann. We're all part of the same strange world. They say we're the strong ones—the Danann, that is. But if we don't use our strength to look out for others, then we risk becoming like Odin. *I* risk becoming like him. And I can't let that happen."

Helen looked up at Cedar, and there was a gentleness in her face that Cedar hadn't seen—or noticed—before. "Thank you. I accept your apology, and I will do my part to help bridge the gap between our people. If you don't mind, I would like to stay in Tír na nÓg for a while. I'm sure there is much I can learn here. And now that the jewels have been destroyed, there is no pressing need for me to return home. There will be a queue of scholars wanting my job, and they are welcome to it."

"Of course," Cedar said. "Eden will be delighted to hear that you are staying."

"You were right to try to protect her, Your Majesty. If she were my daughter, I would feel the same way. I hope you understand that I was genuinely trying to help. And if I may be so bold, I believe you will be a new kind of queen—one who rules with her heart, not her sword. And that's something that the Tuatha Dé Danann have not had in a very long time. This 'strange world,' as you call it, will be the better for it."

CHAPTER 20

Cedar felt strangely calm as she approached the Hall the next morning. No guards had been sent to escort her, so she wondered if the Council had taken her abdication seriously. It didn't really matter to her; she had done what needed to be done, and if giving up the title of queen was the price she had to pay, it had been well worth it.

She had left her hair down and was wearing a simple dress of spring green. The gold dress that had been made for her in Asgard was tucked away in the back of her wardrobe. She thought it might look good on Eden someday. She ignored the curious glances of those she passed as she made her way to the courtyard. Who knew what rumors were circulating about her now?

The Council was waiting for her when she arrived, seated in their circle of chairs in the center of the courtyard. They stood as one when she entered, and bowed to her.

Rohan was the one who greeted her. "Welcome, Your Majesty."

"I'm not the queen anymore. I abdicated, remember?"

"Ah, yes, about that," he said. "I hope you do not mind, but I took the liberty of convening an emergency session of the Council. After a great deal of discussion and, might I add, even more soul-searching, we have unanimously agreed to refuse to accept your abdication. We hope you will continue to do us the honor of being our queen."

Cedar looked at the faces around the circle, a mix of pride and anticipation and sheepishness. "I don't understand," she said. "You opposed me every step of the way. You thought that saving the Unseen was a waste of our time."

"We were wrong, to put it mildly," said Rohan.

"Most of us have been here for a very long time, Your Majesty," said Gorman. "And for most of that time, we have had no contact with other beings or races. Under Lorcan's rule, life became a matter of survival, and most of us grew accustomed to looking after ourselves before all others. It won't be easy to change, but if we want to live on as a great race, then change we must. And you are by far the best one to lead us there."

For a moment, Cedar was speechless, but then she gathered herself. "Thank you," she said. "It would be my honor."

After the Council meeting, in which Cedar described her encounter with Thor and Odin in great detail, she walked home with Rohan. "How did you convince them?" she asked.

"It wasn't hard," he said. "*You* convinced them. They respect you, even if they don't show it at times. You have all the attributes of our greatest leaders—they just look a little different in you because of your upbringing on Ériu. Your tenacity about the Unseen . . . well, it made us all reconsider our position—myself included. And then when Brighid died, it was something no one thought possible. You and she are quite alike, I must say."

"Really?" Cedar asked. "How?"

"Out of all of us, the two of you were the only ones who were willing to risk your own lives to save the Unseen," he said gently.

"And she paid with hers."

"She did," Rohan agreed. "But it wasn't in vain. The two of you have had quite an impact on the Tuatha Dé Danann. You should hear them talking. They're already saying you're the greatest queen

Tír na nÓg has seen in centuries. Lorcan did a lot of damage. People are excited about this new direction we're taking."

Cedar was silent as she thought about what Rohan had said. She didn't feel like she was leading them in any particular direction—she was just trying to do the right thing. But maybe he was right—maybe it was time for her to stop being a reluctant queen, time for her to really determine what she and the other Tuatha Dé Danann could accomplish for good in the universe.

"Where are all my guards?" she asked, noticing that they were alone.

"Ah, yes. I think it will be fine to relax the security a bit. You've proven that you're quite capable of taking care of yourself."

Cedar said good-bye to Rohan once they reached their house. She found Finn sitting in the wicker swing in their room, staring out at the pond, no doubt thinking of Brighid. She took a deep breath and walked toward him.

"How did it go?" he asked, straightening up and smiling when he saw her. She sank down onto the chair next to him and filled him in on the Council's change of heart. He didn't seem surprised.

"You have that impact on people," he said. "You certainly had it on me."

She reached over and took his hand.

"Are you still upset with me for trying to stop you?" he asked. "I wouldn't blame you if you were."

"I was—I am—hurt," she admitted. "I've always felt like we were in this together, or at least that's how it should be. But you stood against me earlier. You and everyone else."

He opened his mouth to respond, but she put her fingers on his lips. "Which just proves that I am sometimes wrong, and that you love me enough to tell me so."

She could feel his lips curve against her fingers. "I do love you. And even though I did think you were wrong, I truly would have gone with you."

"I know. I don't think I ever doubted that."

"So what do we do now?"

"Well, now that I'm queen again, I've made the executive decision that I need a vacation," she said.

"You deserve it," he agreed. "Where do you want to go?"

Cedar looked around the room, her eyes settling on the large white bed. "I thought we might start over there," she said, her eyes twinkling. "And then see where it takes us."

∽

Cedar tiptoed around the edge of the giant bush, stopping to inhale the scent of the enormous yellow flowers hanging from it. She heard a muffled giggle and froze. "I guess no one's here," she said loudly, a grin spreading across her face. She darted behind the bush, her hands outstretched, but she was too late. Squealing with laughter, Eden went tearing across the field. Cedar gave chase. "I'm going to catch you!" she yelled. She was within arm's reach when the air in front of Eden flashed, and she disappeared. Cedar followed her through the sidh before Eden had a chance to close it and swept her daughter up into a hug.

"Hey!" Eden dissolved into laughter as Cedar held her upside down and tickled her.

"You'll have to be faster than that if you want to beat me," Cedar said.

"I didn't want to close the sidh on you and cut you in half!" Eden said between shrieks.

"Uh-huh," Cedar said, setting her back down. "Okay, now it's my turn."

"You're too easy to find!" Eden said. "You can't close them!"

"It's true," Cedar admitted. "Okay, you win. But that reminds me. I have an important job for you."

"You do?" Eden said, her eyes lighting up at once.

"Mmm hmm. I'm letting the druids go home, and I'll need some help making the sidhe back to Ériu."

"Cool!" Eden exclaimed. "I can totally do that! And . . . do you think . . . ?"

"Yes?"

"Do you think maybe we could go for a chocolate-chip bagel, like we used to?"

Cedar squeezed Eden's hand as they started walking back home. "I think that would be just about perfect."

EPILOGUE

The fire on the topmost point of the Hill of Tara was large enough to be seen by half of Ireland. Three times as tall as a person, it burned in a spectacular bouquet of reds, oranges, and yellows. Smaller fires dotted the hillside all around it, a tribute to Brighid, whose own flame had been extinguished. The druids had enchanted the hillside for the night, so that curious human eyes would be averted while they mourned their friend.

There was no body to bury, no remains to burn. But Cedar had insisted they do something to honor Brighid's life, her sacrifice. And so, with Irial's help, they invited everyone whose lives Brighid had touched, whether or not they knew it. The response was overwhelming. Most of the Danann came, and many of the druids. But what was truly remarkable was the outpouring of support from the Unseen. They showed up in droves, each group sending a delegation bearing gifts and tributes to the fallen Elder who had ensured their survival for hundreds of years, and to the queen who had freed them when the curse had fallen at last.

It was a gathering the likes of which had not been seen for millennia. Gods and druids and magical beings of all kinds ate and drank and cried and danced together between the flames, under a canopy of stars. Cedar wandered among them, hand in hand with Eden and Finn. She accepted words of comfort and gratitude from the Merrow, who had apparently forgiven the Danann for Nuala's treachery. She smiled at Syrna, who had Irial pressed up against the trunk of a hawthorn tree, oblivious to the rest of the world. An old man, who turned out to be Logheryman's brother, thanked Cedar for saving his life, though it had been too late for him to make amends with his brother. He had been brought to the celebration by Maggie, and was wearing what looked to be a hand-knit sweater. Cedar saw Abhartach too, and she kissed his tattooed cheeks. He grumbled so much it almost covered up the fact that he was exceedingly pleased to see her. And throughout the evening, she lifted glass after glass in toasts to Brighid, Eden, and herself.

Eden laughed in delight when a troop of pixies surrounded her and dragged her off to the nearest fairy circle for a dance. Cedar and Finn watched her run off with them, sharing an indulgent smile.

Toward the end of the evening, a flash of red hair caught Cedar's eye from behind one of the small fires. She blinked, thinking it was a trick of the flame. But then there he was—a tall, still figure with a large stone hammer gripped in one hand.

"Where are you going?" Finn asked as she moved toward the newcomer.

"I think I see . . . Just give me a second." Finn turned to speak with a púka, and Cedar made her way toward the edge of the gathering.

For a moment, they regarded each other silently. "How did you get here?" she finally asked. "I thought Bifrost was closed. I thought you were trapped."

Thor shook his head. "Bifrost *was* closed, but not forever. When the jewels failed to work for Odin centuries ago, his madness overtook him, and he threatened to find Brighid and force her to tell him the truth. I did not doubt Brighid's strength . . . but my father's fury was not to be taken lightly. And so I pled with Heimdallr, the guardian of Bifrost, to destroy the bridge so that my father could not reach Midgard." He closed his eyes for a moment, and then looked back down at Cedar. "Heimdallr paid with his life when Odin discovered what had been done. But even with all his power, he could not rebuild the bridge without the key, which Heimdallr had entrusted to me. Odin thought it had been destroyed along with Bifrost. He could not reach her."

"Thor," Cedar said, her voice anguished. "*That's* why you never came back. You trapped your father—and yourself—in Asgard to keep her safe. And she never knew."

"It wouldn't have mattered," he said. "She was right to hate me. I betrayed her."

"Brighid didn't have room in her heart for hate," she said. "I knew her well, and I'm certain she would have forgiven you." Cedar felt a tug on her dress and looked down to see Eden, who was staring up at Thor with large brown eyes. Cedar smiled. "Thor, this is Eden. In her *true* form."

Thor looked slightly horrified for a moment, but then he bent down and shook Eden's outstretched hand. "Hello," Eden said. "My mum told me that we've met before, but I don't remember. So it's nice to meet you."

Thor's eyebrows were raised, but he smiled. "And it's nice to meet you, too, little one. You will be a very brave and beautiful lady when you grow up."

"Cedar, look!" Jane, Felix, and Finn had joined them. Jane was pointing to something hovering in the air just behind Thor's left shoulder. "That wispy thing! It's what I saw right after Brighid died. You don't think . . . ?"

They all turned to look where Jane was pointing. A white flame the size of Cedar's palm was floating through the air toward them. As they watched, transfixed, it floated in front of each one of them. As she felt it pass by her, Cedar experienced a burst of warmth and joy unlike anything she had ever felt before. Judging from the others' reactions, they were feeling the same thing. Eden was giggling, and Jane was laughing and crying at the same time. Felix and Finn were taking great steadying breaths. And Thor . . . he reached out his hands, and the flame rested gently on them. "I'm so sorry," he whispered. Then the flame rose up into the air once more and touched him on the lips before soaring toward the huge bonfire in the middle of the Hill. They saw it disappear into the flames, and a cascade of sparks shot high into the sky and then fell in a shower among them. And then it was over, and all the fires on the hillside went dark.

Cedar's voice was strong and clear in the darkness. "Come. It's time to go home."

ACKNOWLEDGMENTS

Many thanks to my husband, Mike, for his patience, support, and never-ending well of good ideas and helpful feedback, and to my girls, Lauren and Willow, for being the inspiration behind Eden and a hundred other stories I can only hope to find time to write.

I owe Jason Goode, Sarah Cook, and Janelle deJager a world of thanks for being good enough friends to read an early draft of this book and give me their honest and very helpful feedback. Thanks to them, you've read a much better book. And thanks to my cousin Sarah for exploring Inis Mór (and Dublin . . . and everywhere in between) with me, even though we didn't find any real selkies, and to Charis and Mark Henderson for hosting us. Once again, I'm so grateful to Chris Hansen for sharing his expertise on storytelling with me and pushing me through the door into this wonderful new world.

As always, thanks to my stellar editor, Angela Polidoro, and the great team at 47North, who are always such a pleasure to work with: David Pomerico, Britt Rogers, Justin Golenbock, and all the others behind the scenes who are working to bring authors and readers together.

ABOUT THE AUTHOR

Jodi McIsaac grew up in New Brunswick, Canada. After stints as a short-track speed skater, a speechwriter, and a fundraising and marketing executive in the nonprofit sector, she started a boutique copywriting agency and began writing novels in the wee hours of the morning. She currently lives with her husband and children in Calgary.